Sadie was different. How could he forget?

"I'm so sorry. Yo[...] the way you loo[...] don't let anyone [...]"

"Can you tell you[...] [...] that?"

"If you want me to, I will happily do so."

She let out a defeated breath. Her shoulders sank. "I don't know what I want anymore," she said before going into the restroom and letting the door close behind her.

Owen was going to lose her if he didn't get his act together. Jonathan didn't know if he wanted that to happen or not. It was possible he wanted both for very different reasons. One much more selfish than the other.

Dear Reader,

When I got the idea to write a series about stopping weddings, this story was one of the first ideas that popped in my head. What could possibly go wrong when two brothers fall in love with the same woman? Sadie Chapman thinks she's found a great guy. Owen is everything she could ask for in a future husband—handsome, rich, generous, funny. Enter his brother, Jonathan. He's everything his brother is and unexpectedly more.

Jonathan is at a crossroads in his life. He's finally digging himself out of the dark hole he's been in since his wife died. He wants the best for his young daughter and isn't always sure what that is. When his family convinces him to spend the summer in Florida, he finds purpose in saving his brother from making a big mistake and marrying a woman he barely knows. He expects to open his brother's eyes, but perhaps it will be Sadie who opens his heart!

I hope that you enjoy this next installment of the Stop the Wedding! series. I love weddings, but it sure is fun to see how many different ways I can mess them up.

Happy reading!

Amy

HEARTWARMING

His Brother's Bride

———

Amy Vastine

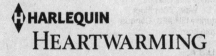

HARLEQUIN®
HEARTWARMING™

ISBN-13: 978-1-335-88971-3

His Brother's Bride

This edition published by arrangement with Harlequin Books S.A.

For questions and comments about the quality of this book,
please contact us at CustomerService@Harlequin.com.

Harlequin Enterprises ULC
22 Adelaide St. West, 40th Floor
Toronto, Ontario M5H 4E3, Canada
www.Harlequin.com

Printed in U.S.A.

Recycling programs
for this product may
not exist in your area.

Amy Vastine has been plotting stories in her head for as long as she can remember. An eternal optimist, she studied social work, hoping to teach others how to find their silver lining. Now she enjoys creating happily-ever-afters for all to read. Amy lives outside Chicago with her high-school-sweetheart husband, three teenagers who keep her on her toes and their two sweet but mischievous pups. Visit her at amyvastine.com.

Books by Amy Vastine

Harlequin Heartwarming

Stop the Wedding!

A Bridesmaid to Remember

Grace Note Records

The Girl He Used to Love
Catch a Fallen Star
Love Songs and Lullabies
Falling for Her Bodyguard

Chicago Sisters

The Better Man
The Best Laid Plans
The Hardest Fight

The Weather Girl

Visit the Author Profile page
at Harlequin.com for more titles.

In memory of my mother-in-law, Joan Vastine,
who passed away on July 6, 2019.
Rest in peace, sweet lady.

CHAPTER ONE

"MARRY ME."

Sadie Chapman stared down at the ring nestled in the black ring box. That emerald-cut diamond had to be at least three carats and was surrounded by a halo of diamonds. It was gorgeous and exactly what she'd dreamed of being offered someday by the man she loved.

Owen Bradley was charming and sweet, but they had been dating barely two months. Sadie wouldn't commit long term to a movie-streaming service without spending a couple of weeks carefully evaluating her usage during her free trial month. How could she possibly answer this kind of question without some time to think about it?

Time was in short supply, however. At least according to Sadie's mom. Her mother loved to mention how at Sadie's age, she'd been happily married for years and already had both of her children.

"I know it seems sudden," he said, kneeling in front of her on his kitchen floor. He had invited her over for a relaxing night in and had even cooked her dinner. She was ready to do dishes, not accept a proposal. She had on black leggings and an oversize Goodman Elementary School T-shirt for Pete's sake! This was not engagement-night attire. She had expected him to pop open a bottle of wine, not pop the question.

"We haven't been together long," he continued. "But I can't remember ever feeling this way about anyone. I think about you when we aren't together. I hate saying good-night when our dates are over. You're an amazing woman and I want to spend the rest of my life with you."

Well, he seemed quite certain. The thumping in her chest was distracting. Sadie needed her brain to work as hard as her heart. What did she want in a husband, and did Owen meet those requirements? Owen was a professional golfer and successful enough to afford this big house, his fancy car and that enormous diamond ring. He was funny and had never been anything but respectful. He had good taste in food, fashion and diamond rings. Based on the little she knew about him, he certainly had the potential to be a good husband.

"Marry me, Sadie."

As she stared into his big blue eyes, she heard the door open behind her.

"Do you know one of your garage doors is open?" someone shouted from the mudroom. "Riley, hit the button to close the garage."

Sadie turned her head and watched as a man in a Boston College sweatshirt and a face that hadn't seen a razor in a few days set a large blue duffel bag down. He made eye contact with Sadie first before turning his gaze on Owen.

"Oh my gosh. I didn't… I know I said we'd be here tomorrow, but we decided to drive straight through. Are you? You are. I am so sorry." He spun around with the horror of his embarrassment written all over his face. "Back to the car, Riley."

"I'm tired!" a little voice whined from the mudroom.

"Uncle Owen needs a minute."

"Uncle Owen only needs an answer." Owen touched Sadie's hand to regain her attention.

Sadie had so many questions that she had

forgotten her answer. She closed her eyes. Why were his brother and niece here? Did he have any other siblings? She knew he was close to his parents, but she had never met them. Shouldn't they have at least met each other's families before they got engaged?

A thousand thoughts zipped through her head in a few seconds. There was only one that mattered, though. Did she want to marry Owen?

Sadie had hoped to be married before she was thirty, but thirty had come and gone. Teaching was her passion and she'd thrown herself into her work instead of searching for a life partner. She loved her students but dreamed of raising a family of her own someday. She'd been a bridesmaid in so many weddings and had been a guest at plenty of baby showers. Maybe it was her turn to be the guest *of honor* at one of those things.

Owen was exactly the kind of man she pictured herself falling in love with. Successful. Charismatic. Good-looking. Getting engaged would also get her mom off her back. That was perhaps the cherry on top of this diamond sundae.

"Yes," she answered, opening her eyes. The

grin on his face made her feel like she'd won the lottery. Owen hopped up and wrapped his arms around her, lifting her feet off the ground.

"She said yes! Did you hear that, Riley? Jonathan?"

"Congratulations." A chagrined Jonathan came back into the kitchen hand in hand with a little girl with dark hair and a bright pink backpack.

"I'm tired," Riley repeated, leaning against her dad.

Owen set Sadie back down. "Sadie, this is my brother, Jonathan, and his daughter, Riley. Jonathan and Riley, this is my fiancée, Sadie."

Jonathan had eyes the same shade of blue as Owen's. "Nice to meet you, Sadie. We're really sorry about interrupting the big moment."

"No apology needed. It's nice to meet both of you. You look about the same age as the students in my third-grade class," she said to Riley.

The little girl pressed against her dad's side and said nothing.

"I think the endless hours in the car have

taken a toll on this one." He smiled down at his daughter. "She just finished third grade and is usually much more talkative than this."

Owen took Sadie by the hand. "Can we get this ring on before you change your mind?" His nerves caused him to shake. Sadie found that endearing. Owen placed the engagement ring on her finger.

An engagement ring.

Sadie was not expecting to leave tonight wearing an engagement ring. Her mother would be ecstatic. Her friends at school would never believe it. They had heard about Owen, but no one would believe he had proposed already. They all had said he sounded like a catch. Sadie decided to add that to the list of reasons why saying yes was the right thing to do.

"You two are in the middle of something and we weren't supposed to be here until tomorrow. I can get a hotel room for the night if—"

"No, you two are staying here," Owen said, cutting his brother off.

"Are you sure? I don't want to interfere any more than I have."

Owen nodded his head. "You're staying."

Jonathan tried to let go of his daughter but she clung to him. He picked up his bag with one hand and kept his grip on Riley. "We are both exhausted and ready for bed. You won't even know we're here."

Owen gave Sadie a kiss on the cheek. "Let me help them get settled and I'll be back down before you can miss me."

He was generous and helpful. Two more traits that boded well for Sadie in the future. She had made the right decision to say yes. She would continue to tell herself that.

Owen showed his brother upstairs and she gave her new ring—her *engagement* ring—a closer look. The ring fit her perfectly. He was observant or a really good guesser. Either way, it was a plus. She wouldn't regret this.

"Owen sure knows how to pick 'em."

Sadie startled. Jonathan walked into the kitchen and opened the refrigerator. Was he talking about her?

She bristled. "Excuse me?"

He closed the fridge and uncapped a bottle of water. "I'm sure the ring is pretty amazing." He took a drink and wiped his mouth with the back of his hand. "Owen doesn't do anything halfway. He only goes all out."

The ring. Of course he was talking about the ring.

Sadie glanced back down at the diamond on her finger. "It's beyond amazing."

"I know we just met, but I feel like it's my duty to warn you about something."

Sadie bit down on her bottom lip. Anxiety tightened her shoulders. Was he about to tell her all the things she didn't know about Owen? She wasn't sure she wanted to hear it. Of course, if it was bad, she needed to hear it.

"My brother believes in love. He believes in happy-ever-after. But he's had his heart broken before and I don't want to see that happen to him again."

Sadie relaxed and a smile spread across her face. Thankfully, she hadn't misjudged Owen. "Is this your if-you-hurt-my-brother speech?" she asked.

"I guess it is."

"I'm no heartbreaker," she assured him.

He gave a sharp nod. "Good to know." Jonathan gulped some more water. "I mean no offense, but Owen didn't even mention you guys were in a serious relationship. I'm sort of shocked he was ready to take things to the next level."

An uneasy feeling churned in her stomach. It was alarming that Owen hadn't mentioned to his brother that he was proposing. Jonathan also didn't need to tell her how fast things were moving. "I might be just as shocked as you are. I hadn't been thinking about marriage until he asked me."

Jonathan set his empty water bottle down on the white granite countertop. "You didn't know he was going to propose?"

"No idea," she admitted.

He scratched the back of his head, his expression perplexed. For some reason that made Sadie nervous.

Owen appeared. "Your daughter needs you to tuck her in. I don't do it right." He narrowed his eyes at his brother. "You aren't down here trying to steal my girl away, are you?"

Jonathan threw his hands up. "Don't worry, little brother. Riley is the only girl I want in my life. I'm going to get out of here, so you two can enjoy the rest of your evening together."

"It was nice to meet you," Sadie called after him.

He nodded and took off. Owen gently

placed his hands on her upper arms. "What do you say we get out of here and get some dessert at Chez Louis to celebrate?"

As much as Sadie loved dessert, she was not dressed appropriately to walk into Chez Louis.

"I can't go out like this."

Owen wouldn't be deterred. "Then we'll go to my favorite ice-cream place. I've seen a woman in pajama pants there before."

Ice cream was Sadie's favorite thing in the whole world. Owen knew exactly what she needed. There was no doubt. Agreeing to marry him was the smartest thing she'd done in a long time.

GETTING ENGAGED TO someone he barely knew was the dumbest thing Owen had ever done. Jonathan could not wrap his head around it. What was his brother thinking?

Sure, this Sadie woman seemed lovely. She didn't appear to be too high-maintenance. Her brown hair had been French braided down both sides like Mindy used to do to Riley's hair. She definitely had a girl-next-door vibe going on. And she was a teacher? Goodness. How did Owen go from a socialite like Courtney to an elementary school teacher? There was no way he would be happy with someone so…normal.

It was a good thing Jonathan left Boston and came down to Florida when he did. Something was majorly off. Three months ago, Owen was completely devastated when Courtney broke things off with him after they had been together for three years. Jonathan had spent more than a few nights on the phone, trying to talk Owen down. Courtney was the one, he had said. He'd sworn he hadn't realized how much he loved her until he lost her. He'd been willing to do anything to get her back.

Jonathan pinched the bridge of his nose. How did Owen go from that to so in love with this Sadie woman that he wanted to marry her in the blink of an eye?

Something was amiss and Jonathan would find out what it was.

"Daddy, I'm thirsty," Riley said from the bed. He had hoped she was asleep, but he had known better.

"I'll get you a little bit of water. Hang on." He didn't want to go downstairs and risk interrupting the lovebirds again. He prayed there was a cup in the bathroom. No such luck.

He crept down the stairs only to find no one was there. Owen and Sadie had left. Relieved, he went into the kitchen to get a drinking glass. Unfortunately, the request for water would probably be only the first of many reasons his little girl wouldn't get a good night's rest.

Since losing her mom over two years ago, Riley struggled with going to sleep. Her bedtime routine had gone from being thirty minutes long to sometimes a two- to three-hour ordeal. Staying asleep was also a challenge. Nightmares used to wake them both more than Jonathan cared to admit. Now, Riley seemed programmed to get up multiple times in the night.

He hurried back upstairs. "Don't drink too much," he warned as he handed her the glass. Needing to use the bathroom would be the next excuse to stay up.

Riley took a sip and held out the cup for him. "Why was Uncle Owen so happy about that lady saying yes?"

"Good question," he said under his breath. He sat on the edge of the bed and got Riley tucked back in. "Uncle Owen asked her to marry him and she said she would."

"They're going to have a wedding?"

"I think so."

Riley rolled onto her side and slipped her hands between her pillow and her cheek. "Will I get to go to the wedding?"

"I would think so. You're Uncle Owen's favorite niece in the whole world."

"I'm his only niece, Daddy." She was sharp even though she was tired.

"True, but even if you weren't the only one, you would still be his favorite." He rubbed her back as her eyes began to flutter.

"I didn't get to go to your wedding when you married Mommy because I wasn't born yet."

Jonathan snickered softly. "That's usually how it works."

Riley couldn't hold her eyes open any longer. "I can go to your next wedding, though."

Everything inside him ached at the same time. Jonathan would never get married again. That wasn't the way he was built. He had ever been in love with only one woman. He'd married Mindy the same summer they graduated from college and couldn't imagine ever being with anyone else.

Riley's breathing slowed. Maybe the long trip had truly worn her out. Jonathan sat next to his daughter until he was sure she was asleep. Once he was certain, he headed back downstairs to get the rest of their stuff out of the car.

Owen had a nice house. Actually, Owen had nice *everything*. The open-floor plan made the downstairs feel even bigger than it already was. Owen had an enormous gourmet kitchen that opened up to a two-story living room with a fireplace—not that he really needed one of those in Jupiter, Florida. He had a formal dining room, which looked like no one had ever eaten in it, and a study that he seemed to use more as a trophy room than an office.

Jonathan's little brother was doing quite well for himself. He had placed rather respectably in the last couple of tournaments he played in, which meant he'd earned plenty of money to afford to live like this. All their dad could talk about was how Owen had the potential to be one of the world's best.

Jonathan golfed, but he wouldn't consider

himself much of a golfer. Owen, on the other hand, had shown potential at a young age and that meant Devin Bradley was gung ho about getting his son out on the links as much as possible. For Jonathan, playing golf was the only way to guarantee he'd get to spend time with his father and brother on the weekends when the boys were growing up.

Jonathan wasn't envious, though. He was proud of his brother and considered his own accomplishments just as important. Riley meant more to Jonathan than any trophy or accolade could. He had been married to the love of his life. He had a consulting job that allowed him to work from home so he could be with his daughter, which was especially helpful after the accident. Had it not been for that blasted accident, life would have been pretty perfect.

Jonathan heard the garage door first, then the laughter. His brother was home and he needed to make himself scarce. He headed for the stairs just as Owen and Sadie appeared.

"Everything okay?" Owen asked. "You guys need anything up there?"

"All good. Riley fell asleep faster than she has in forever."

Owen chuckled. "I told you Florida was the place for you to be. I'm always right, brother."

"Always right. That's a good one." Jonathan started up the stairs.

"Hey, before you go up, can you take a picture of us?" Owen held out his phone for his brother. "I need a good one for Instagram."

Sadie laughed. "Great. All of your adoring fans can see you're engaged to a woman who looks like she hung out with a bunch of eight- and nine-year-olds all day."

"You did hang out with a bunch of eight- and nine-year-olds most of the day. It's one of the things I love about you." Owen gave her a kiss on the cheek. Jonathan had to admit, they were cute together. "And we have to get the word out since it's going to be a short engagement."

"What's that mean?" Jonathan met this woman one hour ago. Owen had known her for only a couple of months. "How short are we talking?"

Owen threw his arm around Sadie's shoulders. "We talked about it and we want to get married this summer. I was going to take off a couple weeks in August, which is perfect."

"This summer? It's the end of May, and

you want to get married in August? This August?" That did not give Jonathan much time to figure out what was going on with his brother and to stop him from making a huge mistake.

"That's the one," Owen replied, staring back at his brother through narrowed eyes. "Are you okay?"

"Don't you think you two need a little more time to get to know each other and make the proper arrangements? Have Mom and Dad even met Sadie yet?"

Owen pressed his lips together and let out a frustrated huff from his nose. "Can you excuse me and my brother for one minute, sweetheart?"

Sadie looked like she was about to cry, which, in Jonathan's defense, was not his intention. Owen grabbed Jonathan's arm and led him into the foyer.

"Listen, I get that you weren't expecting this—"

"Not expecting it?" Jonathan whisper-yelled. "I didn't even know you were dating someone seriously, Owen. That's a lot different than not expecting that you decided to take the plunge. I didn't even know there was anyone to plunge with."

"I know," Owen defended. "I haven't been broadcasting this relationship all over the place. I also know that's sort of unusual for me, but I want this badly. So if you could lay off about time and how much of it we should take, I would really appreciate it."

"What about Sadie? Women usually need a little more time to plan the biggest day of their lives. Are you rushing her a bit?"

"Why wait when you know it's right? And Sadie will have plenty of help planning the wedding. I'm going to hire her the best wedding planner in all of Florida. Plus, she's low maintenance. She just wants to get married. None of the other stuff matters."

None of the other stuff mattered? Why was that? Maybe all of this was happening so fast because Sadie needed it to be happening that fast.

"This is a huge commitment, Owen. It's not something you should rush into. That's all I'm saying. You don't want to think she's an easygoing, low-maintenance person only to find out that she's a lot needier than you imagined."

Owen slapped his hand down on his brother's shoulder. "Don't worry about me, Jon. I know what I'm doing. I love her. She loves me. What could go wrong?"

That was a loaded question that Jon couldn't begin to answer. "If she's pressuring you into making some big gesture—"

Owen cut him off. "No one is pressuring me. I am marrying Sadie in August. We'll have a dinner at the club I can meet her family and she can meet ours. Don't worry about this. I know what I'm doing."

That was a familiar line Owen liked to use, but Jonathan had experienced too many instances where it was clear that Owen actually had no idea what he was doing. When the boys were teenagers and Owen still wasn't old enough to drive, he convinced Jonathan to give him the keys to the Volvo their dad had handed down to Jonathan when he turned sixteen. He wanted to sneak out and impress Molly Unger, who was two years older and in Jonathan's class, by showing up with wheels. He had sworn to Jonathan that he knew what he was doing. Needless to say, the younger Bradley brother ended up backing into another car in a convenience store parking lot and Jonathan was grounded by their dad for a month because he should have known better than to let Owen drive.

Jonathan wasn't going to make that kind of mistake again. He would do whatever it took to stop his brother from getting his heart broken again.

CHAPTER TWO

ALWAYS POLISHED AND SOPHISTICATED, Candice Chapman stood to greet her daughter.
Sadie was still trying to get used to her short
hair. Her mother had won the war against
cancer, but her long blond hair had been lost
in the battle. "How are you, sweetheart?"
her mother asked as she wrapped her arms
around Sadie.

Her cheeks were pink and her skin glowed.
There were no more purple circles under her
eyes or lovely floral scarves tied over her
head to hide her baldness. It was such a relief to be past all that.

"Well, look who finally made it." Paul, Sadie's older brother, didn't bother to get up.
"You called this family meeting and then
are unsurprisingly ten minutes late. Typical
Sadie."

"Leave your sister alone," their father said,
coming up from behind her. Bruce Chapman

had been waiting outside the restaurant Sadie had chosen as neutral ground until she had arrived. He didn't dare engage the other two without her there. Family mediator was her accepted role since the divorce.

Sadie hugged her mom back. "How are *you*?"

"I am better than ever," she reported, pulling back. "I went to yoga this morning and a man no older than your brother asked if I wanted to join him for a smoothie afterward."

Paul groaned. "Please tell me you said no. One stepparent my age is enough."

Sadie's father frowned and she couldn't help but feel bad for him. Five years ago, Sadie's father left their mother and, a short six months later, married a woman twenty years younger. That made Bianca closer in age to Sadie and Paul than their parents. As much as the divorce had hurt them all, Sadie loved both of her parents equally. Her older brother had had trouble accepting their father's choices after the split and liked to be as passive-aggressive about it as possible.

Their mom put her hand over her heart. "Unlike your father, I know better than to marry someone almost half my age. That doesn't mean I won't let someone buy me a smoothie when they offer."

Her dad gave her the "why-did-you-make-me-come?" look. Sadie needed to change the subject. The diamond on her finger felt like it weighed a hundred pounds. She was surprised that her mother hadn't noticed it right away. "Would you be okay with me marrying someone half your age?"

The space between her mother's eyebrows creased. Sadie held up her left hand.

"Is that—?" Her mother covered her mouth.

Paul's eyes went wide. He stood up and grabbed his sister's wrist to get a better look. "How? Are you kidding us with this? How big is this thing? Since when are you ready to get married?"

"Owen popped the question last night. We decided we want a short engagement, so there's lots to do, Mom."

Tears welled in her mother's blue eyes. "Oh, Sadie!" She threw her arms around her once more.

"Is there a reason why this Owen didn't bother to ask me for permission before popping the question?" her dad asked.

"Did you ask Bianca's father for permission?" Paul snipped.

"Don't start with me, son."

Paul folded his arms across his chest. "Start what? It's a simple question."

Sadie stepped in between her dad and brother. "Let's sit down and talk about it over lunch like I planned." Everyone took a deep breath and sat. "I feel bad that Owen hasn't met all of you yet. With his tour schedule, it's been hard to find a time to get everyone together, but I know he really wants to get to know everyone important to me."

"How long have you two been dating?" Paul asked. "I swear I only just heard about this guy a couple weeks ago and you're already engaged?"

"Do not give her a hard time," their mother said. "We've been waiting a long time for this."

Mother probably longer than daughter. The only thing worse than holding her mother's hand through the cancer treatments had been listening to her lament the fact that she might not ever get to see her only daughter get married.

"We've been dating for several weeks,

thank you very much. I'm not here to go into the details of our courtship. We're planning a short engagement. I need to make sure everyone can work with our timeline."

"How short are we talking here?" Paul asked, hiding none of his cynicism.

Sadie straightened her shoulders. She had to brace herself for their reaction. "Owen is going to take some time off from the tour in August, so we were thinking the first."

"August first?" Her dad's voice was loud enough to get the attention of people a few tables over.

"As in two months from now? You cannot get married in two months to a guy you haven't even known for two months." Her brother was taking this news as well as Owen's brother did.

"Let me get a look at the ring," her mother demanded. "I'll decide if this Owen is the one or not."

"Goodness, Candice. You can't judge a man based on the ring he proposes with," her dad said.

Paul actually agreed. "Yeah, when Haley and I got engaged, I was a poor college student. That didn't make me the wrong man for her."

"You made up for it by getting her that diamond necklace for your ten-year anniversary." Candice was all about the bling.

Sadie held out her hand for her mom to get a good look. Her mother's jaw dropped, making Sadie laugh as she folded her hands in her lap. "Owen wants to host a dinner so both sides of the family can meet before the wedding."

"I hope that means Bianca will be invited," her dad said.

"No," her mom said with a scowl at the same time Sadie said, "Of course."

"Perfect. I won't have to stop this wedding. You'll chase this guy away as soon as you put Mom and Bianca in the same room together," Paul said with a smirk.

Four years ago, when Paul's wife, Haley, had been pregnant with their first child, Candice had refused to invite Bianca to the baby shower she and Sadie had hosted. Bianca, in retaliation, had thrown her own baby shower and had done everything in her power to outdo Candice. Since then, Sadie's mom had not been allowed in the same room with Bianca for fear there could be a catfight.

Her mother glared at her father from across the table. "You will inform your wife-child not to speak to me or speak about me during any of these wedding events. I will not have her ruin this for our daughter."

"The only one acting like a child is you."

"Don't talk to Mom that way," Paul said, coming to her defense.

"Stop it," Sadie said with enough oomph to get them to listen. "We are all adults, including Bianca, and I would hope we could manage to get through one dinner together without making a scene." This was the exact reason Owen was not invited to this luncheon to share their good news. These three needed firm boundaries set before she could present them to her future husband.

The thought that she could have a husband in two short months gave her pause. How was this happening? It was unlike her to jump in head first. She couldn't let anyone in her family know she had some apprehensions. Her mother wouldn't hear it and her dad and brother would jump all over it and feed all her fears.

Paul shook his head. "I can't believe you are okay with this, Mom. She's marrying someone you haven't even met yet. Isn't that a bit alarming?"

"I'm alarmed," their dad chimed in. Of course their negative opinion on Sadie's engagement would be the one thing her dad and brother managed to agree on.

"He should have at least asked for Mom and Dad's blessing before asking you to marry him. Something is not right with this guy."

Sadie's face felt hot. First of all, getting someone's blessing could easily be construed as getting someone's permission. She was a grown woman marrying a grown man. They didn't need her parents' permission to get married. Given her brother's reaction to the news they were dating, his disapproval was shocking.

"This guy? When I first told you I was dating Owen Bradley, you thought it was the best thing ever. You asked me to see if he could get you a tee time at some golf course."

"TPC Sawgrass is not some golf course," Paul argued as if Sadie knew anything about golf.

"Okay, you're making my point for me.

You were impressed before you met him. Why would wanting to marry me make him any less impressive?"

Paul's shoulders slumped. "I was impressed you were dating a professional golfer. I figured I would get to meet him and maybe play some golf with him before I had to watch Dad walk you down the aisle."

"Oh, leave your sister alone," their mom said to Paul. "I'm sure she can give you a list of reasons why she wants to marry Owen. Your sister has always been a cautious and conscientious person. She isn't entering into this lightly."

"You got a list?" Paul asked Sadie. He cocked his head to the side, waiting for her to answer.

Luckily, Sadie had been making a list since Owen had asked to marry her. "I have a long list of reasons to marry him, thank you very much." She listed them off, using her fingers to count them. "He's kind, generous, successful, has good taste in everything, is a good brother and son, he's observant, funny and he loves ice cream as much as I do."

"See?" their mother said. "She could think of all that right off the top of her head."

Paul still seemed unconvinced. "I'll leave you alone if you can tell me the number one reason you want to marry him," he said.

Sadie had to stop and think about it. She had rattled off so many good traits, she wasn't sure which one was the best. Being kind was important. Her brother might like that he was generous the best. But what truly convinced her to marry him?

"Sadie, the fact that you have to think about this is concerning me," her father said, breaking her concentration.

She anxiously spun the ring around her finger and frowned. "I know exactly what's most important. He's a good man. He's a good man who will take good care of me the rest of my life."

"And you love him," her mother added.

Sadie felt her stomach knot. Love? Oh goodness, she hadn't even thought about love. She hadn't even said those words to Owen yet. She could attest to falling in love with him. Close enough.

"Of course, Mom. We're in love. Is there any other reason better than that to get married?"

Paul shook his head. "No better reason.

You should never marry someone you aren't one hundred percent in love with, Sadie. And he better be completely and totally head over heels for you. I don't want you to marry someone who ends up running off with someone half his age as soon as you start getting wrinkles."

Their dad let out an exasperated sigh. Their mother scowled. "I do not have wrinkles."

Sadie tried to control her expression. "Owen and I are totally in love, so no worries."

"Paul, ask the waitress for a pen," her mom said, digging in her purse and pulling out her pocket calendar. "We need to start making a to-do list. Two months is not much time to get everything done, but luckily, you have me to help."

Thankfully, her mother was over the moon about a wedding. The other two would be won over as soon as they met Owen. The love would work itself out. There was no reason she wouldn't fall in love with Owen...eventually.

THE GUIDE IN the aviary adjusted the wire-rimmed glasses on her face. "Even though birds are usually the hunters and bugs are the prey, sometimes the opposite is true. Believe it or not, the praying mantis has been known to make a snack out of these little hummingbirds."

Jonathan set Riley back on her feet after lifting her up to get a good view of the hummingbird exhibit. She stuck out her tongue and scrunched up her face in disgust. "They don't look like they taste very good."

"I can think of something that tastes better," Owen said. "Let's go get some cotton candy."

Palm Beach Zoo was the perfect first stop on this vacation for Riley. She loved all kinds of animals, and this place delivered on some of the best. First stop had been the American pink flamingos before they discovered the zoo also had Chilean flamingos. After taking pictures in front of both, they had decided to escape the obnoxiously hot Florida sun for a few minutes by going inside the aviary.

"I have an interesting fact about the praying mantis," Jonathan said. "The female eats the male after they mate. I think Mother Nature's giving us a clear message."

Owen was busy typing his own message on his phone. "Oh yeah, what's that?"

"It's an obvious warning that no creature should jump into any relationship too quickly. Bad things will happen."

Owen slipped his phone into his pocket, a shocked expression on his clean-shaven face. "Wow, really? Are you insinuating that my fiancée plans to eat me as soon as we get married?"

Riley's face twisted in confusion. "What's a fiancée? Is it a bug?"

"No, silly girl. Sadie's my fiancée. And I think we all agree she is clearly not a killer bug." Owen directed his last comment toward his brother.

Jonathan smirked. At least he got his brother's attention. More than anything, he wanted his brother to think about what he was doing. The only explanation for this unusually fast engagement had to be that he was making decisions based purely on emotion instead of reason.

"Sadie is coming here to meet up with us, by the way. I sure hope we won't be having any other extra lessons on animal behavior that might offend my beautiful fiancée."

Jonathan tried to play innocent. "I wasn't trying to offend anyone. I was sharing a fun fact."

"Here's a fun fact," Owen said, taking Riley by the hand and leading her toward the concession stand. "You two are going to love living in Florida. I don't understand why your dad didn't pack up everything before coming down here."

How quickly the tables had turned. From a conversation one brother didn't want to have to one the other brother didn't want anything to do with. Jonathan had not made any decisions about moving. He certainly wouldn't be pressured into it by his little brother. Unlike Owen, Jonathan liked to think about all the pros and cons of his choices before making a major life decision.

"We agreed to come down for the summer to help you and so I could investigate the *possibility* of moving back. Florida has always been a great place to visit, but we're not making any major life changes anytime soon."

"Don't you want to live close to Uncle Owen and Grandma and Grandpa?" Owen asked Riley. "You know how much your grandma loves to spoil you."

Riley looked to her dad. He could see the hope mixed with concern in her eyes. She didn't want to say the wrong thing, but he could tell she wanted to say yes. She was always so cautious, overly aware of his reaction to everything since the accident.

"It would be superfun to live by them. Right, Riley?" He tried his best to sound upbeat. She smiled up at him with those big brown eyes and nodded. "But Boston is still home."

"I don't know what there's to think about. Your family is here. Your job allows you to live anywhere you want. There's nothing tying you to Boston other than a mortgage. Sell your house and come back home!"

Easy for him to say. Jonathan felt like there was a boulder pressing down on his chest. He still felt undeniably tied to Boston. It was where he and Riley had made all of their memories with Mindy. It was where his wife was buried. Leaving there would mean leaving Mindy behind. He wasn't sure he was ready to do that yet.

"What color cotton candy do you want, Riley?" Owen asked, pulling her attention from the nearby cranes and their long, skinny legs with knees that bent the wrong way.

"Pink!"

Pink was her favorite color. If she could live in a pink world, she'd be happy. What Jonathan wouldn't do to see Riley happy, truly happy. She had struggled with so much sadness over the last couple of years. He'd noticed that even when she smiled or laughed, her whole heart didn't seem in it.

"You want some?" Owen asked Jonathan.

There was no way Riley would be eating the entire bag of sugar her uncle planned to buy her by herself. "I'm good," he replied.

"I'm going to get Sadie some. She's got a major sweet tooth. What color should I get her?"

"Pink!" Riley was nothing if not predictable.

"What's Sadie's favorite color?" Jonathan asked, curious if his brother even knew that detail about his fiancée.

Owen adjusted the visor on his head. "I bet she'd like the purple one."

The man selling the concessions pulled down pink and purple bags of fluffy candy floss. Owen handed him some cash and gave

Riley her bag. Jonathan reminded his delighted daughter to say thank you.

Owen told her it was his pleasure just as his phone chimed with a text. His face lit up with a wide smile. "Sadie's here. Let's go meet her by the fountain."

There had been no mention of Sadie joining them when they headed out this afternoon. According to Owen, she was telling her family about the engagement. Without him, which was odd. Wouldn't they want to meet the man she was supposed to marry in a few months?

"Is purple her favorite color?"

Owen's head turned in Jonathan's direction. His eyebrows pinched together. "What?"

"Is purple Sadie's favorite color?"

"Why do you care what color's her favorite?"

"I don't care, but I bet you can tell me Courtney's favorite color just like I can tell you that Mindy's favorite color was turquoise."

Owen's jaw tensed and his eyes narrowed. Jonathan had hit a huge nerve. "You need to stop. Right now."

It was probably wrong to bring Courtney

into this, but there was a point to be made. It wasn't that long ago Owen had been lamenting that he regretted not asking Courtney to marry him. Jonathan couldn't understand how he could have learned enough about this woman to know that she was truly the right person for him.

"I'm not trying to make you mad."

"Well, please don't start trying because you're doing quite a good job with very little effort apparently." Owen picked up the pace and left Jonathan and Riley trailing behind him.

"He sounds really mad," Riley said. Her tongue was already stained bright pink from cotton candy that was also sticking to her fingers.

Jonathan took the bag from her and pulled off a bit for himself. The sugary goodness melted on his tongue. "Your uncle just hates it when I'm right."

Owen took off running as soon as he spotted Sadie. He lifted her off her feet and kissed her like there was no tomorrow. Jonathan had to avert her eyes from the PDA. His brother was clearly trying to make his own point right now.

Jonathan could only stare at her once his brother's mouth was not attached to hers. Her hair was pulled back into a ponytail and she wore jean shorts and a plain T-shirt, and had running shoes on her feet. Nothing was designer. None of it would be seen on a runway. She didn't appear to be wearing any makeup, not that she needed it, and instead of a fancy, overpriced purse, she had a drawstring bag strapped to her back. She was the complete opposite of every woman and girl Owen had dated his entire life.

"I hope I haven't missed all the fun," Sadie said with cheeks the color of apples.

"You didn't," Riley assured her. Jonathan was surprised she attempted to be so outgoing. "We only saw the pink flamingos and some other birds that get eaten by bugs who eat their fiancées. It's good you aren't a bug because I don't want you to eat my uncle. He bought you cotton candy. You can eat that!"

The look on Sadie's face was priceless, but Jonathan felt sort of bad. Owen was almost too shocked to speak. When he finally gathered his thoughts, he handed her the purple bag of cotton candy. "You can thank my brother for these amazing fun facts. We don't have to walk around the park with him if his sense of humor annoys you as much as it annoys me."

Sadie's gaze moved from Jonathan to Owen and back to Jonathan. The way she tried to read him reminded him of Riley. She wanted to know if she was welcome or not. Guilt weighed down his shoulders. It truly wasn't his intention to make Owen mad. All he wanted to do was look out for his brother's best interest. He needed to spend some time with Sadie and Owen if he was going to be sure she wasn't right for him.

"I promise to keep all my fun facts to myself the rest of the day. I would not want Sadie to think I am annoying."

"I would never think that. I love fun facts. I'm a teacher. I spend all my time trying to think of ways to make facts fun. Don't feel like you can't say stuff because I'm here."

Her anxiety was palpable. It wasn't hard to tell that today's goal was to win over her future in-law.

"Don't worry about him." Owen glared in his brother's direction. "Jonathan has no trouble speaking his mind. It's one of his less attractive qualities. Where should we take Sadie first, Riley?"

"Wanna see the otters?" Riley asked.

Jonathan noticed some of the tension leave Sadie's face. "I would love to see the otters. They're my favorite."

"Your favorite animal is an otter? My favorite is a tiger." Owen took her and Riley by the hand but stared hard at Jonathan. "I'm told it's so important for us to know these things about each other. Good thing we have our entire lives to discover all of our other favorite things."

Jonathan was going to keep his mouth shut the rest of the day. Better to be quiet and observe rather than speak and annoy. If he was going to figure out if Sadie was the one, he would need to be less vocal about his fear that she wasn't.

CHAPTER THREE

NEGATIVE TEN. THAT was where Sadie would rate her chances of impressing Jonathan on a scale of one to ten. She wasn't an overly confident person to begin with, so throw in the pressure of gaining the approval of the most important person in Owen's life and she was sure she would fail.

Sadie got tongue-tied around new people. She wasn't flirty and witty like some of her friends. Sadie was and always would be much more comfortable standing in front of a room of eight- and nine-year-olds, who hung on her every word and thought she was the smartest person they'd ever met.

Thankfully, Jonathan had Riley. She was Sadie's dream audience, and the little girl's curiosity was contagious. She wanted to know everything Sadie knew about every animal they saw.

"Is that a leopard?" Riley asked, pushing

her hair out of her face as they neared the cat's enclosure. The breeze had kicked up and Riley's dark locks were flying all over the place.

Sadie always kept an extra hairband in her wallet. She took it out. "Would it be okay if I gave you a ponytail like mine?" Riley nodded and let Sadie gather all that hair up. "I know those look like leopards because they both have spots, but that's a jaguar."

"That has to be a leopard. It looks nothing like the Jaguar in my garage," Owen said with a playful smile.

She tried not to roll her eyes. When they first met, Sadie had been nervous to even sit in his expensive car. It must have cost more than she made in an entire year. "We're talking about the animal, not the car. Now that you can see with all that hair out of your eyes, let's read what the sign has to say about it."

Riley skipped over. She stared at the sign for a second and turned to Sadie. "Can you read it?"

The teacher in her couldn't help herself. "Let's read it together. You start."

Riley pressed her lips together and squinted

her eyes a bit. "Jaguars are the..." She paused. She glanced up at Sadie.

"Largest of the cats in the Americas," Jonathan finished for her. "Of all the big cats, only the lion and tiger are bigger."

Sadie had to bite her tongue. As much as she wanted to inform him that if he continued to jump in and read words that tripped Riley up, it would actually make learning to sound out words harder for the little girl, that probably wouldn't win her any brownie points.

"Look what it says about them being similar to leopards," she said, pointing to that part for Riley.

"Jaguars are sim...simi..."

Jonathan came to her rescue again. "Similar to leopards but are much more muscular and powerful."

Sadie couldn't hold back any longer. "It's okay if it takes her a couple tries to get it. I'm used to being patient with a new reader."

"Reading's not her favorite. She loves being read to, but it's a lot of pressure to read aloud."

Riley's gaze fell to the ground. "I stink at reading."

Sadie's teacher heart hurt. She hated it when kids put down their abilities so early in their learning. In today's world of instant gratification, they assumed they were supposed to know it all before they'd even been taught.

"Lots of people think reading is hard when they first learn to do it. I am so happy to hear you love listening to stories. Books are magic to me. They can teach you things you didn't know or take you to places you've never been. I love listening to stories, too."

"You do?" Riley didn't seem convinced.

"I listen to audiobooks all the time. It's my favorite thing to do when I'm in the car. You want to know what my favorite book is?"

"What?"

"*Charlotte's Web.* Have you heard of it?" Riley shook her head. Sadie loved being able to introduce new generations to a book that she had loved since she was Riley's age. "Oh my goodness! We'll have to read it while you're here. It's the best."

"Does it have animals in it?"

"Does it have animals in it? It's all about animals. You're going to *love* it."

Jonathan cleared his throat. "Doesn't the S-P-I-D-E-R D-I-E at the end?" He rattled off the letters so fast that even if Riley knew how to read those words, she would have been confused.

"Yes, but—"

"That's not the book for her. I would have thought a teacher would be more sensitive." Jonathan took his daughter's hand and pulled her away. "Come on, Riley, I think I see some monkeys up ahead."

Owen put his hand on Sadie's arm as she started to go after them. She wanted to explain that she meant no harm, that the story ended much happier than perhaps he remembered.

"Don't bother. Ever since they lost Riley's mom, he's been so overprotective. He spends every waking moment trying to protect Riley from every little thing, as if that's even possible."

Sadie had known Jonathan's wife had died in a tragic car accident a couple of years ago but hadn't thought her favorite children's book would trigger something. She hadn't meant to stir up negative emotions.

"I never would suggest Riley read something that could retraumatize her," she said in her defense.

Owen rubbed his hands up and down her

upper arms. "Of course you wouldn't. He's overreacting. I agree with you, I think Riley would love that book."

Sadie felt like a failure. This was worse than simply making a bad impression. "I'm pretty sure your brother hates me."

"He doesn't hate you. He's judgmental. A little bit of a know-it-all. Always has to be right. Basically, your typical annoying big brother."

His description made Sadie laugh. She had one of those, too. Hopefully, Paul wouldn't be so tough to win over in the end. Owen had his interesting career and long list of accomplishments to help sell himself as Mr. Right. Sadie would have to work a lot harder to show she wasn't a terrible teacher who loved to make children cry.

"Come on," Owen held out his hand. "Let's go see the monkeys. I love their music. Did you know that they outsold the Beatles back in 1967?"

Sadie burst out laughing. "You are so weird."

JONATHAN NEEDED A minute or two to regroup. He didn't need Sadie trying to force Riley to read when all his daughter wanted to do was enjoy a nice summer day at the zoo. Why did teachers have to be so pushy?

The worst part was she sounded exactly like Riley's third-grade teacher back in Boston. That woman had wanted Riley to get special reading services. Jonathan had declined because his daughter didn't need special services. Riley was one of the smartest kids he knew. Reading might have been a little more difficult for her, but maybe they needed to stop pressuring her so much.

"Dad, why can't I read the book with Sadie?"

"You wouldn't like it."

"She said it has animals in it. I love animals."

"It's for older kids. You can read it when you're older."

Her eyebrows pinched together. She looked so much like her mother when she did that. "I'm not a baby. I'm going into fourth grade. I can read older books."

No one was more aware of how fast she was growing up than Jonathan was. "I know you're not a baby. I'm just saying I don't think you would like it. It has too much sad stuff in it."

"If Sadie likes it, I think I will like it, too."

Oh boy. Jonathan suddenly could envision his future and teenage Riley telling him she could do this or that because everyone else did it. He was not ready for that. "Check out those monkeys," he said, pointing at the two monkeys hanging from a rope strung across the enclosure. He hoped changing the subject would work this time.

Owen and Sadie strolled up hand in hand. So much for them getting the hint that he needed some space.

"Can you take a picture of us?" Owen asked. "I need a couple good photos to post online."

"Since when are you all about posting on social media?" Jonathan didn't have any social media accounts. He didn't understand people's fascination with it. Courtney used to post every five seconds. In fact, Owen used to complain that she thought she needed to take a picture of every meal she ate as if people cared what she had for breakfast, lunch and dinner.

Owen threw his arm around Sadie's shoulders. "I've got a beautiful fiancée to show off. Can you take a picture of us or what?"

Jonathan took his brother's phone and snapped a couple pictures for him. Sadie's smile faded as soon as the photo session was over.

"Do you want me to take some pictures on your phone so you can post on all your accounts, too?" he offered.

Sadie shook her head. "I have a Facebook account so I can see what's going on with all of my high school and college friends, but I don't post much on there."

She really was the exact opposite of the kind of woman Owen usually fell for. It also meant that it would be harder for him to do some snooping. He had planned to team up with his mother, who was secretly the queen of internet stalking. If Sadie didn't have anything to stalk, how would they figure out why things were moving so quickly between her and his brother?

"Can we go to the gift shop?" Riley asked as they approached the little marketplace. Racks of T-shirts and a huge box of stuffed animals were outside to lure all the children inside.

"Of course we can," Owen said, leading the way. "Uncle Owen will get you anything you want."

"Within reason," Jonathan called after her as she and Owen nearly sprinted inside. Jonathan and Sadie lingered outside while she looked at some stuffed monkeys in one of the outdoor sidewalk displays.

"He's excited to spoil her. He takes his job as uncle very seriously," Sadie said. *At least he took something seriously.* "He's actually really glad both of you are here. He seems to think he can convince you to move back to Florida permanently."

"Yeah, he's been bugging me about it. I don't know why he suddenly thinks I'm going to make a huge, life-altering decision just because he asked me to."

Sadie ran her hand down her ponytail. "Yeah, he has a way of doing that. Some of us are easier to convince, I guess."

"Did he need to *convince* you to get engaged? I know you said you weren't expecting a proposal, but you want to be engaged, right?"

Her eyes went big. "Yeah, of course! I'm

happy we're engaged. Your brother is great. He's a good man."

Something wasn't right. Jonathan couldn't put his finger on it, and it was driving him nuts. They silently walked around the displays for a few minutes. Sadie shook a stuffed giraffe so its floppy legs appeared to be dancing in front of a toddler in a stroller. The little boy squealed with delight.

"He's adorable," Sadie said to the mom.

"And a handful," the mom replied, sounding a bit haggard. "That's why he's strapped into the stroller. It's the only way I can keep track of him."

"Full hands mean a full heart. So much better than empty."

The woman gave her a sheepish smile. "I suppose you're right."

Sadie was right. As hard as it was to be a single parent at times, Jonathan couldn't imagine a world without Riley in it. What she did to fill him up was worth way more than whatever energy she depleted.

The woman moved on and Jonathan moved closer to Sadie. "Have you and Owen talked about having kids?"

Sadie shook her head. "No, not really. Like

I said, we barely talked about marriage until he proposed."

"Probably a good idea to get on the same page about that, don't you think?"

"I can tell Owen loves kids. He's so good with them. He came to school to surprise me with lunch one time and got to meet my class. He was hilarious, answered all their silly questions. I think he'll be a great dad."

Jonathan knew his brother liked being an uncle, but last he had heard, Owen was in no hurry to have his own. Children didn't exactly fit into his lifestyle. Maybe that had changed since meeting Sadie. Jonathan didn't want to speak out of turn.

"Whose idea was it to get married so fast?"

"Owen has the time off in August, so he thought that was the best time." She fidgeted with the stuffed animal in her hands even though she tried to sound nonchalant.

Jonathan pulled a pink T-shirt off the rack. On sale, they still wanted twenty-five dollars. Good thing Uncle Owen was paying. "I'm sure my brother will have time off next August, as well. I mean, he's playing golf almost every week this summer. That's why Riley and I are staying at his house. We wouldn't be imposing and we could house-sit while he's gone. Why not give yourselves some time?"

"Time." She let out a humorless chuckle. "What I've learned about time over the last year is that there are no guarantees when it comes to how much any of us have."

That was an interesting answer, but Jonathan wouldn't get to ask a follow-up question because Riley and Owen were on their way out of the gift shop with more than one bag full of stuff and a giant stuffed tiger that didn't look like it would even fit in the car for the ride home.

"What in the world?"

"Don't say it," Owen said.

"You bought my daughter a tiger? I thought tigers were your favorite, not hers."

"They are. Riley thought I should have one. She got other things for herself."

"This is yours? Why am I carrying it?"

"Sadie drove separately. Tanya the tiger can go in the back seat of your car and I'll drive to Mom and Dad's with my lovely fiancée." He handed the oversize tiger to Jonathan before walking over to Sadie and kissing her on the cheek. Owen ignored him and pulled out a little stuffed otter. "We got you something, too."

Sadie put her hand over her heart. "Aw! You two are so sweet."

"They didn't have any life-size ones, but Riley thought this one was perfect for you."

They were cute together. Jonathan couldn't deny it, but he still had lingering doubts that either one of them truly knew what they were getting themselves into.

"Dad, Uncle Owen got me this pink flamingo." Riley slipped a headband with a bright pink flamingo attached to it on her head.

"It's very…pink. I can see why you like it." Something Owen said needed to be addressed. "Wait, why are you going to Mom and Dad's?"

"We're all going. Mom just called and invited us all over for dinner."

Sadie's face blanched. "I have to meet your parents? Today?"

Owen put his arm around her. "Don't worry. They can't wait to meet you. My mom is so excited about our engagement."

Jonathan thought that was real funny because he had been there when Owen called to drop the bomb on his parents that he was engaged. Their dad hadn't had much to say while their mom had had about a million questions. She had many of the same concerns as Jonathan. He couldn't wait to have dinner with them. No one was better at sniffing out the truth than Beth Bradley.

CHAPTER FOUR

Why did meeting the parents feel more like heading into a lion's den? As a teacher, she'd survived many parent/teacher conferences, but talking to a third-grader's mom about how their son was doing in math was a lot different from talking to a grown man's mother about why she was worthy of the woman's son's heart.

"You have a lovely home, Mrs. Bradley." Owen's mother would get along well with Sadie's. They both could stage houses for a living. Sadie felt like she was sitting in a room straight out of *Better Homes and Garden* magazine.

Owen's mom set a tray of drinking glasses and a pitcher of lemonade on the coffee table. "Please, call me Beth. We're going to be related in a couple months. No need to be so formal."

Jonathan picked up the pitcher and began

to pour drinks for everyone. Riley happily accepted a glass and let out a loud belch.

"Riley Marie!" her grandmother exclaimed. "Where are your manners?"

"You are definitely your father's daughter," Owen said, holding his hand out for a high five.

Riley slapped hands with her uncle. "Excuse me, Gramma."

Jonathan appeared to be fighting the urge to laugh. He was so much less intimidating when he wore a smile.

Sadie crossed and uncrossed her legs. She wanted so badly to give herself a good sniff. She couldn't help but wonder if she smelled terrible. She feared the combination of zoo and sweat was surely lethal to noses everywhere.

"I'm sorry that we didn't have any time to clean up after our visit to the zoo. I don't usually show up to meet my future in-laws looking like I just came from the gym." She tucked a lock of hair that fell out of her ponytail behind her ear.

Beth's interest was piqued for all the wrong reasons. Her head swung Sadie's way. "How many future in-laws have you met with?"

"Oh, no, no, no." Sadie's face was on fire. "I've never had future in-laws before. You're the first, I swear. I meant I don't usually meet new people looking so disheveled."

Ugh. Did that sound vain or did that make her sound like she simply took pride in her appearance? How she looked wasn't that important, but making an effort to be presentable was.

"Well, we understand you all came from the zoo," Beth said, making Sadie feel so much better. "But I am used to Owen bringing home girlfriends who somehow managed to look flawless day or night. I used to wonder if Courtney had a secret posse of makeup artists follow her around. I don't know how she managed to look like the real-life version of a filtered Instagram photo at all times."

From better to worse in that matter of two seconds. Sadie knew there was a former girlfriend, but Owen did not talk about her. It was not very reassuring to know she was basically some kind of supermodel.

Owen stiffened a bit next to her. "Mom," he said with a shake of his head.

Jonathan offered Sadie a glass of lemonade. "I think being low maintenance is never a bad thing," he said. She downed her drink much like Riley had, hoping it would help her swallow the lump in her throat.

"Owen tells us you're a schoolteacher," Mr. Bradley said from his leather recliner. He had silver-gray hair and the same blue eyes as his sons.

"I am. I teach third grade."

"Could any of your students burp as loud as Riley can?" Owen asked, prompting Riley to attempt another one.

Jonathan cleared his throat and gave Riley a pointed look. She quickly stopped her silly behavior. Her grandma stood up. "Why don't you help me get dinner ready before you get yourself into more trouble, Little Miss Riley."

"I can help," Sadie offered. She went to stand and accidentally bumped the coffee table. One of the glasses of lemonade tipped over and spilled onto the wood floor. She immediately began to profusely apologize. Not only was she less glamorous than Owen's ex, she also managed to be more clumsy. She would bet big money that Courtney had never soiled Beth's beautiful home.

"Jonathan, grab a towel from the kitchen," his mom said, picking up the knocked-over glass and using her hand to stop the flow of lemonade from continuing onto the floor.

Sadie followed Jonathan into the kitchen, hoping she could actually be of some help. He snagged a towel out of one of the drawers.

"We should get one a little wet or the floor will be all sticky."

"Good call." He tossed her a second one.

Sadie held the towel under the water faucet. It would have been nice if Owen had prepared her a bit better for this meeting. She was not ready for this. Maybe she wasn't ready for any of this.

"I didn't think it was possible to make someone like me less than you do, but something tells me your mom will be encouraging Owen to think twice about this engagement after tonight."

Jonathan seemed genuinely surprised by the thought she let escape out of her mouth. "Have I made you feel like I don't like you?"

Sadie shook her head, not wanting to continue the conversation she hadn't meant to start. "Ignore me."

He came up beside her and placed a gentle hand on her shoulder. "You're fine, Sadie. It takes a lot more than some spilled lemonade to make my mom dislike you."

She squeezed the excess water from the towel. "Well, the night is still young. I'm sure I can mess up some more."

"Hey, I know this is stressful. I'm sure you weren't too thrilled that my brother decided to spring dinner with the parents on you with no warning, but you should know Owen doesn't understand those feelings. He's always been the most popular person in the room. He has no fear, no anxiety because everyone likes him. He doesn't get it that that's not everyone else's reality."

Sadie had to remind herself not to cry even though it was nice to hear someone could see things from her perspective. She was so mad that Owen didn't think about how she would feel. He didn't even consider that she would need some advanced notice before meeting his parents.

"You also haven't made a negative impression."

The tears threatened anyway. "You're being nice to me right now, but I can tell you don't like me. I've been getting negative vibes from you all day, and I am pretty good at reading people." Jonathan's face had given away his emotion all day. He was probably terrible at poker.

"Jonathan! What is going on in there?" his mom shouted from the other room. "I need a towel!"

"Great," Sadie rushed out to clean up the lemonade. "More reasons."

JONATHAN FELT LIKE a heel. Honestly, he was more worried about Owen's impulsive behavior than he was about Sadie being a bad person. There was no doubt she was sweet and kind. She seemed to have a good head on her shoulders. Lacked a little confidence, but maybe that was because he was giving her a complex.

He followed Sadie out to the living room with the dry towel in his hands. They helped his mom clean up the spill and Jonathan offered to take the towels to the laundry room.

Owen was waiting in the hall when he came out. He stood with his arms crossed over his chest. Pictures of them as little boys hung on the wall behind him. His brother wasn't a kid anymore, though.

"Why did Sadie look like she was about

to cry? Did you say something to her in the kitchen?"

"I told her not to worry about Mom. She thinks everyone in this family hates her except for you."

Owen gave him a little shove on the shoulder. "Yeah, I wonder who could have made her feel like that. All the passive-aggressive comments need to stop. Can you just be nice to her? She's not like other women I've dated, and that's not a bad thing."

It wasn't. It might have been the best reason for Jonathan to give his blessing in the end. Maybe Sadie's humility would rub off on Owen. "How about you help her out a little more with Mom? Tell her to ask Mom about her garden. You know how proud Mom is of that. Give her a fighting chance."

Owen dropped his arms to his side. "That's a good idea."

"She feels really overwhelmed. You didn't give her enough warning that she was going to be in this position. I know you have no fear that you won't win over everyone in her family when you meet them, but Sadie isn't you. She's got a bit more self-doubt than you do."

"She wouldn't have so much self-doubt if

Mom didn't bring up Courtney. What was that about?"

"You know how Mom felt about Courtney." Their mom had loved Courtney and was heartbroken when she broke up with Owen. She had assumed they were going to get married. It was probably hard for her to imagine Owen with someone else, especially someone she didn't know at all.

Owen's head dropped and his hands went to his hips. "Yeah, well, hopefully Mom remembers how I felt about Courtney. I can't talk about her. I *really* don't want to talk about her in front of Sadie."

Gone was Mr. Overconfident. If there was one thing that completely deflated Owen's ego, it was the reminder that Courtney left him.

"I'll talk to Mom. You need to go hold your fiancée's hand and make her feel comfortable around Mom and Dad."

"You're going to be nicer?"

"I haven't been mean, have I?"

"You haven't been nice or mean. You've been indifferent, and to someone trying to get to know you, it can feel mean."

Jonathan was impressed with Owen's empathy. Maybe he wasn't completely oblivious to how other people might feel. They returned to the living room to find Sadie watching television with their dad. He had on some golf tournament and was sharing with her all of his insights into each player.

"This guy has needed to work on his short game for two years now. He can't chip to save his life. I don't know how he expects to win a major when he can't chip."

"Do you think golfers in general spend too much time working on putting or at the driving range when they should be practicing chipping?" Sadie asked. It was kind of cute to hear her trying to bond with their dad. She apparently didn't need any coaching to cue her that letting the man talk about golf would completely win him over.

"Well, I think you need to work on whatever you need to work on. I used to tell Owen that he couldn't neglect one for the other. They are all equally important. When we used to go out and he'd miss a putt, I would make him practice that same putt ten more times. Same thing when he'd flub a chip or get stuck in a trap. Ten drives off the tee if that's what he needed. These pros get complacent. They figure a bad shot is just a bad shot. But if they don't put in the time to correct it, they end up like this guy—unable to chip for two years."

"He was the best coach I ever had," Owen said, taking a seat next to Sadie. He took her by the hand and gave it a squeeze. She let her head rest on his shoulder for a second.

It was good to see her smile. Jonathan pulled his gaze away from them. What in the world made him think that? That was his brother's fiancée. He shouldn't be thinking about her beautiful smile.

Jonathan hightailed it into the kitchen, where Riley was helping her grandma put the finishing touches on dinner. He had noticed how amazing it had smelled in here when he came to get the towels earlier. His mom was the kind of cook who made him miss those days he lived under her roof. She was roasting some kind of meat in the oven with some garlic potatoes that were surely to die for.

"Can I help?" he asked.

"Of course you can, sweetheart." His mom made room for him at the kitchen island. "You can butter the top of the rolls before we put them in the oven."

Riley stood on a stool with one of his mom's aprons tied around her little waist. She was busy plucking grapes off the vine and dropping them in a bowl that was already half full of strawberries and blueberries.

His mom handed him a basting brush and a bowl of melted butter. "I think I know what's going on with you-know-who and you-know-who."

No one was better at talking without saying anything than his mother.

"Oh, yeah? What did you find out exactly?" Sadie had made it clear she wasn't on much social media and what she was on, she didn't post much.

"Well, you-know-who doesn't have an Instagram, but she does have a—"

Jonathan had to interrupt. "Facebook, but she told me she's not really on social media. What could you have possibly learned from someone who doesn't go on there very often?"

His mom laughed. "Just because she doesn't post often doesn't mean she doesn't post at all. In fact, to me that means that what she does post is more meaningful. She doesn't just post for the heck of it."

Now his curiosity was piqued. "What did she post?"

She glanced at Riley, who wasn't paying attention before continuing. "I think her mom has C-A-N-C-E-R. She was asking for lots of prayers a few months ago when her mom went in for a scan."

That made some of what Sadie had said over the last couple of days make more sense. Her comments about time not being guaranteed had to be inspired by her mom's illness. Was she hurrying to get married because she was worried her mother was dying?

"But it's not her social media that made me take pause."

Jonathan knew Owen had been posting a bunch recently, but he couldn't imagine what would have grabbed his mom's attention. "He's been more active lately."

"No, not him. *Courtney*," she whispered.

"What? I thought you were told to unfollow her after they broke up. He was very adamant about it."

"What else can I do, Gramma?" Riley asked.

"Why don't you take these appetizers out to our guests." His mom opened the refrigerator and pulled out a platter with cubed cheese and a variety of meats. She added some crackers and put a handful of the grapes in the center. "Tell Grandpa that this is not the white cheese that he likes. Tell him to stick with the orange kind."

Once Riley was out of the room, Jonathan pounced. "Why are you still following her?"

"Because she didn't unfollow me and she was the one who broke up with him. I thought maybe she would come back to him, so I muted her instead of unfriending her."

"Muted?"

"It's when you're still friends, but their posts don't show up in your feed. The only way I can see what she posts is if I go to her page on purpose."

Jonathan's mother was a sixty-one-year-old social media expert. He, on the other hand, was lucky if he could remember his login.

"So what is she posting that makes you think you know what's going on with Owen?"

"She's engaged."

It took only those two words to blow Jonathan's mind. Courtney had dumped Owen because he wouldn't commit. It wasn't surprising that she had turned around and agreed to marry the very next guy she dated. What was surprising was Owen's reaction to it. There was no way he didn't know. There was no way that asking Sadie to marry him wasn't in response to Courtney's engagement.

"That is the worst reason ever to get engaged. Are you going to say something to him? He can't marry Sadie because Courtney found someone else."

His mom put her hand up and shook her head. "No way. I'm not telling him I know anything about it. You know your brother. If we tell him he can't do something, he'll try that much harder to do exactly that."

She was so right. Owen had always been driven to prove all of his critics wrong. It was why Jonathan hadn't come right out and said he shouldn't rush into this marriage. It was why he only tried to raise some questions he needed his brother to ask himself. Owen needed to feel like whatever he did was his idea and no one else's.

"Did you notice that he purposely chose a woman who is the exact opposite of Courtney? And that he's been spamming his social media with pictures of him and Sadie?"

"He wants Courtney to see."

His mom nodded. "That's what I think."

"What does he think is going to happen? Courtney will see that he's engaged and come running back to him? She's not going to do that. She's going to be upset that he's only been dating Sadie for over a month and was able to commit to her."

"It's good that you're here, sweetheart," she said, leaning against him. "Hopefully, you can get him to open up to you eventually."

"Eventually?" Jonathan felt an enormous amount of pressure. "I think we need to get him to open up as soon as possible. Preferably *before* he gets married. And on top of that, he's not even going to be around the next two months because he's trying to get as many tournaments in as possible."

"If anyone can do it, it's you."

He wasn't sure if knowing what had prompted his brother to get down on bended knee was a good thing or bad. The truth meant that Owen would not only be making a mistake that could hurt him, but now there was the potential that he could be misleading Sadie into a revenge marriage.

"We need to be nicer to Sadie. If she's not the reason for this superspeedy engagement, she doesn't deserve the scrutiny. Not to mention, if he thinks we like her, he won't think he needs to prove us wrong."

"I'm always nice," his mom said with feigned offense.

"Be nicer." Jonathan's stomach growled loud enough for them both to hear. "How long until dinner?"

"I need a few more minutes," she said, setting the temperature on the second oven. "Why don't you go snack off the cheese platter."

Jonathan rejoined the rest of the crew in the living room. Owen and their dad were watching the golf tournament while Sadie sat cross-legged on the floor with Riley. She was dealing out some playing cards and explaining the rules of Gin Rummy. The smile on Riley's face was priceless.

"Can three play this game?" he asked, taking a seat between them.

"Absolutely," Sadie replied. She dealt him his own hand.

"Don't beat me, though, Dad."

"Don't beat you? You want me to let you win?"

"Yes."

Sadie and Jonathan both cracked up at her honesty.

"Oh my gosh, Sadie," Owen said from the couch. He pointed at the television.

The nightly news was on and the breaking story was about a giant sinkhole that had opened up and swallowed a town house in a neighboring city. The newscaster said the residents in the affected town houses as well as some from the surrounding area were being evacuated while they monitored the sinkhole.

Sadie hopped to her feet, and her hands flew to her head. "That sinkhole ate my house!"

CHAPTER FIVE

SWALLOWED. HER HOME had been swallowed up by the ground. It was like her end unit had been ripped right off the building. The roof was in pieces. Walls had collapsed into the nine-foot-deep and thirty-five-foot-wide sinkhole. She could see the cornflower blue quilt that covered her bed because the second floor was now at ground level.

The city had placed officers in charge of keeping people from getting too close. Sadie wasn't even allowed to get any of her stuff because the ground was too unstable. The sinkhole had eaten not only her unit, but the street between her building and another. That other building had lost its end unit, as well. This was some sort of horrible nightmare.

"This is unbelievable," Jonathan said, holding tight to Riley's hand as they stood a few feet away from the police caution tape.

"Everything I own is underground. Everything." Sure, insurance would cover the cost of what she would lose for good, but she literally had nothing but the clothes on her back until they allowed her to enter what was left of her home. "What am I going to do?"

"You're going to move in with me," Owen said matter-of-factly.

"What?" Jonathan said at the same time Sadie shook her head no.

"I can stay with my mom or my brother. You don't have to—"

Owen wrapped his arms around her. "I don't have to do anything, but you're my fiancée and I'm going to take care of you. When you're my wife, I'll be pledging to be there for you in good times and bad. This is about as bad as it gets. No reason for me not to start being there for you a couple months early."

Sadie wanted to cry. His kindness was almost as overwhelming as the disaster that lay before her.

"Don't be sad. You can read your favorite book to me every night!" Riley said all bright and cheerful.

"That would definitely make me feel better." Sadie forced a smile for the little girl's sake. She wasn't sure that anything could make her feel better after all that had happened today.

"Let's go," Owen said. "We need to take you shopping for some of the basics. A new toothbrush at least?"

A new toothbrush was the tip of the iceberg. "You guys should go back to your parents' house and eat dinner. I feel so bad that your mother went to all that trouble and I ruined it."

"You didn't ruin anything," Jonathan said. His support was unexpected. "Our mom completely understands that you had to come check things out."

"But I didn't need to drag you guys with me."

He chuckled. "You didn't drag us. We came because we wanted to see for ourselves what happened."

"Why don't you and Riley go back to Mom and Dad's for dinner and Sadie and I will see you back at home," Owen suggested.

"I want to go shopping with Sadie," Riley said.

"Why don't we all stop at the store," Jonathan proposed. "You're going to need all the help you can get. This has to be overwhelming. We can order some pizza and pick it up on our way back to Owen's. We'll make it up to Mom another day."

After the day she had had, Jonathan's kindness meant even more than Owen's. She had been certain he hated her, but maybe there was hope she could earn his approval after all.

SAUSAGE AND MUSHROOM pizza never tasted so good. Sadie's stomach had been growling out of control for the last hour. She thought she might pass out from hunger while they waited in line for the cashier to ring up her two carts full of basic necessities.

"Thank goodness it's the last week of school. I don't know what I would have done if I had needed to lesson plan this week." Sadie had three days of school left before summer break. The last three days were filled with cleaning out desks and cubbies as well as field day and class picnics. She wouldn't have to worry about grading homework or preparing her students for assessments.

"You still have school?" Riley asked with a mouthful of her cheese pizza.

"I do, but only for a couple more days. We didn't get out as early as you did."

"Can I come to your school? I want to see your classroom."

"Well, that's up to your dad." Sadie looked to Jonathan, who was reaching across the table to snag another breadstick from the box.

"You want to go back to school already?" he asked his daughter. "Summer vacation just started!"

"Yeah, Riley. Wouldn't you rather go to the pool than school?" Owen asked. "You and your dad were going to come to the country club with me this week. Grandma was going to hang out at the pool with you while your dad and I play some golf with Grandpa."

"I have to play golf every day this week?" Jonathan didn't seem too excited by that idea.

"Have to? You mean are fortunate enough to be allowed to?"

Jonathan took a bite out of his breadstick and then pointed it at his brother. "Just because you prefer to spend every waking moment on a golf course doesn't mean that I do."

Owen's eyes widened and his jaw dropped open. "How are we related?"

Jonathan and Owen reminded Sadie of her

and her brother. They were similar in a lot of ways but so different in others.

"Well, Jonathan and Riley are more than welcome to stop by my classroom. This week is a little out of the norm, but you guys could come at the end of the school day and I could show you around."

"Please, Daddy," Riley begged.

"If you want to visit the school, we can visit the school."

"My teacher had a tent in the room for us to read or draw in. And she had a pretend campfire. It was so cool. Do you have that?"

Sadie shook her head. "No tents in my room, but I love that idea. I might have to steal it for next year. The current theme in my room is baseball. Thanks to my dad, I'm a huge baseball fan."

"Marlins or Rays fan?" Jonathan asked.

"Cubs."

"Cubs? How did that happen?"

That was often the reaction she got from people when they heard who her favorite team was. "My dad grew up in Chicago and he has been a lifelong fan. I don't think I have seen the man cry harder than the day the Cubs won the World Series."

"Interesting," Jonathan said, sitting back in his chair. "I love baseball. I grew up a Marlins fan, but I would probably be kicked out of Boston if I didn't say I now only root for the Red Sox."

"It's on my bucket list to see a game at Fenway."

He leaned forward, placing his elbows on the table. "It's pretty awesome. I would totally take you to a game if you came up to Boston."

Her dad would be so jealous. "I'm going to take you up on that. I've been to every iconic baseball park except for that one."

Owen reached over and placed his hand on hers. He played with her diamond ring, rocking it side to side on her finger. "I'll take you to a Red Sox game if you promise to go golfing with me."

Guilt swept over her. She had completely left Owen out of this conversation. She hadn't even thought about the fact that if she was up in Boston for a game with Jonathan, Owen would probably be there, too.

"I'm not sure why you would want to play golf with someone who won't be any good at it, but I'm willing to try your favorite sport if you're willing to come to mine."

Owen leaned in and kissed her on the cheek. She could feel Riley's and Jonathan's eyes on her. The PDA made her uncomfortable all the sudden.

Jonathan averted his gaze and scratched the back of his head. "If you can get my brother to enjoy any other sport besides golf, you'll be a miracle worker."

"Well, love makes you do unexpected things," Owen said. His grin was wide and toothy. Sadie smiled back, but an uneasy feeling settled in her stomach. She stared down at the ring on her finger. *Love* was a big word, one she needed to get used to hearing and saying because she was about to get married.

This was real.

"CAN I CALL Sadie Aunt Sadie?" Riley's nose and cheeks were slightly sunburned even though he had slathered her up before he left her in his mother's care at the country club pool. His mom must have forgotten to reapply as he asked her to.

"That's what you get to call her after she marries Uncle Owen. Maybe we should wait until then."

What he really wanted to say was that she

shouldn't get too attached to the idea of her becoming her aunt because after everything Jonathan had learned over the last twenty-four hours, he was more than certain that this wedding not only shouldn't happen but wouldn't.

Having Sadie in the house made getting Owen to open up about how he felt about Courtney's engagement difficult. Jonathan didn't want to bring up that name within earshot of Sadie. He had no intentions of hurting her feelings. The poor woman had enough going on, he wasn't going to add to her stress by making her think she had to worry about Owen's ex.

"If any of her students are still at school, I'm going to tell them she's my aunt anyway."

"How come?"

"Because I bet they wish she could be in their family, but she gets to be in mine."

"Ah, I see." Jonathan finally got it. "You want to make her students jealous. That's not very nice, pumpkin."

"It is nice. It's nice to Sadie. I bet she's happy she's going to be my aunt."

"Well, that is probably true." Riley wasn't the only one he was worried might become too attached. Sadie seemed like the type to get emotionally invested in people, especially kids.

Fairmont School was not in the nicest part of town, but it was clear that the community took pride in its elementary school. The grounds were well maintained. There were large bunches of petunias in oversize planters outside the front door. The playground could have used a face-lift, however. Only three of the four swings had seats. There were two basketball hoops, and neither of them had a net. The main play set was in desperate need of some paint.

Riley held her dad's hand as they walked up to the main entrance. The security door buzzed and unlocked, letting them in before Jonathan could press the call button.

An older woman with a round face and remarkable smile greeted them from behind the front desk. Her eyes lit up when Jonathan announced they were there to see Sadie.

"Are you who I think you are?" she asked, getting to her feet and peering down at Riley.

"I'm going to be Sadie's niece."

"Oh, she told me that the most awesome

girl was coming to our school for a visit. Riley, right?"

Riley nodded, beaming with pride.

The woman shifted her attention to Jonathan. "I would call Sadie to come down and get you, but we've had a little issue with a student who didn't get picked up at the end of the day. If I give you my best directions, are you willing to attempt finding her room on your own?"

"Sure. How hard can it be?"

Famous last words.

It could be extremely hard when there were normal stairs that led to a second floor all over the place but another set of stairs that went only halfway up and transported you to some kind of secret hallway that was magically not connected to the first or the second floor and could be reached only by cutting through the gym and past the kitchen connected to the cafeteria. That was where Sadie's classroom was located, of course.

"Are you sure this is the way?" Riley asked as they walked by a skid of boxes labeled SPORKS that was blocking most of the hallway near the kitchen.

Jonathan spotted the hidden stairwell. "I

think this is it," he said, hoping he wasn't wrong.

Bright red lockers lined the walls of this new hallway. Baseball cutouts were taped to a row of them with students' names written on them in the most perfect handwriting.

"Baseball-themed lockers must mean we're getting close."

Sadie popped her head out of the room on the right. "You made it! Julie was worried you guys would get lost."

"Sadie!" Riley let go of Jonathan's hand and dashed over to her soon-to-be-or-not-to-be aunt. She wrapped her arms around her and hugged Sadie tight. The image of his daughter showing this kind of affection to a woman other than her mother put a lump in his throat.

"Come on in, guys. Riley, this is one of my most creative students. Her name is Vivian and she's going to be hanging out with us for a little bit while we wait for her mom to come pick her up. Viv, this is Riley. She just finished third grade in Boston. Remember how we looked that up on the map?"

Vivian nodded, her blue eyes as large as saucers. She was a slight, wispy little thing.

Her pale blond hair looked like it hadn't been washed in a few days. Her clothes were clean but a couple of sizes too big, emphasizing her tiny frame.

"Vivian was just about to help me check my markers and see which ones need to be recycled. Would you like to help her?" Sadie asked Riley, who was more than willing and quickly took a seat next to Vivian. Sadie gave both girls a piece of paper and set three bins of markers and one empty bin in front of them.

The girls got busy pulling caps off and testing markers. Sadie motioned for Jonathan to join her by her desk. The baseball theme was in full effect in the classroom. The reading nook in the corner was called The Reading Dugout. One of the bulletin boards exclaimed HOME RUN and was covered in student work. Sadie had a sign on the front of her desk that read Coach Chapman.

"I'm sorry. I didn't expect to still be working when you guys got here. Vivian's mom was supposed to pick her up and we're having a hard time getting a hold of her. The principal is trying to reach Viv's grandmother. I said she could hang out in here until someone comes to get her instead of making her sit in the office."

"No worries. Riley was actually hoping there would be some students here to brag to about having you as an aunt."

Sadie pressed her hand over her heart. "Oh, that's so sweet."

Jonathan pointed at the baseball field on the board behind her. Students were given a classroom job that was listed in the different positions on the field. The pitcher was the teacher's helper, first base was the weather watcher and the right outfielder was the paper passer.

"I wish I had teachers who made school this fun when I was Riley's age. I would have liked it better for sure."

"I have the advantage of something called Pinterest. Our teachers had nothing to rely on other than their own creativity back in the olden days."

"Any news on your town house today?"

"They want to wait another twenty-four hours before they open anything up to residents. I'm worried that because my unit is in the sinkhole, I won't be one of the lucky ones who they let get inside their home, though."

He felt bad for what she was going through. He couldn't imagine having everything he owned sink into the ground. She was rolling with the punches pretty well. She'd stayed level-headed, didn't subject anyone to dramatics. Her resilient nature was admirable.

"Well, if you need any help, you've got me and Owen."

She gave him a grateful smile. "Thank you. You guys have been so gracious. You came here to spend the summer with your family and now you're stuck with me. I want you to know that I want you to feel free to ask for your private family time if you need it."

"Owen would say you're part of the family, too."

"Not officially for a couple of months," she said, opening her desk drawer and pulling out four lollipops. "Can Riley have one?"

"Sure. But I get the grape one."

She handed him the purple-wrapped sucker and walked over to the girls to give them their pick of the others. Not surprising, Riley picked the pink strawberry one.

"My daughter is going to want to move here and repeat third grade if you keep being so nice to her," he said when Sadie came back with the blue-raspberry lollipop in her mouth.

"She's a sweet girl. Vivian is usually close to mute, but look at the two of them laughing together."

The girls had started drawing funny pictures on their papers. They would each take turns adding something to it with a new marker. Whatever it was had them giggling nonstop. Seeing Riley so carefree made Jonathan want to freeze this moment forever. It had been so long since he had heard his daughter be so joyful.

"Sometimes I think wounded hearts recognize each other," Sadie said.

Jonathan pulled his gaze away from the girls. "What do you mean?"

"Vivian lost her dad a year ago. She's had a really hard time adjusting. And unfortunately, unlike you, her mom is really struggling to hold it together. This isn't the first time she's forgotten to pick Viv up."

Jonathan glanced back at the happy-go-lucky girls. He never would have imagined Vivian would have been as heartbroken as Riley. Of course, no one would know that Riley had night terrors. People who didn't know her well wouldn't know that when she smiled, it wasn't like how she used to smile when her mom was alive. People might not notice the way she preferred to stay close to Jonathan and didn't ever ride in a different car from him.

"Miss Chapman?" a voice came over the intercom.

"Yes?"

"Vivian's grandmother is here to get her. Can you bring her to the office?"

"Sure thing." Sadie grabbed Vivian's backpack off the student desk close to hers. "Riley, do you want to walk with us?"

Riley looked to Jonathan. She clearly didn't want her time with her new friend to end, but she was always worried about leaving Jonathan behind.

"We all can go. Maybe Vivian can show us a shortcut back to the office."

The girls were happy to have a few more minutes together and held hands as they led the way to the office. All Jonathan could think about as they followed behind the girls was that Sadie's comment about wounded hearts meant that she saw Riley's scars as well as Vivian's. He wondered if she could see his, too. And if she had her own.

CHAPTER SIX

THE ONE NICE thing about Owen's house being so huge was Sadie didn't have to feel like she was intruding all the time. There was plenty of room to spread out. He also had an awesome pool, which was where she decided to spend her very first day of summer vacation after getting off the most stressful phone call with her insurance agent.

She stretched out on one of the lounge chairs and started making a list of things she needed that hadn't crossed her mind the other day when she was shopping for essentials.

Bathing suit. The tank top and shorts she bought the other night would have to do for today, but a bathing suit would be needed for the rest of the summer because the water was calling her name.

Thank-you notes. She needed to write thank-yous to parents and students for the generous end-of-the-year gifts she had received. One of the moms had gotten all of the kids to stamp their thumbprints on a canvas in the shape of a giant heart and it read, "It takes a big heart to shape little minds." Gifts like that made Sadie a little weepy.

Tissue. There was not one box of tissues in Owen's house. Did he never have to blow his nose? Did the man not make boogers?

Sadie had cried last night when she thought about poor Vivian and the crisis her family was clearly in. Her grandmother had been so ashamed and apologetic when she picked her up on Monday. The next day, Vivian said her mom and grandma got in a big fight that night and now she wasn't allowed to go to her grandma's anymore. Sadie had a feeling that would change as soon as her mother needed Viv's grandmother's help. On the last day of school, Vivian had hugged Sadie so hard and told her she was the best teacher she'd ever had.

Sadie hadn't realized that there was no tissue until it was too late. She had been forced to get up and go into the bathroom, where she blew her nose into toilet paper. He may have had the softest, thickest toilet paper ever made, but it wasn't the same as a tissue.

Her phone chimed with a text.

Here. OMG this place looks like a mansion!! I can't believe you live here!!

Mariana was the other third-grade teacher at Fairmont. She and Sadie became fast friends when Mariana started three years ago.

Come around back. And I don't live here for real yet.

It was weird to be staying here as a guest when she would probably be moving in after the wedding. She and Owen hadn't talked about where they would live once they got married, but considering her house was nothing but rubble, it was safe to say it wouldn't be there.

Mariana somehow opened the back gate with her arms full. She had flowers in one hand and two oversize bags hanging off the other. Sadie got up to help her.

"What is all this?"

"I got you sympathy flowers for your loss. I know you loved that town house. And the bags are full of stuff I figured you probably didn't think about buying because you've been so overwhelmed."

Mariana was the sweetest person alive. Sadie took the flowers from her and gave her friend a one-arm hug. "You are so thoughtful."

"Oh, don't start. You would have done the same for me. Who are you kidding?"

Sadie put the flowers on the little side table by her lounger. Mariana went to the patio table and began to pull items out.

"Thank-you cards because if I know you like I do, you're already freaking out that you haven't sent these out." Mariana set them down and took out some pens next. "A set of colorful pens because something tells me your fiancé only had blue and black and we both know you are not black and blue, you are a rainbow."

Sadie laughed. Mariana did know her too well. That would have been the next thing on her list.

"Next up, we have Vitamin Water because it's really the only thing you like to drink in the morning, but I'm betting you were too self-conscious to buy things to keep in his kitchen."

"I mean, what am I supposed to do? Ask him if I can have some space in his pantry and refrigerator for the things I like to eat and drink? That seems so weird."

"It's your pantry and refrigerator now, amiga. You should be able to put things you like in there. Which is why I also got you these." Mariana set the box of Cinnamon Toast Crunch cereal and the bag of Jolly Ranchers next to one another.

"You're going to make me cry. Did you bring tissues? Because my boyfriend doesn't believe in them."

"Boyfriend? I think you mean fiancé." She grabbed Sadie's hand and sighed at the sight of the giant diamond on her finger. "I cannot believe you're engaged."

"Neither can I." Sadie stared down at the ring, as well. It was so big. Bigger than anything she had ever seen in real life.

"He seems to be doing pretty well for himself. You won't be like me and Alfonso, eating boxed macaroni and cheese and learning to live without air-conditioning until the temperature reaches eighty-five degrees in the house."

"You don't turn on your air-conditioning until it's eighty-five in your house?"

She nodded. "I walk around in my underwear most of the time unless we're expecting guests. But it looks like I will be spending the summer at your pool this year."

Sadie was so grateful for friends like Mariana. The woman was barely making ends meet and she went shopping for Sadie anyway. If all the woman wanted in return was a chance to sit by the pool, Sadie would make sure that happened. "You're welcome anytime. As long as Owen's okay with that. Do you think I should ask him before I invite people over?"

Mariana's dark eyebrows lifted. "You are going to be the man's wife. This is going to be your home. If you have to ask if you can have guests over, we need to talk about your definition of a healthy relationship."

Sadie couldn't wrap her head around this being her home. She currently was staying in one of the guest bedrooms because they had decided that it was important to wait until they were married to share a bed. That clearly added to her feeling like this was more temporary than permanent.

She couldn't exactly complain about anything, though. It was nicer than the house she grew up in. He had it decorated beautifully, but it wasn't the way she would decorate. Exactly how was she supposed to feel like she had ownership when everything was his?

"Owen isn't like that. I didn't mean to make it sound like I'm some sort of submissive. I meant I'm still a guest, not an equal partner in ownership."

"If you're really serious about marrying him in August, you better start changing your mind-set."

"I'm trying. Look at me, I'm hanging out by the pool, aren't I?"

"In a tank top and shorts?"

"I didn't think about a bathing suit when I was shopping for essentials."

"I figured you didn't." She pulled out one more surprise from her bag of goodies. A hot pink bikini.

Sadie could feel her cheeks turning the same color as that skimpy bathing suit. "Are you kidding me? I thought you knew me so well until that!"

Mariana held it up to herself. "Do you know what I would give to be able to rock a bikini like this? You are beautiful and fit, amiga. You need this. You deserve it."

The French doors opened and Riley came running outside with Jonathan right behind her.

"Hi, Sadie!" Riley shouted as she ran by and jumped right into the pool.

"She has been begging to come out here. If we're interrupting, I can tell her to get out. We can always swim later," Jonathan said.

"Oh goodness, she's more than welcome to swim. I don't own this pool," Sadie replied, earning an eye roll from Mariana. "Jonathan, you remember Mariana from school."

The two of them had met briefly on Monday when Mariana stopped by to say goodbye on her way out of school.

"Hi, Mariana."

"Jonathan, we need your opinion." She held the bikini up to herself again. "Do you think Sadie could pull this look off?"

Sadie was ready to jump in the pool fully clothed just to avoid hearing him try to get out of answering this question. Obviously, Jonathan wouldn't want to offer up an opinion on her looks. He was too much of a gentleman for that.

She snatched the bikini away from her friend. "Don't answer that," she said to Jonathan before stuffing the suit back in the bag. "I will go shopping for a bathing suit later today. One that makes me feel comfortable. Thank you very much."

Jonathan seemed more than relieved to not have to answer Mariana's question. "I'm going to supervise Riley. You two enjoy your visit."

Jonathan sat down at the edge of the pool. Sadie turned her back to him and Riley. "That is my fiancé's brother. Can you please be appropriate?"

Mariana laughed and shook her head. "Let's go get you a bathing suit. I'm not sunning myself by the pool next to you in street clothes."

SADIE AND HER friend left in a hurry. Jonathan wasn't sure if it was because he and Riley came out or not. For the last couple of days, the only time Jonathan saw Sadie was when they ate dinner and Riley's bedtime. She seemed to be trying to keep her distance.

"Dad, watch this," Riley said. She took a deep breath and then attempted to do a somersault in the water. She came up with her hair all in her face. She tried her best to push it away, but it wasn't as easy when it was wet. "Did you see it?"

"That was awesome, sweetie."

"Watch me swim all the way from here to over there," she said, pointing to the far side of the pool.

"I'll be watching. Don't worry." Riley had taken swim lessons back in Boston since she was three. Well, except for the year after Mindy's death when Jonathan could barely get his act together to get himself in the shower once or twice a week.

Once he'd pulled himself out of that pit of darkness, he began to try to reintegrate them both back into the life they'd had before the accident. Some things had been more successful than others. Riley had missed swimming the most and excelled when she got back in the water.

Jonathan sat on the edge of the pool with his legs in the water. His brother was so lucky to have a pool in his backyard. In Florida, it wasn't that uncommon, but in Boston it was rare. Being able to swim outside year-round might have something to do with it. This was a definite plus for moving to Florida. Riley would love it. And if he couldn't find a place with a pool, they could always come over to Uncle Owen's house to swim.

As long as Aunt Sadie wasn't sitting by it in a hot pink bikini. Jonathan wished he could erase the image of that from his brain. Sadie wanted to marry his brother. He shouldn't ever be focused on how attractive she was or how drawn he felt to everything about her.

She was his brother's fiancée. She should feel comfortable around him. So far, he thought he had been successful in making her feel welcome. He had tried being nicer to her. He had let her start reading *Charlotte's Web* to Riley, who, not surprisingly, *loved* it. This was not the right time to begin to have these feelings when he was around her. Given the already messy circumstances surrounding this engagement, Jonathan did not want to be the reason his brother's engagement fell apart. It was one thing to make Owen aware of the reasons why he should slow things down. It was another to have feelings for her. To have improper thoughts. He wouldn't do that to his little brother.

"Did you see how fast I was?" Riley asked

when she made her way back down by the shallow end.

"I saw. You were superfast."

"I wish Sadie could have seen me."

An unusual ache hit him in the chest. Was he the reason Sadie had left? If he hadn't seemed mortified over a bathing suit, would Sadie have stayed and hung out with them? He couldn't think that way. She might have had plans to go out with her friend instead of staying home. Maybe they were getting lunch. That was normal behavior for two adult women.

"You're going to have lots of chances this summer for Sadie to watch you. Try your best to have fun without her here."

"It's going to be hard," the nine-year-old complained.

It was a little frightening how attached Riley had become in such a short time. Sadie was the first woman she had been around in a long time. Jonathan hadn't dated or sought the support of many female friends over the last few years. Maybe he had isolated his daughter more than he realized.

It wasn't until he and Riley were enjoying peanut butter and jelly sandwiches and apple slices that Sadie and Mariana returned. They both came out dressed for the pool. Thankfully, Sadie had returned the pink bikini and bought herself something that covered a little more skin. She had a colorful sarong tied around her waist and her brown hair piled on top of her head in a sloppy bun. He loved how easy-going she was.

"How's the water, Riley?" Mariana asked as she shed her white cover-up.

"It's good," Riley replied while chewing her food.

"Manners, missy. No one wants to see your lunch after it's in your mouth," Jonathan reminded her.

Mariana dived right in, popping up with a big smile on her face. "That will cool you off real quick!"

Sadie was a bit more cautious. She walked over and dipped her toe in. "How can it possibly feel cold? It's been in the mideighties every day for a couple weeks."

"It's not cold once you get all in. Jump. Come on," Mariana encouraged.

"I don't jump. I like to ease my way in."

Mariana splashed some water up at her.

"Oh, come on. Don't be a baby. The water is the perfect temperature."

"Don't splash me."

"Jump in," Mariana said. When Sadie refused, she tried to get Riley involved. "Riley, give Sadie a push. She needs to take the plunge."

Funny that Sadie was willing to take figurative plunges but not real ones. Maybe Jonathan had been going at this all wrong. Maybe it wasn't his brother he needed to convince to slow down. Maybe it was Sadie.

"Riley, don't even think about it," Sadie said, making her way over to the pool steps.

Mariana kept up the splashing. "If you think it's so cold, why would you torture yourself and make it take longer to acclimate. Jump in!"

Sadie untied her sarong and tossed it on one of the loungers. Jonathan had to avert his gaze. Those thoughts he wasn't supposed to be thinking were definitely being encouraged by how amazing she looked in her new bathing suit.

"Okay, that's it. You asked for it." The next thing Jonathan heard was a loud splash. He turned to see Sadie and Mariana wrestling in the water like children.

Riley pushed back her chair. "Can I be done with lunch? I want to play with them."

"Okay, but be careful. They look a little rowdy."

Riley shouted, "Cowabunga!" before jumping in.

The three of them splashed around, squealing with delight, giggling and taking turns dunking one another. Sadie picked up Riley and threw her as far as she could. Jonathan sat up, concerned that Riley would come up unhappy, but all his fears disappeared when she popped back up with the biggest smile on her face. Riley was having the time of her life.

"Dad! Come help me! We have to dunk Sadie."

Jonathan wasn't so sure that was a good idea. There was no way he could get in the water and put his hands on Sadie. He had another idea, though.

"I got your back, Riley. Hang on!" Owen had a deck box that was full of pool toys. If memory served him right, there should be the perfect water fight weapon in there. He opened the lid and there it was right on top. "Oh, you ladies are in big trouble."

Owen had bought these water shooters that acted like big syringes. You sucked the water up by pulling out the plunger and shot it out by pushing it back in. Jonathan went to the far end of the pool and loaded his shooter up.

"That is not fair. We're unarmed!" Sadie shouted.

"Life isn't fair, Miss Chapman. Deal with it!" With that, Jonathan shot her in the back of the head with a steady stream of water.

Riley hooted and hollered, cheering like he had just scored the winning touchdown.

"You can't do that to my friend," Mariana said, swimming over to him. She tried to splash him before he could reload, but she was too late. He shot her with the next water blast. She had to duck underwater to get away.

He bent over to reload, losing sight of his next target. Before he could finish, he heard the pitter-patter of bare feet on wet concrete.

"Dad, watch out!" Riley yelled a bit too late.

Sadie wrapped her arms around him and used her momentum to send them both into the deep end. "You deserve this," she said as they went in.

The cold water took his breath away. He came up for air and tried to wipe water out of his eyes. Where had his sunglasses gone? Sadie didn't stop there. She started splashing him in the face.

"Stop," he tried to say through the relentless water. He finally ducked down and swam for her. He grabbed her around the legs and lifted her up, letting her fall into the water.

Jonathan had water up his nose and his eyes burned from the chlorine, but Riley's laughter made it all worth it. Sadie jumped on his back, her arms and legs wrapped around him. She was like a spider monkey that he couldn't get off him. He dunked himself, knowing that would take her down, as well. When they came back to the surface, she was in front of him instead of behind him. He put his hands on her waist and their eyes met. His heart skipped a beat without permission. What was wrong with him?

"Hey, who said you could have fun without me?" Owen's voice boomed. Jonathan couldn't have let go of her faster. He didn't know what was going on. Sadie affected him like no other woman had since Mindy.

Sadie was off-limits, though. Didn't his heart understand that?

CHAPTER SEVEN

SADIE COULD HAVE qualified for the US women's swim team considering how fast she swam from one side of the pool to the other when Owen showed up. Not that she had been doing anything wrong. It just felt like she had been doing something…potentially wrong.

Had she been flirting with her soon-to-be brother-in-law? Sadie didn't flirt. Or at least when she tried to, it was a disaster. Maybe that wasn't what just happened. They had been playing around. Like a family. Mariana had been there. She had splashed him, too. Of course, Mariana hadn't made physical contact and pushed him in the pool. She hadn't jumped on his back. He hadn't grabbed her and looked at her like he wanted to…

No, no, no. Sadie had to be misreading the situation. He had looked at her like he wanted to dunk her. That was what she saw. They were playing around. It was completely innocent.

Sadie got out of the pool and grabbed her towel. "Hi, how was your meeting?" she asked Owen before giving him a peck on the cheek.

"It was good. You guys look like you're having a blast. It makes me happy to see you fitting right in."

"You remember my friend Mariana, right? She teaches third grade with me," she added when he made a face that told her he had no idea who she was.

"Right! Hey, Mariana. Excited about summer break?"

"I'd be more excited if I got to live here like Sadie. You got any more guest rooms?"

"The inn is officially full," he replied. "Sorry."

"You could kick out Jonathan. He's a cheat and scoundrel."

Sadie's heart rate accelerated. "What? He's not a cheat."

"He shot both of us with that water shooter when we were unarmed. He doesn't play fair," Mariana said as she towel-dried her dark hair.

Owen chuckled. "I grew up with the man.

He's always been like that. Jon will do whatever it takes to win. He once took my putter out of my bag before we went golfing in an attempt to beat me."

Jonathan got out of the pool. He had swim trunks on but was wearing his T-shirt when Sadie had pushed him in. Soaked, he took it off and wrung it out. "That's a lie. I didn't intentionally remove it so I could beat you."

"He didn't beat me, by the way. Even without my putter, I beat him."

Jonathan flicked some water from his wet shirt at his brother. Sadie had to force herself to not stare at his chest. She focused her gaze as high on his head as she could.

"I wasn't trying to beat you. There was a spider sitting above the door to the house in Mom and Dad's garage. The thing was the size of my palm. I needed something long enough to reach it and your golf bag was right there. Only, when I went to kill it, it leaped down on its own and scared the heck out of me. I had to run for my life and I threw the putter at him to stop him from chasing me."

Sadie and Mariana locked eyes and busted out laughing. It was actually pretty cute that he was scared of a spider.

"Sweetheart," Owen said to Sadie. "I think you may need to come with me to North Carolina tomorrow because it sounds like my brother cannot be trusted to be the man of the house and keep you safe from spiders."

"The good news is that I am an expert in spider removal. I promise to keep Jon and Riley safe from all the spiders."

Owen slid his arm around her waist. "You could come to North Carolina just because you want to be with me."

"I would, but you scheduled that meeting for me with the wedding planner tomorrow." She leaned away from him a bit so she didn't get him wet. "My mother would be devastated if we didn't go."

"The wedding planner. I forgot. Well, I wouldn't want you to miss the meeting with the person who is going to help us get married." He placed a kiss on her lips. The muscles in Sadie's shoulders tightened. She was embarrassed by the PDA again.

"Can I meet the wedding planner?" Mariana asked. "The only planners I had for my wedding were my mother, my aunt, my mom's cousin and Alfonso's sister. None of them were very good at it, but they all thought their ideas should have been featured in *Brides* magazine."

Sadie remembered how stressed Mariana was two years ago when she was in the throes of wedding planning. Sadie wondered if it was because she had too many people involved with too many different opinions. Sadie needed this process to go smoothly. Perhaps the fewer opinions the better. Her mother wouldn't appreciate the competition either.

"Trust me, you do not want to get in the middle of my mother and whatever plans she has for this wedding. You'll be much safer planning my bachelorette party as my matron of honor."

"I get to plan your bachelorette party?" Mariana clapped her hands. "Can I do anything I want?"

"*Anything* feels a bit too broad. Let's go with you can do anything I approve of."

Jonathan placed his hand on Mariana's shoulder. "Why do I get the feeling that those parameters greatly limit your options?"

Sadie's eyes narrowed. "Are you calling me boring? I am not boring. I am just not wild.

I like to be a positive role model for my students in and outside of the classroom."

"You talk to me later, Mariana," Owen said. "Money is no object when it comes to my girl and her bride tribe having the time of their lives. If you want to go somewhere— Vegas, LA, San Diego. Wherever or whatever you think up, I'll make it happen."

Jonathan's face scrunched up. "Bride tribe?"

"It's a thing," Owen defended. "People not old and out of touch like you know what it is."

Mariana was loving this idea. "Oh! We could make shirts and cool drinking glasses with Bride Tribe written on them."

Sadie, on the other hand, found it all a bit overwhelming. "You will not pay for me and my friends to go anywhere." She looked pointedly at Mariana. "And we don't need any bride tribe swag."

"I am impressed that my brother has decided to settle down with someone so sensible. Based on his dating record, I never would have guessed it," Jonathan said, and Sadie felt Owen stiffen beside her.

"I think I'm going to go put my suit on," Owen said, stepping back toward the house.

"Seems like everyone was having way more fun in the water than out. Oh, and I call dibs on drowning my brother when I get back."

"Hey, now." Jonathan had poked the bear and then seemed surprised that he angered him.

"Did I say drowning? I meant dunking. I have dibs on *dunking* my brother."

OWEN SURE DIDN'T like it when Jonathan brought up the women from his past. He hadn't had a lot. He wasn't that kind of guy—changing girlfriends with the seasons. He had had only a handful of girlfriends in his lifetime. He had no reason to be sensitive about the number of women in his past.

Jonathan knew that wasn't what bothered his brother when he brought it up. What bothered Owen was that it was noticeable how different Sadie was from those others. Owen may not have had a lot of girlfriends, but he definitely had a type.

First, they were always blonde. Second, they were never seen in public without the perfect outfit and hair and makeup on point. Third, they were all about being pampered. Jonathan wasn't judging. If someone wanted to swoop in and pay all his bills and wine and dine him, he'd have a hard time saying no. He didn't have an issue with the fact that they liked how much Owen did for them. His issue was that they rarely seemed to be the type who found ways to give back.

Sadie was different. Her default was to give rather than take. Maybe that was why Owen had fallen for her. It certainly wasn't a bad thing to be in love with someone who was kind and generous. Someone who didn't seem to have a superficial bone in her body. Jonathan just wasn't totally convinced that his brother had realized that about Sadie yet.

In some ways, he felt like he knew Sadie better than Owen did.

"I know you were trying to be sweet and generous, but I'm not comfortable with you paying for me and friends to take a trip to Las Vegas."

"Why? What is so bad about that?"

"It's not bad. It's just asking too much from you. And traditionally, the groom doesn't pay for the bachelorette party."

"Well, when the bride's friends are teachers in a low-paying district with husbands who have jobs that pay by the hour, I'm pretty sure it's okay for the groom with lots of money in the bank to chip in."

Jonathan didn't mean to be eavesdropping. He had been coming downstairs to get a glass of water and to let Sadie know Riley was ready to do some bedtime reading. He didn't walk into the kitchen when he heard them having this argument. Although, he was beginning to think he should make himself known and save his brother from saying something more offensive than he already had.

"Did you just say what I think you said?" Sadie sounded ready to blow. Jonathan wasn't sure there was coming back from this level of frustration. "First of all, how much money my friends make and what kinds of jobs their husbands have is none of your business. Secondly, you know nothing about my friends or their husbands, so I'm not sure where you get off thinking they need your charity."

"That's not what I meant—"

"I don't care what you meant. That was rude. And second, since when is the only measure of a good time how much money was spent? I think we all had fun in the pool today and that didn't cost anyone a thing."

"Really? I didn't have to pay for this house? For that pool? I understand that it feels free to you, but I definitely paid for it."

Oh boy, things were going further south than Jonathan thought they would. He decided that stepping in would at least send them each to their own corners to nurse their wounds for a minute or so.

Jonathan stepped into the kitchen and the look on Sadie's face was heartbreaking. "Hey, Riley's ready for some *Charlotte's Web* when you are. No rush or if you aren't up for it tonight, I can read it to her."

"No, I'm ready." She tossed the dish towel down on the island. Owen put his hand on her arm, but she jerked away without a word to him.

Jonathan opened up the cabinet by the refrigerator and got himself a glass. He filled it with water from the refrigerator door. His brother stood at the island with his head in his hands.

"Everything okay?" Jonathan asked, knowing it wasn't. Maybe this would help Owen open up to him a little bit.

Owen stood up straight. "Since when is it such a terrible thing to be nice to someone?

When did it become a crime to open up your checkbook so someone else can have a good time?"

"I don't know if she thinks it's a terrible thing. I think you're forgetting that Sadie isn't impressed by expensive things."

"She sure seemed impressed when she saw her engagement ring," Owen mumbled.

"Stop. That, that attitude right there is part of the problem. It sounds elitist..." Owen wanted to interrupt but Jonathan clarified, "... I know you aren't, but you sound it when you talk like that."

"She's so sensitive about the weirdest stuff. I can't keep up," Owen said with a sigh.

Jonathan pinched the bridge of his nose. "Well, you better figure it out because it doesn't magically get better just because you put a ring on her finger and say I do."

"I'm trying. She just doesn't think like anyone else I know, and I'm not a mind reader." He leaned against his kitchen counter. It wasn't like Owen to admit defeat. He was the one who never gave up.

"If you try harder to remember exactly what you said—she doesn't think like anyone else you know—maybe you'll have a better chance of getting it right next time."

"You're not going to say it?"

Jonathan furrowed his brow. "Say what?"

"That this kind of thing is a good example of why I shouldn't rush into this marriage."

He had not said that on purpose. Jonathan was done pushing his brother to slow things down. He was going to focus his efforts on the one in the relationship with more doubts, but it was good that his brother was finally seeing the light.

"Looks like I don't have to say anything. You thought it anyways."

Owen pushed off the counter. "I may have thought it, but I don't believe it. Sadie and I are going to get married. I will figure her out and we will be happier than any other couple."

"I hope so. I wouldn't want anything less for you, little brother."

"I've got to go pack." Owen walked past Jonathan, his eyes narrowed with suspicion. "I know you're up to something."

"I'm not up to anything," Jonathan said with a laugh.

"You're a terrible liar, Jon. Always have been."

Jonathan finished his glass of water and refilled it to take upstairs for when Riley asked for water to delay bedtime. Being prepared was key when it came to his daughter.

Once he reached her door, he found himself eavesdropping once again. Sadie was sitting next to Riley on the bed. Her legs were stretched out on top of the bed covers. Her cheeks had gotten a little sunburned today in the pool. She hadn't been very good about reapplying sunscreen on herself even though she had reminded Riley to do it twice. Her hair was down and it fell over her shoulders. It looked soft to the touch.

"Who is your favorite character so far?" Sadie asked.

"I think it's a tie between Charlotte and Wilbur. Charlotte is so nice and calms Wilbur down when he's upset. She's a good mom."

"She is."

Jonathan's alarm bells went off. This was why he hadn't wanted them to read this book. He didn't want Riley to fall apart when she got to the end and the mother figure went away like her own did.

"What happened to Wilbur's real mom?" Riley asked.

"Well…" Sadie pursed her lips "…they don't really say in the story, but I think we can assume that she was sold at another fair. That was the purpose of the farm, to raise animals to sell. Wilbur's mom probably got turned into some bacon and ham. Maybe some pork chops, too."

"What?" Jonathan almost stepped in to stop this conversation, but then Riley started to laugh. Dumbfounded, he stayed just outside the door. "I didn't know that pork chops came from pigs!"

"Bacon, ham and pork chops all come from pigs. That's why they took Wilbur to the fair. To sell him to someone who wanted ham."

"So his whole family got turned into ham except for him?"

"Probably."

"That's sad."

"It is sad, but thankfully Wilbur had other people who stepped up and took care of him."

"Fern and Charlotte."

"Right. It's sad to lose someone but good to know we have others who love us and will be there for us."

"Like how I have Daddy. And Gramma and Gramps. I even have Uncle Owen and you."

"Aw. You definitely have me," Sadie said, giving Riley a hug.

Jonathan took a step back and pressed his fingers to his eyes to hold back the tears. His heart felt so heavy in his chest. He worried all the time that he wasn't enough for Riley, that growing up without a mother somehow put her at a huge disadvantage.

Hearing her acknowledge how much she was loved by so many people meant the world to him. It also made moving to Florida something he truly needed to consider. It clearly made Riley happy to have all this family around.

He took a deep breath and tried his best to pull himself together before going in the room.

"You guys finished reading for the night?" he asked.

"We are," Sadie said, setting the book down on the nightstand.

"No, I want to read a little more," Riley protested.

Jonathan sat on the edge of the bed and fixed her covers. "Of course you do, but you've had a very busy day. You have to be exhausted."

"I'm not even—" she yawned "—tired."

Sadie and Jonathan exchanged a look and fought to hide their laughter.

"I think you're more tired than you realize," Jonathan said.

"I will see you in the morning. Good night, sweet girl." Sadie bent down and gave Riley a kiss on the forehead.

"I need a drink. I'm really thirsty."

Jonathan held up the glass of water he brought with him for this very excuse to extend her bedtime routine. "Ask and you shall receive."

Riley took the tiniest of sips and flopped back down. "Can Sadie stay and say bedtime prayers with us?"

Jonathan glanced over at her. She had been making her way to the door. She stopped and smiled. "Of course," she said. She came back over to the bed and knelt next to Jonathan, folding her hands like Riley did.

Riley recited her prayer and then began her special requests. "God bless Mommy in heaven and Daddy on earth. God bless Charlotte and Wilbur. I hope they stay friends forever. God bless Gramma and Grampa and Nana and Papa. God bless Uncle Owen. Thank you for making him fall in love with Sadie so she can be part of our family forever. And God bless her. Amen."

"Amen," Jonathan and Sadie said at the same time. Sadie wiped under her eye and cleared her throat.

Jonathan leaned over and gave Riley a kiss. He followed Sadie out and shut off the light. "Sleep tight, sweetheart," he said before closing the door.

"She's so special," Sadie whispered. "You've raised a really wonderful little person in there."

"Thank you." Given how often it felt like he had no idea what he was doing, it was nice to hear that someone who was somewhat of an expert on kids Riley's age thought he was doing a good job.

Sadie gave him a small smile. "Have a good night." She turned to go down the hall to her bedroom, but he reached out and touched her arm. She stopped and he could have sworn he felt her shudder slightly.

"I appreciate how well you're handling the questions she has about the story. I wouldn't have read it to her because I wouldn't have known how to answer them, but you're amazing. She's able to talk about it and still sleep at night, which for her is a big deal."

"As terrible as it was to lose her mom, she's okay because she knows you're here for her." She placed her hand on his shoulder, and the contact set off a spark he wasn't expecting. "You're a good dad."

The door to the master bedroom opened, and Sadie quickly dropped her hand. "Can we talk?" Owen asked, clearly speaking to Sadie.

Sadie folded her arms in front of her. "Sure." She stepped around Jonathan, looking up at him through those thick lashes. "Good night, Jon."

"Good night."

Owen opened his arms and Sadie walked right in. "I'm sorry if I was being a jerk. I didn't mean to sound like a stuck-up snob. I promise to stay in my lane moving forward. Can you forgive me?"

"Of course."

Jonathan forced his feet to move. This was one conversation he didn't want to overhear. Right before he shut his door, he could hear his brother kiss his fiancée. *His* fiancée. Jonathan needed to stop his stupid heart from letting him forget.

CHAPTER EIGHT

"HERE ARE THE colors I was thinking." Sadie's mother had actual fabric swatches in
her purse.

Chelsea LeFleur's wedding planning business, Ever After, had been featured in the
Palm Beach Post and on the local news recently. She was an up-and-comer who had
her finger on the pulse of what was what in
today's Palm Beach-area weddings.

"That's lovely. However, I'm not sure we're
ready to discuss colors yet. There are some
other things we need to focus on first."

"Colors are the foundation of any event!
How are you going to choose anything without knowing what the colors are?"

Chelsea gave Sadie's mother a tight smile.
"Because we're working on such a short timeline, it actually makes more sense to talk
about location first. Where we're going to
have the ceremony and where you'd like the

reception. All of the more exclusive places are already booked, as are many of the mid-range places."

Her mother frowned. "I don't believe that."

"Well, we can agree to disagree. To help me guide you effectively, I need to know how big of a wedding we're looking at. How many guests? How big will the wedding party be?"

"Small. Mostly family. Some close friends."

"You're marrying a professional golfer. Are you sure he doesn't want to have more people at his wedding?"

"It's *our* wedding, and Owen and I talked about having just family and close friends. It makes me happy because I don't think I want to be on display for hundreds of people, and it makes him happy because now his wedding will be 'exclusive.' And our wedding party is only going to consist of a matron of honor and a best man."

"Okay, that helps me a lot. I'd love to hear what you were thinking for the ceremony because I got the impression that the reception was already handled."

"We haven't decided on anywhere yet." Sadie's mom turned on her phone and began scrolling through her text messages as if she may have missed one where Sadie told her where they were having it. "Have we?"

"When I spoke to your fiancé, he made it clear that because he is a member at Jupiter Beach Country Club, he should be able to call in a favor. They have a couple rooms that would work depending on the size of the guest list."

"Well, we need to see that venue before we agree to it. Have you been to his country club?"

Sadie had been there twice. Owen had taken her there for dinner on their first date. He had also tried to give her a golf lesson on another date.

"I've had dinner there. I don't know that I saw the rooms where they might hold receptions, but it was very nice. And it's an important place to Owen, so if he wants it there, we should have it there."

Sadie's mom wasn't going to let it go. "Well, I'll need to see it before we decide. Can you get us in for a walk-through or do we need to ask Owen?"

Chelsea sat forward in her chair and rested her elbows on the table. "I can get you in anywhere you want, but maybe you should check with Owen. As a high-profile member, he would ensure you got their very best customer service."

"So what you're telling us is that you don't have much of a reputation in this business yet."

"Mom!" Sadie knew her mother was going to be difficult. She didn't expect her to be straight-up rude.

"She's the one who said—"

Sadie cut her off and spoke directly to Chelsea. "I will talk to Owen when he gets back from his tournament. Although, I'm sure once my mother sees the clubhouse, she'll be more than happy to sign off on that as our reception site."

"Excellent. Church wedding and, if so, do you already have a church in mind?"

"We were thinking an outdoor ceremony," her mother chimed in again.

Sadie hadn't ever mentioned wanting to have an outdoor wedding. Not that she had a strong opinion about where it should happen. Still, it would have been nice if her mom asked her before she spoke for both of them.

"Did you have somewhere in mind?"

Sadie's mom pulled a list out of her bag of

tricks. "These are in order of preference. If we have it at the Botanical Gardens, we could cut back on our flower budget and spend that money elsewhere."

Chelsea perused the list, shaking her head ever so slightly. Sadie could feel her mother's aggravation growing.

"I can almost guarantee none of these places will have any openings on a weekend in August."

"I'd still like you to check," her mom snapped back.

"I can do that, but it will probably be a waste of our time. If you're thinking you want to get married somewhere that will kind of naturally serve as not only the location but as the decor, I have some places you might want to look at. They are some lesser-known spots but equally as beautiful."

"That sounds great," Sadie said before her mother could complain.

The rest of their meeting continued to be just as contentious with Sadie's mom trying to outplan the wedding planner. When they finished, Sadie had been tasked with creating a Pinterest board to fill with things that matched the aesthetic she was leaning toward.

Chelsea kindly took the fabric swatches Candice had brought along with her and promised that after viewing the wedding board, she would put some ideas together for their approval.

"I'm not sure she's the right person for this job," Sadie's mom said as they got in the car.

"Mom, we are not hiring another wedding planner."

"I don't know why you need a wedding planner. There isn't much that she's doing that you and I couldn't do on our own."

"I appreciate all your help, but because we don't have a lot of time to plan everything, having a professional do some of the legwork will be a godsend. We can focus on the important things like what I'm going to wear and going to all the local bakeries and tasting lots of cake."

Her mom laughed. "You and that sweet tooth of yours."

"I want this to be a pleasant mother-daughter experience. Can you please trust Chelsea will do a good job?"

Candice sighed and rolled her eyes. "I don't know if I can fully trust her to do as good of a job as I could do, but I will try to keep some of my more negative opinions to myself."

"Thank you," Sadie said, reaching over and patting her mom's hand. As difficult and embarrassing as her mother had been during that meeting, it meant so much to have her here to do this planning. There had been times during her mother's cancer treatments that Sadie had feared Candice wouldn't be around for these major life events. She swore to herself that she would never take their time together for granted again.

"So you're not going to have your brother stand up in your wedding?"

"I'm sure that Paul will be relieved that he doesn't have to wear a tux and stand the whole ceremony, and I'm even more sure that Haley will appreciate that Paul will be able to help her with the kids."

"How are things going at the house with Owen's brother and niece there?"

Sadie wasn't sure how to answer that question. They certainly weren't going badly, but she wasn't sure that they were going well either. Mainly because she was struggling a little with wishing that sometimes Owen could be more like his brother.

"Your silence is making me think that there's a problem. You know that you can always come stay with me if things are a little too crowded over there."

Sadie shook her head. "Everything is fine. Jonathan and Riley are great. Riley is the sweetest little thing. She's so curious about things and loves to do crafts, so we're getting along splendidly."

"And the brother is coming around about the wedding being so soon after Owen proposed?"

"He's been more supportive lately. More so than Paul, who keeps texting me words of advice. Today's was don't sign a prenup. His positive attitude is so helpful."

"Oh, don't listen to your brother. I don't know what he's so worried about. You're in love with a rich, attractive, successful man who seems to come from a good family. As long as you believe that he's as equally in love with you, what could go wrong?"

Love. That was something Sadie had avoided thinking about. The more time she and Owen had spent together, the more confused she got. He had some amazing qualities. He was funny and fun loving. He treated her like a princess. But there was another side. Sometimes he was a little entitled. He didn't always read people very well, and that lack of empathy sometimes made him come off as aloof.

Jonathan, on the other hand, was good at reading others' emotions and was cognizant of how his actions might impact others. He was even aware of how Owen's actions impacted Sadie. He was a good dad. He was able to find a good balance between being fun and being firm. Riley had boundaries. Owen often put fun before everything else.

She couldn't tell anyone about all that, though. If anyone else heard what she thought, they might get the impression she was falling in love with Jonathan instead of Owen. That would be the stupidest thing she could let happen. If she fell for Jonathan, she would lose them all.

"SAY THANK YOU to your grandmother. She did not need to buy you all of that." Jonathan was hoping his mother got the hint that she went overboard with the clothes shopping she had done with Riley this afternoon.

"Thank you!" Riley gave her grandmother

a big hug. Jonathan wished his mother understood she would never need to buy Riley's affection. The child was dying to give it away.

"You are so welcome. I had fun today. We need to do it again real soon."

"Go take all your bags up to your room, okay?" Jonathan said to Riley, who was more than happy to oblige. His child had a strange love for organization. Her closet was completely color coordinated. It looked like a rainbow when you opened it up.

"I know you think I spoil her, but isn't that what a good grandma does?"

"She would have felt spoiled if you bought her half as much." Jonathan poured her a glass of lemonade and grabbed a soda out of the fridge for himself.

"I hear you and I will try to do better next time." She took out a metal straw from her purse and stuck it in her lemonade.

"I'm so impressed with your environmental consciousness."

"I've joined this group that's trying to raise awareness of the amount of plastic we're dumping into the ocean. If you saw how much plastic we pick up off the beach every week, you'd be sick."

"Well, I love that you are practicing what you preach."

His mother had a tendency to take up causes and then lose interest because she didn't get to see the fruits of her labor often enough. Hopefully, this would be different.

"How are things going with your brother? I've been wondering if having Sadie under the same roof has made him more or less willing to acknowledge how he's really feeling."

Jonathan knew she would ask. He had been contemplating what he was going to tell her about Sadie. If he wasn't careful, she might get the impression that he had stronger feelings for Sadie than Owen did. That would be disastrous.

"If he was here more often, maybe. I still think that they should take it a little slower." For Sadie's sake more than anything. The more he'd gotten to know her, the more he could tell she was typically more cautious about things and that she wasn't so sure where she fit into Owen's life just yet.

"They need to break up, Jonathan. He's not over Courtney."

"I know you're a big Courtney fan, but

have you stopped to think that maybe it's not a bad thing that Owen has moved on with someone like Sadie?"

His mom looked skeptical. "She seems very nice. Your brother needs someone with a little more spunk than sweetness, though."

"Trust me, she stands up to him. She puts him in his place when he deserves it. I think she could make him a better man."

Now her interest was piqued. "Really? I wasn't aware that your brother wasn't already a great man."

Jonathan dipped his chin. "I love Owen, but we all know his ego can get in his way sometimes."

"And you think that Sadie is going to help him keep his ego in check?"

"She might. Like I said, I think they should take more time to figure this out, and I have a plan."

"You have a plan?" She leaned forward. "I can't wait to hear this."

"Instead of confronting Owen or waiting for him to open up to me about how he feels about Courtney, I'm going to focus my attention on Sadie."

"What is that supposed to mean?"

"I'm going to help her listen to that little voice inside her head that already thinks they're moving too fast. I'll convince her to push the wedding back. I feel like they need a little more time to work out the kinks. To make sure they can work them out before they say vows in front of God and everyone they love."

His mother frowned. "I'm not sure why you think that's going to work."

"Trust me, Mom."

The front door opened and there were voices in the foyer. A few seconds later, Sadie and an older woman walked into the kitchen.

"Oh, hi!" she said. "I didn't know your mom was coming over. Hi, Mrs. Bradley."

"Hi, Sadie. It's nice to see you again."

"This is my mom, Candice. Mom, this is Jonathan and Beth Bradley."

Everyone got acquainted. Jonathan offered Sadie and her mom something to drink.

"I would love a rosé," Candice said, setting her large purse on the kitchen table. "Wedding planning took a lot out of me today."

"What were you guys doing for the wedding?" his mom asked.

"We had our first appointment with the wedding planner," Sadie explained.

Jonathan was on the hunt for a rosé. His brother had a wine cooler in his butler's pantry and surprisingly had a bottle. The man had a bottle of everything. Owen was nothing if not always prepared to be the host with the most. He got that from their mom.

"I'm not a huge fan of this planner, but if Owen thinks she's the best then we're going to trust him," Candice said.

Jonathan handed her a glass of wine and sat down across from her. She looked well. Jonathan and Sadie had not had a heart-to-heart about her mom's battle with cancer yet. Maybe she'd had cancer but was in remission.

"It's hard when you're working with such a tight timeline. These two and their race to the altar," Jonathan's mom said, obviously checking to see what Sadie's mom thought about the short engagement.

"It's quick, sure, but I know my daughter and she doesn't make any decisions without thinking them through. She must be madly in love with your son and believe your son is in love with her to go through with this." She took a sip of her wine. "Don't you trust your son's judgment?"

"Owen has always been someone who knows what he wants and doesn't give up until he gets it."

"Well, there you go. Everything will work out, then. The wedding planner acted like we were going to have all these troubles, but if we have someone as determined as Owen and as certain as Sadie, it will go off without a hitch."

Jonathan jumped in the conversation. "The planner thought you were going to have trouble getting married so soon?"

Sadie shrugged. "She just said it will be difficult to get into certain venues, but she also said she would find us some alternatives that will be just as good or better."

"Better than I picked out? Pfft!" Candice said.

"We're going to trust, remember?"

"I trust she'll find something. I don't think it will be better than the places I found for you, though."

Sadie had her hands full. It was also clear that her mother was perfectly fine with the fast engagement because she believed her daughter wouldn't make a major life decision without thinking things all the way through. Jonathan knew different, though. He could see the uncertainty on her face and hear it in her words.

"If you need any help, I'm more than willing to lend you guys a hand," Jonathan's mother offered.

Sadie sucked in a breath. "That's so kind of you, Beth."

"We're going dress shopping next time. If you want to join us, you're more than welcome," Candice said.

"I would *love* that. Have you thought about where you want to look? I know this great boutique in Palm Beach. I could set up a fitting."

Jonathan wondered what his mom was up to. There didn't seem to be a good reason for her to know about bridal boutiques. She had two boys.

"That would be great. Thank you." Sadie had no idea what she was getting herself into either.

After some more small talk, the two moms left. Jonathan's mom had reported Riley was fast asleep in her bed. Apparently all that shopping had taken its toll. Sadie stayed in the kitchen with Jonathan instead of running off to her wing of the house.

"I actually managed to have a normal visit with your mother. I didn't embarrass myself or have to rush off because of a massive disaster."

"You're funny. I told you that my mom wouldn't hold any of that against you. Your mom was nice."

Sadie laughed and the sound made Jonathan aware of his heart beating. "I love my mom, but she is very opinionated. She really hates the wedding planner. I thought I was going to have to separate them during our meeting today."

"She does seem like a tough lady. I'm guessing she's not someone you want to cross."

"Absolutely not. Just ask my dad about that one."

"Your parents aren't together anymore?"

"Divorced five years ago. He got a new wife and she got cancer. She's a little bitter about it."

Jonathan took a seat on one of the island

stools. "That's a lot to happen in five years. I think she kinda has a right to be a lot bitter."

Sadie came around the island and sat down next to him. Her knee touched his. It shouldn't have been a big deal, but for some reason he couldn't stop focusing on it.

"Thankfully, she beat the cancer and is working on accepting my dad's new wife."

"Impressive."

"Actually, that's a total lie. She will probably never accept Bianca. The woman could rescue a bunch of orphans from a burning building and my mother would spread the rumor that Bianca started the fire in order to look like a hero."

Jonathan cringed. "Yikes. Divorce is rough."

"It has been for my family. It's my biggest fear."

"Getting a divorce?" Sadie nodded. "Why would you be thinking about a divorce before you even get married?"

"Because it can happen even when you don't want it to. My mom didn't want to be divorced, but my dad did. She wanted to work on things, was willing to go to counseling, but he was done. He wasn't in love with her anymore."

"That's the scary part about love. You have to trust that the other person will fight for what you have as much as you will. Of course, I also know that even if you both love each other something fierce, one of you can leave. I didn't want to be a single dad. I'm fairly certain that Mindy didn't want to die. But here I am and she's gone."

Sadie put her hand on his leg and he wanted to run away and move closer at the same time. "I'm so sorry for your loss. I can't imagine losing the person I thought I was going to spend a long life with."

"It sucks. It really sucks."

"I feel like that's an understatement."

"It is." The cracks in Jonathan's heart that would never be fully healed ached as a reminder.

Sadie climbed off her stool. "Can I give you a hug? I feel like we both need a hug right now."

Jonathan knew he should say no because his emotions were all over the place at the moment, but something about her offer was undeniable. He stood up and let her wrap her arms around his neck. He wrapped his around her waist. In her embrace, he felt understood. She made it okay to be not okay. She didn't tell him not to be sad or that he should be over it by now. She just held him. It was such a comfort.

"Dad?" Riley's voice turned the comfort into guilt.

He jumped away from Sadie, and quickly tried to deflect. "You're awake. Do you want a snack?"

"Were you sad?" Riley had always been in tune with Jonathan's feelings.

"No, I'm fine, honey."

"Was Sadie sad?"

"No one was sad," Jonathan asserted. If Riley knew he was thinking about Mindy and it made him sad, she would dwell on it for days.

"Are you in love?"

Jonathan hadn't thought about her going there. His brain froze and no words would come out of his mouth.

"I was sad," Sadie blurted out. "I was sad about my mom and dad fighting and your dad gave me a hug."

"What were your mom and dad fighting about?"

"What *don't* they fight about?" Her joke went right over Riley's head. "They fight about everything. That's why I was sad."

"I'm sorry," Riley said, coming over and putting her arms around Sadie's waist. "I'll give you a hug, too. Two hugs are better than one."

Sadie hugged Riley back and made eye contact with Jonathan. *Are you in love?* That was a question he didn't dare answer because he was sure he might answer in a way that would ruin everything for everyone in this room right now and the one who wasn't.

CHAPTER NINE

"I LOVE YOU."

Sadie stared hard at her reflection in the mirror. They were three words. They shouldn't be so hard to say, especially to the man she was supposed to marry in a month and a half.

"I love you."

Why did the words taste weird? How was that even possible? Words didn't have a taste.

"I love you."

Sadie was bound and determined to say those words to Owen today. She was going to prove to herself that her relationship was real. Like her mother had said last week—she must be in love with him or she wouldn't have made the decision to marry him.

"I love you."

Owen was taking her to a charity golf outing at his country club and they had invited Jonathan, Riley and all of the parents to join them for dinner afterward. All the parents including stepparents. Well, there was only one stepparent, and she was coming, much to Sadie's mother's dismay.

"I love you."

It was getting easier. She could do this. Owen had been nothing but wonderful this week. He came back from his tournament feeling good. He had finished in the top three. His highest finish this year. His father said that boded well for his chances next week when the purse was almost $10 million dollars. Owen had explained that the purse was how much money was distributed among the players. Owen made money even if he didn't win. If he won, he would go home with a little over a million dollars. In her opinion, no one should be a millionaire for playing a good round of golf, but she didn't make the rules.

There was a knock on the door. "You almost ready?" Owen asked from the other side.

"I'm coming." She checked her reflection one more time. She could do this. They had been officially engaged for two weeks. She should be able to tell him she loved him. "Ready to go," she said as she opened the door.

"Are you sure you want to wear your hair like that?"

Her hand went right to her ponytail. "I thought I'd wear a hat. If we're going to be in the sun all day, I'll need the shade."

He stared at her for what felt like a long minute. "It looks better down, but a hat could work. You should wear one of mine so my we can promote another one of my sponsors. Where is your change of clothes?"

"I didn't know I needed a change of clothes." Sadie didn't have that many outfits to begin with, and she had no idea she had to come up with two today.

Owen chuckled. "Well, you can't exactly wear that to dinner."

Sadie looked down at her outfit. Owen had bought it for her specifically for this event because she didn't own any golf gear. She had assumed what she had on was good enough to wear all day since the scalloped skort and polo shirt were pricey.

"What am I supposed to wear to dinner?"

"Don't you have a dress? I keep forgetting that you don't have your whole wardrobe."

"Dresses weren't high on my priority list

when I went shopping for everyday clothes. I have a cotton maxi dress. It's very casual."

"Let me see," he said, heading for her bedroom at the end of the hall.

"Going to the country club is stressful for someone not very fashion forward like me." She went to her closet and showed him the blue maxi dress with the anchor print.

"Do you have shoes that could dress it up by any chance?"

She cocked her head. "Owen, I own one pair of sandals, one pair of tennis shoes and the new golf shoes you bought me. Again, heels weren't really part of my emergency everyday-wear fund."

"We'll stop on the way to the club and get you what you need. Come on," he said, storming out of the room.

"Don't people wear this kind of stuff inside the clubhouse? Does everyone bring a change of clothes? Did you bring a suit?"

"I keep certain outfits in the locker room to wear for different events. Most of the members do." He sounded frustrated. Not exactly how she wanted their day together to begin. Especially since she was planning to use the *L* word today.

He stormed through the house to the garage. They passed Jonathan and Riley, who were sitting in the living room.

"Don't be late for dinner," Owen said as he stomped on.

Sadie waved while she tried to keep up. Jonathan gave her the are-you-okay? look and she shrugged and kept going.

Everything Owen did until they got to the country club was in fast mode. He drove fast, he shopped fast and he paid fast. Sadie didn't even get to try anything on. Owen walked into Bloomingdale's, snatched six dresses off the rack and asked the woman behind the counter to grab nude heels in Sadie's size and ring him up.

"You can try them all on in the locker room. One of them will work," he said when Sadie tried to protest.

When they pulled up to the valet stand at the club, Owen handed all of Sadie's new things to a young man in black shorts and a red polo shirt with the Palm Beach Country Club logo stitched on the chest. "She needs a temporary locker. Please have them remove the tags and steam all of these so they're ready to wear."

"We shouldn't take the tags off until I try them on and decide which one I like."

"You're going to need a bunch of dresses this summer. There are going to be plenty of opportunities for you to wear them all," Owen said to her as he tipped the young man, reiterating, "Please have Veronica take all the tags off."

"No problem, Mr. Bradley."

That was something Sadie would hear the rest of the day—*No problem, Mr. Bradley.* When Owen wanted something, he got it. If the person he asked couldn't get it for him, they immediately went to find someone who could.

It wasn't only the staff, though. Other members seemed to treat him like he was the crown prince. He was actually one of the prizes at the event. Owen had been auctioned off as a team member for the group that had donated the most money.

He tried to explain it to Sadie that it was a scramble, which meant that teams would all tee off their own ball but the next shot got to be wherever the best shot had been hit. Seeing that Owen usually had the best shot, having a pro like him meant they were likely to win the tournament.

Sadie wasn't there to play. They definitely would not benefit from having her on their team. Her purpose seemed to be arm candy. She drove Owen's cart and was also supposed to make small talk, which would have been easier if she'd had anything in common with these wealthy donors.

The whole day had been more a test of her patience than a fun afternoon with her fiancé. Once he finished playing, there was some more schmoozing with all the participants at the bar. She tried to remain upbeat, but no one truly wanted to engage her in conversation. She felt more like an accessory than a person.

She was actually looking forward to her parents showing up, even if things would be tense between Bianca and her mom. Hopefully, they would behave themselves in front of Owen's family, especially around Riley. If she was being honest, she couldn't wait for Jonathan to get here.

A dangerous thought floated through her head. Things would have been different today if she had spent it with Jonathan instead of Owen. It would have been better. He wouldn't have made her feel like she was only something to look at.

"Why don't you head on down to the locker room and get prettied up for dinner," Owen said, leaning close.

Something about that made her skin crawl and her face flush hot. Part of her wanted to tell him to enjoy dinner by himself. The other part wanted to refuse and show up to dinner exactly the way she looked now.

She wouldn't make a scene, however. She would go down to the posh locker room, try on six dresses, fix her hair and makeup and show up to dinner with a smile on her face. If she was going to marry Owen, she would need to learn to play this role.

"Do you think Sadie will like my dress?" Riley asked while they waited for the stoplight to turn green.

Owen had asked him to not be late, and here he was, *late*. His mother had already texted him twice. He should have realized that Riley would want to do her hair fancier than usual. She wanted braids, which wasn't Jonathan's strong suit. Four attempts, three

YouTube tutorials and a few tears later, and Riley was ready to go.

The light changed.

"Knowing Sadie like I do, I would say she is going to love your dress. Do you think she'll like my tie?"

Riley giggled. "She'll love it. She loves us."

Jonathan's physical reaction to those three little words was so strong that he almost ran off the road. He couldn't think about Sadie and not feel. That wasn't right and it wasn't productive. It wasn't like he would ever be anything other than her brother-in-law.

They were twenty minutes late when they pulled up to the valet station at the club. Riley jumped out and took Jonathan's hand. She was becoming quite the little lady. She definitely wasn't a baby anymore.

"I see Gramma."

Jonathan scanned the room until he spotted the right table. His parents were each flanked by Sadie's parents. She had been so worried about how they would all get along during dinner. There were two open spots next to Sadie's stepmom. Owen was in the next seat and seemed to be holding court. All eyes were on him while he told some story, surely something about golf. On his left was Sadie, and she looked absolutely gorgeous.

Sadie had on a hot pink halter dress and wore her hair down. He had to look away; otherwise he might never be able to tear his eyes away. Why would everyone be looking at Owen when they could be staring at her?

"Sorry we're late!" Riley said as she approached the table. They all had salads and drinks. It wasn't surprising that Owen wouldn't wait.

"Finally!" his mother said.

"So glad you could finally make it," Owen said. "We've only been waiting for a half hour."

"Twenty minutes. And it looks like you ordered without us."

"Riley, your braids are awesome," Sadie said.

Riley beamed. "Thank you."

"You're welcome. My family has been waiting to meet you." She pointed across the table at her dad. "This person right here is my dad. Dad, this is Riley and her dad, Jonathan."

Sadie's dad was tall, like professional-basketball-player tall. He had a head full of dark hair that was graying at the temples.

"And this is Bianca. She's my dad's wife."

The infamous Bianca. Stepmom extraordinaire. She looked like she could pass for Sadie's sister rather than her mother. She had blond hair like Sadie's mom. Jonathan imagined Sadie's mom probably looked a lot like her twenty years ago. No wonder Candice hated her.

"And this is my mom."

"Hi, Riley. I really wanted to meet you the other day at the house, but you were fast asleep when I was there. Nice to see you again, Jonathan," her mom said.

Jonathan could tell that she was mentioning having been at the house on purpose. Sadie had said her mom loved to one-up her dad anytime she could.

"Great to see you again, Candice. Nice to meet you all. You have raised a wonderful daughter, so I expect we'll all get along spectacularly if you can stomach listening to my brother talk endlessly about his golf game."

Owen laughed in an exaggerated manner. "My brother is just jealous because he can barely hit the ball a hundred yards off the tee."

"There's more to life than golf, right?" Sadie asked.

Jonathan had to hold in the guffaw begging to burst forth.

"Golf is a big deal in this family," Jonathan's dad said, coming to Owen's defense as usual. "You need to be ready to eat, sleep and breathe golf if you're going to marry this guy."

"Don't worry, Dad," Owen said. He put his arm around Sadie. "She was great today. The guys on my team thought she was a doll."

"She's not a doll, Owen. She's a grown woman," Jonathan snapped. It was annoying to hear his brother talk about her like she was some kind of prop.

"It's a saying, Jon. Relax. I am more than aware that my fiancée is a grown woman. What's your point?"

"It's rude when you talk about her like she's something you possess instead of someone. She's a person, an incredible person."

Sadie cleared her throat. "Thank you, Jonathan. I appreciate that more than you know."

"Yes, thank you, Jonathan. She is an incredible person who was raised by me. As a stay-at-home mom, who dedicated her life to her family so her husband could make a name for himself in his career, I appreciate the fact that you recognize how amazing she is."

Sadie's dad set his drink down. "This isn't about you, Candice."

"Well, actually the amazingness of our daughter is about me, barely about you and has nothing to do with *her*."

"I never claimed to have anything to do with who Sadie is. Don't put words in my mouth," Bianca said, not sitting back and letting Candice talk about her.

"Mom, let's not do this," Sadie said as calmly as she could probably muster.

"I'm pretty sure Owen was just referring to how charming she was during the event he was a part of today," Jonathan's dad interjected. "We're all saying the same thing. No reason to argue about it."

"I'm not arguing. I just think my brother should talk about Sadie in a way that doesn't demean her. I don't think he even realizes how he sounds sometimes."

Owen shifted in his seat so he was facing Jonathan. "What is your problem all the sudden?"

Sadie put a hand on Owen's arm. "I'm sure there's no problem. I think he's simply pointing out that sometimes the way you say things makes it sound like I'm arm candy instead of your future life partner."

Jonathan was proud of her for standing up for herself and calling him out on his behavior.

Sadie's mom picked up her drink and tipped the glass in her ex-husband's direction. "Unfortunately, men tend to put looks above everything else. Her own father thinks that's more important than a person's character."

"Okay, Candice. That's enough."

"You don't even know my character because you're the one who is so stuck on my looks," Bianca challenged.

"We have new guests!" The waitress appeared just in time to save the day. She took Jonathan and Riley's order.

Jonathan noticed how mortified Sadie looked. He wanted to apologize for starting the argument. All families had their idiosyncrasies. His family was a perfect example.

She didn't need to be any more self-conscious than Owen did.

Once the waitress left, Owen, their dad and Mr. Chapman went back to talking about golf. It may have been a less interesting conversation, but it was much safer.

"Daddy, I have to go to the bathroom," Riley said.

"I can take her," Sadie offered, pushing back her chair before he could even say that wasn't necessary.

"I need to wash up before the food comes. I can take her," Jonathan said.

"You can't take her in the men's room. I'll go so she can go in the ladies' room." She was on her feet and not taking no for an answer.

Jonathan excused himself and the three of them left the dining area. Riley immediately took Sadie by the hand.

"Your dress is so pretty," Riley said in obvious awe. "We're like twins."

"I wore it because I knew pink was your favorite color. I didn't choose it, though. Your uncle went in the store, bought six dresses that he liked and made me try them on here in the locker room with a bunch of women that I don't know." Her tone was upbeat, which probably left Riley thinking all that was totally fine, but Jonathan understood exactly how angry she was. "I love your dress, too, but I want you to know you are more than how you look. You are smart and kind. You are strong and funny. You are resilient and empathetic. You're amazing. Don't ever forget that."

Oh, Owen. He really had a hard time reading Sadie correctly. She wasn't like Courtney, who would have felt like a supermodel trying on dresses he bought for her in front of strangers.

"I won't forget," Riley promised.

Sadie pushed open the ladies' room door. "Go on, honey. I'll be right there." Riley went in while Sadie lingered a minute.

"I'm so sorry my brother did that to you."

"It wasn't just your brother. What kind of place is this? Do you know how many times a man told me today that I was a 'pretty little thing' or 'a natural beauty' or 'another one of Owen's hotties'? Not one of them wanted to know that I'm a teacher. No one asked me what I thought about anything going on in the world. I was literally treated like my only worth was my looks. It was horrible."

Jonathan was embarrassed to be a man. He didn't understand why some guys thought that was what women wanted to hear. Of course, there were some women out there, like Courtney, who took those things as a compliment. She would have enjoyed all the attention from the men Owen had to play with today. Sadie was different. How did he forget?

"I'm so sorry. You are also so much more than the way you look. Take your own advice and don't let anyone make you think different."

"I wish your brother thought the same way you do."

"If you want me to, I will happily knock some sense into him."

She let out a defeated breath. Her shoulders sunk. "I don't know what I want anymore," she said before going into the restroom and letting the door close behind her.

Owen was going to lose her if he didn't get his act together. Jonathan didn't know if he wanted that to happen or not. It was possible he wanted both for very different reasons. One much more selfish than the other.

CHAPTER TEN

THE TWO SIDES of Owen were hard to reconcile. In certain situations, like at the country club, he was not the kind of man she wanted anything to do with. She did not like it when he treated her like a piece of meat. She was not going to be some kind of trophy wife, and he needed to accept that or they shouldn't get married. She had made that clear during the ride home from dinner a few days ago.

There was another side of him, however. There was the Owen sitting at the kitchen table, eating Frosted Flakes with his nine-year-old niece and talking about her favorite cartoons.

"Which would you rather have, a talking dog or the power to make ice come out of your hands?" Owen asked Riley, who had just shoveled a mouthful of cereal into her mouth. He gave her a minute by answering the question himself first. "I would want the power to make ice. I live in Florida. That could be a very useful skill."

"I would want a talking dog," Riley answered. "I want a real dog so bad, but Dad won't let me get one because he's allergic."

"Well, he must not have heard of these dogs that are hypoallergenic. He could totally get you a labradoodle."

"Dad, can you get me a labradoodle?"

Jonathan stood over by the coffeemaker and rubbed his eye. "I think your uncle should get a dog and then you can play with it anytime you want, but we wouldn't have to do any of the work."

"Dogs are a lot of work," Sadie added. "Wouldn't it be nice if they could talk and then you would know for sure if they need to go outside to go the bathroom or if they just want to chase a squirrel."

"Did you ever have a dog?" Owen asked Sadie.

She appreciated when he was curious and tried to learn something about her. "We had dogs growing up. My mom has an obsession with long-haired dachshunds. We always had one."

"Would you want one of your own?"

"When I think about having a dog, I think about my childhood dog, Beverly, who was a sweetie but stubborn as all get out. She literally refused to follow any commands unless you had a treat in your hand that she could see. She also barked at everything. If a leaf blew across the yard, she would bark at it like it was an intruder coming to kill us all. I deal with third-graders all day. That's enough animals for me."

"Third-graders aren't animals!" Riley said with a giggle.

"You're right, Riley." Owen stood up and grabbed Riley out of her chair. "They're monsters!" He lifted her up and made monster noises, causing her to laugh a deep belly laugh.

This was the Owen whom appealed to Sadie. If he could be awesome uncle and interested boyfriend all the time, she'd be completely enamored.

"She's going to barf Frosted Flakes all over you if don't put her down," Jonathan warned him.

"Don't barf on me!" Owen set her back down on her feet.

"Want the last banana?" Jonathan asked Sadie, tugging the last two apart.

"No, thanks. I don't really like bananas."

Jonathan set the other banana back down. He was dressed like he was ready for the gym in a T-shirt and basketball shorts. "So what's on your agenda for the day?"

"We have our second appointment with the wedding planner. Owen is going this time instead of my mom. Please don't mention that to her the next time she comes over."

Jonathan flashed her a crooked grin. "Didn't want to play referee?"

When he looked at her like that, her stomach did a flip-flop. "I did not. She will be joining me and your mom at the bridal shop your mom recommended next week. I figured that would give her plenty of chances to give me a thousand opinions."

"Your mom just wants everything to be perfect for you."

Jonathan totally got it. Her mom was harmless. Her main motive for her overinvolvement was to get Sadie everything she could want. She just forgot to ask what that was sometimes.

"She wants to make sure she's the only one

who has input so she can take credit for the whole wedding when it's spectacular," Owen said. "Right after she makes everyone aware that Bianca had nothing to do with it."

Sadie's face fell. Owen, on the other hand, didn't get it at all. "Her issues with Bianca are separate from all this."

"She's pretty bitter," he said, making Sadie's blood boil.

"She's got good reason to be bitter. The way my dad handled the divorce and his remarriage caused a lot of hurt in our entire family. On top of that, soon after he remarried, she got the cancer diagnosis. The emotions she has about those two things got welded together, unfortunately."

"That makes complete sense. I'm sure Owen wasn't judging," Jonathan said, his glare aimed at his brother.

Owen put his hands up. "I was not judging. I didn't know the timing of everything in her life. Those would be two big blows."

"Yeah." Jonathan gave his brother a light punch on the shoulder. "Can you imagine if the person you thought you were going to spend the rest of your life with just up and left you and turned around and married someone else almost immediately afterward? Imagine how messed up you'd be if that happened to you."

Owen was the one glaring now. "That would be horrible," he said. "Painful. All you could do is move on and open your heart to someone else. Someone better. Someone who is really the person you want to spend the rest of your life with."

"I can imagine you might find someone better, the best even, but if you haven't given your heart enough time to heal and don't give the new relationship enough time, it could fail like the first one. Sadie's mom has been smart not to rush in given everything going on in her life. She took care of herself first."

The two brothers stared at one another like no one else was in the room. Sadie got the sinking suspicion they weren't talking about her mom. She didn't know much about Owen's past relationships, but some of them had to be serious. Had he thought someone in his past was the one before Sadie became the one?

"You're full of sage advice," Owen said with a little venom in his tone. "I think you might be trying to justify why you've stayed single so long. Your opinion seems based more on your personal experience than Sadie's mom's situation."

"Okay, well, how about we stop arguing about my mom and her reasoning for not jumping into a new relationship because I have no idea why we'd argue about that or why we're even talking about it in the first place." She touched Owen on the arm to get his attention, hoping he'd stop shooting death glares at his brother.

"I don't know why we're talking about it either." Owen kissed her cheek and shook off whatever bad mood his brother was putting him in. "I would much rather talk about where we're going to go for lunch after we meet with the wedding planner."

"I'll go wherever you want. What are you and Riley doing today, Jon?"

"My mom is taking Riley out for a girls-only lunch and to a movie. I'm pretty jealous about that."

Riley ran over and gave her dad a hug. "You can come, too, Dad."

Sadie stared down at her coffee. There was nothing more attractive than a good dad, and she didn't want to think about Jonathan that way. He wasn't someone she could be attracted to, especially as she stood next to Owen.

"You and Grandma are going to have a blast, and then I'm going to meet you at Grandma and Grandpa's for dinner tonight."

"I don't want you to be sad." Riley made Sadie's heart melt. Jonathan had raised such a compassionate soul.

"I'll be fine, sweetheart. I have some work to do."

"Vacation's over already?" Sadie asked. This was the first time he had mentioned work.

"We've been here over two weeks. We may be living in the lap of luxury this summer, but I still have bills to pay back in Boston."

"When are you going to sell that overpriced shoebox you call a house in Boston and buy a place down here?" Owen asked. "Think about how many times you could use Mom as a babysitter. Maybe you'd actually get a social life. Meet someone. Be happy like me and Sadie."

"You two are definitely life goals," Jonathan said with a touch of sarcasm.

Sadie wondered what it would be like if

Jonathan and Riley lived nearby and they became permanent fixtures in her life. The thought of them going back to Boston and seeing them only on holidays made her sad, but having them close—having Jonathan close—made her nervous, as well.

"What do you think, Riley? You want to live in Florida?" Owen picked her up. "We could play grotto monster in the pool all the time. Wouldn't that be awesome?"

She glanced over at her dad. Sadie could tell she was waiting for him to give her the okay to be happy about it.

"What do you think, Riley?" Jonathan said, easing some of her worry. "Do you really want to live near your smelly uncle?"

Riley grinned at her uncle. "Kinda."

"I'm not smelly. Your dad is just jealous that my cologne is better than his."

Jonathan huffed. "I don't wear cologne. I smell this good naturally. I don't require perfume."

Owen rolled his eyes. "Even though you're mean to me and call me names, I'm going to call my Realtor friend to take you out and show you some houses. Not only will she find you the perfect house, she's recently divorced and ready to jump back into the dating scene."

"Don't you dare try to set me up."

"Too late."

"What did you do?"

Owen shrugged. "I may have mentioned my very single brother was in town and he was thinking about moving down here."

"Thinking about it. Not doing it. And just because I'm single doesn't mean I'm looking to not be single."

Sadie set her coffee mug in the kitchen sink. She needed to get out of here. "I'm going to get ready. We need to leave by eleven thirty," she reminded Owen before darting upstairs.

Her heart thumped hard in her chest. She told herself it was because she was anxious to meet with the wedding planner, but she knew that the emotion that had triggered her racing heart was more likely related to thinking about Jonathan dating someone. Someone who couldn't be her.

"HAVE FUN AT the movies," Jonathan said as he closed the car door. He poked his head in the open passenger's side window. "Just remember that if you give her a three-gallon cup of soda, she will need to go to the bathroom about seven times during the movie. If you prefer to see more of the movie and less of the bathroom, I suggest skipping the soda."

"You're no fun, but probably very right," his mom said. "Get your work done so you can join us for dinner."

"I'll be there. I need to make sure you're nice to Sadie."

She looked offended. "I have been nothing but nice. I even arranged for her dress fitting."

"You still make her nervous."

"Well, then be ready to go at five thirty. And dress nice."

"Dress nice? Why would I need to dress nice?"

"No reason. Just do it. Bye!"

Jonathan had to jump back because she rolled the window up. He didn't have time to worry about what his mother was up to. His work was calling and he welcomed it. He needed to think about something other than whether or not he should move to Florida, how he was going to slow his brother's engagement down or how Riley would handle things if he uprooted her from her home.

"Megan is available this afternoon around two," Owen said as he and Sadie walked into the kitchen where Jonathan had set up his at-home office.

"Who is Megan?"

"My Realtor friend we were talking about earlier."

"I'm not meeting with your Realtor friend today, Owen."

"You are. She'll be here at two."

"Owen…"

"Jon. I'm not asking you to marry her. I'm asking you to talk to her about what kind of neighborhood and house you would be interested in. If you find yourself interested in her, all the better."

Everything about that made him feel uncomfortable. He was not going to be pressured into moving or dating.

"I'm pretty sure your brother made it clear that he wasn't ready to do either of those things yet," Sadie said, grabbing her purse off the kitchen chair.

"Yeah, if I wait for Jonathan to be ready, he'll die alone in Boston. He needs to be given a little nudge."

"This feels a little more like a shove than a nudge," Jonathan quipped.

"No one said you have to do anything other than talk to her. Let her find you some potential homes so you can make an informed decision about moving here or not. Isn't that what you're always going on about? You like to think things through rather than trusting your gut like me."

"I don't like being set up. I don't want her to think that I have any plans to date her."

"Relax. She isn't going to pounce on you. She's a Realtor, not an escort. Focus on houses and let the romance happen naturally like it did for me and Sadie. Come, my bride-to-be, let's go see what the wedding planner has picked out for our special day." Owen held his hand out and Sadie took it. Every time he mentioned him and Sadie as a couple, Jonathan's stomach felt twisted.

Sorry, she mouthed as they headed out through the mudroom.

At least she understood how he felt. She seemed to understand everything better than Owen did.

Not that it mattered. She was going to visit the wedding planner with Owen, her *fiancé*.

Jonathan might be able to delay the inevitable by reasoning with her, but that didn't mean that Sadie wouldn't eventually become his sister-in-law. As much as his mom thought that Owen should try to win back his ex, Jonathan thought Sadie would be better for him. She would keep him grounded, something he desperately needed someone to do.

Even if it pained him to admit it, Sadie was a solid choice in life partner. His brother may have acted hastily, but he had chosen a winner. Typical Owen. All he ever did was win, win, win, and he was clearly the winner when it came to Sadie.

Jonathan sat down in front of his laptop and tried to push away all the feelings that were messing with his head lately. Moving to Florida meant being close to family, but it also meant having a front-row seat to the wonderful life Owen could have with Sadie. Jonathan wasn't sure he could stomach that.

His phone rang with a business call, rescuing him from his thoughts about Sadie. Work was a nice distraction. He had a report to write and if he didn't get it finished, he'd hear about it. Jonathan had the easiest going boss as long as deadlines were met.

A couple of hours later, he had completed everything he needed to get done for the day. With no kid to entertain, no lawn to mow, no chores in general, he considered taking a nap. He hadn't taken a nap since before Riley was born.

The doorbell rang and a tall, slender blonde woman stood on Owen's front porch. "Hi, I'm Megan Cooper. You must be Jonathan."

"Hi, Megan. I'm sorry, I totally forgot you were coming." He could kill his brother for setting this up last minute.

"I'm so sorry," she apologized. "Do you want to reschedule?" There she was dressed to kill in a tight-fitting dress and he looked like he'd just rolled out of bed.

There was no reason to live through this awkwardness another day; might as well get it all over today. "It's fine. Come on in," he said, opening the door wider. "I knew you were coming, I just got distracted with some work stuff and didn't make myself present-able before you showed up."

Megan giggled as she stepped in the house. "No worries. You don't need to be dressed up to talk about houses. I need to be dressed up to talk about them, but you're all good."

She had on enough perfume to knock Jonathan out as she walked past him. It made his nose itch. He welcomed her into the living room, not sure what he was supposed to even tell her he was interested in seeing. He wasn't convinced he should move to Florida.

Megan sat down on the couch and took a tablet and stylus out of her bag. "So your brother told me that you are looking for a house in a family-friendly area with good schools that's both close to here and where your parents live. Is that right?"

Leave it to Owen to have that all figured out for him already. "Well, that would be nice, but my budget isn't the same as my brother's budget would be. I'm not sure if I could get all that for what I can afford."

Megan wasn't as enthusiastic about things once she heard what kind of budget Jonathan had, but she did her best to sound optimistic that she could find him something.

"If you're willing to look at some places that need some love and attention, I think I could help you."

"I'm not really superhandy. Plus, I don't usually have the time to do a lot of home improvement with my daughter and all."

"Oh, Owen told me you were a single dad. I think that's awesome." She pushed some of her long blond hair behind her ear. "I have a six-year-old son. I know what you mean about not having time. With all the activities and being the only one home to cook, clean and give him attention, it's exhausting. I wish my ex would step up as much as you do. It's so awesome that you're so involved. So many guys take the easy way out and just do their every other weekend. I mean, come on. They're basically Fun Dad instead of Full-Time Dad. It's sad."

"Well, my wife died. I didn't have much of a choice in being Full-Time Dad."

Her eyes went wide and her cheeks flushed. "I'm so sorry. Your brother didn't tell me you were a widower."

Maybe the next time Owen tried to get Jonathan a date, he'd try to remember that his situation was not the same as someone divorced. He didn't break up with his wife. He didn't fall out of love and want to move on, and neither did she. Mindy died. She died while they were still very much in love with one another.

Jonathan had managed to make this meeting even more awkward than it needed to be. Megan seemed unsure of what to say after the dead-wife bomb had been dropped. Luckily for her, Owen and Sadie got home. Megan was thrilled to see Owen. Sadie, however, seemed unhappy.

"How did things go at the wedding planner?" he asked, hoping that would explain her sour mood.

"Great," Owen said a tad louder than usual. "This is going to be the wedding of the year. Chelsea LeFleur's reputation is well-earned. She is brilliant. If you know anyone who needs a wedding planner, Megan, I strongly recommend her because I am going to be throwing the wedding of the year."

Jonathan didn't know how Owen knew Megan, but it sure felt like that recommendation was for someone very specific. Maybe an ex-girlfriend who was recently engaged?

Sadie's face didn't seem to match Owen's level of enthusiasm. Jonathan wanted to know why that was but wasn't sure how to do that with Megan in the room.

"Well, I'm going to make sure your brother has some houses to look at real soon," Megan said, gathering her things.

Jonathan thanked her for her time and showed her to the door. If Owen had thought this was going to end with him asking her out to dinner, he was wrong. Jonathan wasn't interested in Megan. What he was interested in was why Sadie looked so upset and Owen seemed oblivious.

When she excused herself upstairs, he followed, saying he needed to clean up before going to dinner at his parents'.

"Hey." He touched her elbow once they were upstairs by themselves. "Are you okay? You did not look as excited about your visit to Chelsea's as my brother did."

She definitely forced a smile. "He's not wrong. She's amazing. She came up with some great ideas. We picked out invitations and she's going to get them sent out. My mom will even be happy, I think."

"But…" There was something else.

Sadie seemed to grapple with if she should say it or not. "It's nothing. There's just all these things that have to get done and Owen's not going to be around to help me."

Owen was scheduled to play several tournaments over the next few weeks. He was headed to Connecticut next week, would be in Tennessee over Fourth of July and then up in Illinois right after that. He was trying to play as much as he could so he could take some time off in August.

"You're not alone, though. You've got your mom. You've got Mariana. You've got me."

Before he had time to process what was happening, she gave him a hug. The contact was unexpected but not unwelcome. He put his arms around her and hugged her back.

"Thank you," she said into his shoulder. "I'm feeling so overwhelmed right now."

"And Owen acts like there's not a worry in the world."

She sighed and let go of him. He found himself reluctant to do the same. "He loves to go on and on about how this is going to be the wedding of the year," she said. "I know we have Chelsea giving me options and I have my mom and Mariana to offer their opinion, but I'm the one who has to make the final decision on things. No pressure, right?"

"I get it. You know, you could always tell him that an August wedding doesn't give you the time you need."

"He'd be so disappointed."

"Don't worry about Owen. It's more important to him that you're happy. You don't look happy right now."

She shook her head. "I can't back out."

He couldn't push her on this. She was already too stressed. He couldn't bring himself to make her feel more anxious. "Then, don't stress. You can do this. What do you have to do next?"

"Cake tasting. Chelsea made me an appointment to meet at some sort of famous bakery. Not only do I have to choose flavors, but I have to decide which design I want."

"Cake? Please let me come eat cake. I can handle that responsibility."

"You're so…good," she said as if it pained her.

"Is that a bad thing?"

She blew out a laugh. "No. It's not a bad thing. It's…" She shook her head and didn't finish. "You should go get ready for dinner. Your mother is expecting you to be on time, I'm sure."

Jonathan went to his room to get ready. He needed to figure out how to get her to feel less guilty about postponing this wedding. He didn't want her going through with this if she wasn't ready. He also wanted her to really be sure that Owen was the one. She was a good person who deserved to be loved by the right man.

Jonathan loved his brother, but he wasn't sure Owen was the right man for someone like Sadie. She needed someone more like... Jonathan. Not that he could be the one. He couldn't be the one. He would never do that to his brother.

CHAPTER ELEVEN

"Whose car is that?" Jonathan asked as they got out of Owen's car. Sadie had no idea. She looked to Owen, who simply shrugged. They would have to go inside to find out.

Riley came running as soon as they got inside. She was in her bathing suit and wrapped in a towel. "Guess what Gramma bought me at the movie theater?"

"Don't tell me." Sadie had a pretty good idea that Jonathan might be able to guess based on the fact that Riley's tongue was still bright blue. "I'm going to guess something blue raspberry flavored."

Riley dropped her chin to her chest. "How did you know?"

"I'm your dad. I know everything."

"Riley, don't run while you're wet!" Beth came in through the back sliding door. "Oh, you're here! We're going to eat on the lanai tonight."

"Is someone else here?" Jonathan asked his mother.

Beth smirked. "Come out on the lanai and find out. I'll go help Riley get dressed for dinner."

Sadie could see Jonathan's reluctance right away. He seemed suspicious of his mother, which made her nervous. Who could the mystery guest be?

"Do you really not know who's here?" she whispered to Owen as they headed outside.

His smirk matched the one his mom had been wearing a moment ago. He knew. For some reason that only created more anxiety.

The Bradleys had a lovely screened-in lanai with a dining area and a small pool.

Devin was at the grill. He had a bright red apron on and was busy flipping steaks and chicken.

"Owen!" A silver-haired man with the most golden tan stood up from the table and opened his arms.

Owen's smile broadened. "Mr. Wilder." They embraced and Sadie turned to see Jonathan's face when he recognized the three unfamiliar people around the table. He looked displeased, and now she was going to have a panic attack.

Sitting next to Mr. Wilder was an older woman, who most likely was Mrs. Wilder. Sadie didn't think she was the reason for Jonathan's frown. The issue must have been the gorgeous brunette next to her.

"Mrs. Wilder, Georgina, you're both looking lovely as ever," Owen said. He gave them both a kiss on the cheek.

Who was Georgina to him? An ex? Sadie was going to be sick.

"I'd like to introduce you to my fiancée, Sadie."

The Wilders greeted Sadie kindly. They seemed genuinely happy to meet her. Maybe they were simply family friends.

"Hello, Wilder family," Jonathan said. "It's been a long time."

"Too long," his father added.

Owen pulled a chair out for Sadie and then took the seat next to her. Jonathan seemed to hesitate about choosing a seat.

"Your mother was telling us that you're thinking about moving back to Florida," Mrs. Wilder said to him. "I know she would be thrilled to have her granddaughter nearby."

Jonathan's smile was tight. "My mother is thrilled by many things, some of them more likely to happen than others. Are you in town visiting, Georgina?"

"Not visiting!" Mrs. Wilder exclaimed. "She's in Palm Beach Gardens now."

"You and Harry left Orlando?"

"Harry is still in Orlando," Georgina explained. "The kids and I are in Palm Beach Gardens."

Beth and Riley returned outside. Riley skipped over to Sadie and sat on her lap. Beth reminded her that she had her own chair next to her, which meant that the only open seat was next to Georgina.

Mr. Wilder picked up his drink. "She kicked that jerk to the curb finally. He cheated on the wrong woman."

Poor Georgina looked embarrassed to have her dirty laundry aired out in front of the Bradleys. "Dad, please."

"I'm sorry, sweetheart. You know it's difficult for me to hide my feelings about him. Just think, had you and Jonathan stuck it out after high school, you never would have cried so many tears."

Georgina took a deep, frustrated breath.

"And your grandchildren never would have been born. Beth and Devin wouldn't have their granddaughter. Is that what you would want?"

"Of course not. That's not what I meant."

Beth returned to set a bowl of fruit salad on the table. "Of course that's not what he was saying. We can't change the past. Things happen for a reason. But the future gives us all hope, doesn't it?"

Not Owen's ex. Jonathan's ex from high school. This was an old-fashioned setup. Owen and his mother were awfully determined to get Jonathan to stay in Florida, and they both thought finding him a woman to settle down with was the best way to make that happen.

Jonathan took the seat next to Georgina, the only spot left open at the table. "Seems like our parents have forgotten how worried they were that we would stay together after high school."

"And how relieved they were when we broke up."

The two of them laughed, and Sadie felt a pang of jealousy. She shifted in her seat, trying to pry her attention away from them and their conversation about the past.

"Can I help you with anything, Beth?" she asked, hoping she could go inside and not have to witness Jonathan smile at his ex like his mother's plan was actually working.

"Sure, I could use some help with the salad."

Thankful for the escape, Sadie jumped up and went inside. Beth set her up to chop some vegetables.

"I heard you two were at the wedding planner today. How did things go?" Beth asked, handing Sadie a grater to shred the carrots.

"Chelsea came up with some gorgeous ideas and found us the perfect place to have the wedding. We only have to knock thirty-thousand other things off the to-do list and we'll be golden."

Beth's brows pinched together in concern. "Maybe you two should think about slowing things down. I know Owen wants to take August off and get all this over with, but even if you pushed things back a couple months, that could really relieve some of the stress."

Sadie tried not to take offense to the fact that Owen's mother just referred to her wedding as something her son wanted to get over with. It was also interesting that she and Jonathan had basically said the same thing about the wedding. Why was it that it always seemed that two of the Bradleys were in cahoots with each other?

"We have so much already invested in the August date. I don't think we can postpone anything."

"Oh, sweetheart, you can postpone anything you want. There are no rules for that kind of thing."

There might not be rules, per se, but there were contracts that they had signed that meant they had to follow through with the current dates or they would be out money. Owen's money because he had insisted. Sadie would not let her roller-coaster emotions be the reason Owen would lose all that money.

She put on her brave face. "We'll be fine. I'm overexaggerating how much we have to do. I'm sure if I just gave my mom permission to go wild, she would get everything done in a couple days."

"Can I help, too?" Jonathan asked, joining them in the kitchen.

His mother frowned. "We're fine. You

should be out there catching up with Georgina and the Wilders."

Devin poked his head in. "Beth, I need a plate or whatever you're planning on serving these on."

"The steaks cannot be ready yet," she replied, wiping her hands.

"They are. I'm the master griller, remember?"

Beth handed Jonathan a potholder. "When that timer goes off, pull the potatoes out of the oven. Devin, let me look at the steaks before you do anything." She left Jonathan and Sadie alone.

"So, let me guess—I feel like you weren't expecting your parents to invite your high school girlfriend to dinner."

Jonathan guffawed. "Yeah, you could say that. I love that my family has resorted to trying to hook me up as a way to lure me back to Florida. They don't even bother to ask me why I want to stay in Boston."

"It makes sense to me. That's Riley's only home. It's where you and your wife chose to start your life together. You have a lot of memories there—good and bad."

He placed both palms on the island. "How

is it that we've only known each other a couple weeks and you understand me better than my own family?"

She shrugged. He wasn't that hard to read. He wasn't very good at hiding his emotions. They were always written all over his face. He was clearly still not over losing his wife, and he always put Riley's needs above everything else.

"Georgina seems nice, though. And is very pretty. I can see why your mother would want you to consider getting back together."

"Georgina and I are not getting back together. She is awesome. That's why I dated her in the first place. She's also extremely rigid and hates to compromise. That would be why we broke up. I haven't forgotten why it didn't work even though my parents think I should."

Why did that give her such a sense of relief? Shouldn't she want Jonathan to find someone?

"Well, Owen will be happy to hear that. He's betting on the fact that you'll fall for Megan." It was all Owen could talk about at lunch and on the way home from lunch today.

Jonathan chuckled. "Megan is exactly the

kind of woman Owen used to date. She's very nice, but not my type."

Again there was a flutter in her stomach. "How can you know already? Maybe you should give her a chance."

Jonathan took a step toward her and his eyes were locked on her. "I know exactly what I want. And I know she's not who I want."

The air around them seemed to vibrate with electricity. Sadie's heart raced. Her mouth went dry. She set her knife down. Did he know whom he wanted? Did he have someone in mind?

JONATHAN KNEW EXACTLY what he wanted and he knew it was wrong to think that Sadie seemed to fit the bill. She was the kind of person Jonathan would like to have in his life if he was ever ready to let someone in.

The way she looked at him made him want to believe that she wasn't completely against being that person either. That was a crazy thought. A dangerous one at that.

The timer on the oven went off, breaking whatever spell he had fallen under. He grabbed the potholder and took out the potatoes like his mother had asked.

"Jonathan." His mother sounded exasperated. "Please go back out there. Georgina did not come to dinner to listen to her father and Owen talk about the PGA tour. I've got these," she said, pushing him toward the door.

"Okay, Mom. I'm going. I'm not going to get back together with Georgina Wilder, but I'll go make conversation with her during dinner if it will make you happy."

She stopped shoving him. "Why do you say that? You and Georgina used to be the best of friends as well as boyfriend and girlfriend. Sometimes you get a second chance to make things right."

Did his mother and brother have a bet about who could marry him off before the other? First Owen with the Realtor, and now his mother with Georgina. "Mom, I love you, but you have no idea what you're talking about right now. I am never, ever, ever getting back together with Georgina."

"You're being stubborn."

That made him laugh. "I'm being stubborn? Since when is the goal of life to find me a girlfriend? Is this about trying to get me to stay? You figure if I fall in love with someone, I won't leave and go back to Boston?"

His mom averted her eyes and folded her arms in front of her. "I want you to be happy."

"You want me to be happy in Florida."

She looked up at him, no longer chagrined. "I want you to stay because I hate thinking about you in Boston without anyone there to pull you out of this cocoon you have built around yourself."

Cocoon? Since when did he have a cocoon? "I'm fine, Mom. You don't have to worry about me."

"Ha!" She dropped her arms and resumed pushing him toward the door. "You be sure to let me know how that works out for you when Riley grows up."

It was fruitless to argue with her. All he could do was keep living his life the best way he could. If it made her worried, he couldn't do anything about that.

He rejoined the dinner party and played nice with Georgina, who seemed equally annoyed by the setup as he did. He had a feeling she didn't realize what she was walking into tonight either. Her children were with their dad for the next two weeks, and she was leaving for a short vacation to New York City with some friends of hers this weekend.

Dinner was served and the conversations dwindled a bit while everyone shoveled food in their mouths. Sadie was especially quiet. Every once in a while, she would glance over at Jonathan. He offered her a little smile, hoping it would relax her. He hadn't wanted her to overhear that argument with his mother. He knew she didn't like to be in the middle of the drama.

"So how is the wedding planning going?" Mrs. Wilder asked Sadie. "I don't think you could pay me to try to plan a wedding in two months. It took two months to just finalize the guest list when Georgina got married!"

"There's a lot to do, but we have a fantastic wedding planner and I have tons of help from family and friends. Jonathan's even offered to help me pick out a cake this weekend since Owen is going to be gone."

"It's a real sacrifice, but a best man has to do what a best man has to do even if that is eat chocolate cake."

Sadie's grin was big and beautiful. "Oh, really? Who said we're going to be eating chocolate cake?"

"Don't even pretend we aren't going to at least taste something chocolate. You can choose a boring white cake with white frosting in the end, but let's taste the chocolate cake while we're there."

"I was not planning on picking out a boring white cake. I am much more adventurous than that. I would throw some fresh strawberry in there at the very least."

He loved her subtle sense of humor. "So adventurous. Nothing says bold and daring like sliced strawberries."

"Owen's always loved banana cake," his mom interjected, popping the little bubble he and Sadie had been in for a minute. "I sure hope you'll ask them about something like that since it's his favorite."

The smile was wiped from Sadie's face. "Of course. I didn't know that was your favorite," she said to Owen, who wasn't even paying attention.

"What's my favorite?"

"Banana cake?"

"Well, I love my mom's banana cake, but it never seems to taste the same when I get it elsewhere."

Owen knew how to win brownie points

with his mom. She looked like she wanted to leap across the table and hug him. "Is that true? That was your grandmother's recipe. She would be so thrilled that you love it the most."

"No one has banana cake at a wedding," Jonathan scoffed. Why would she even suggest that? "And Sadie hates bananas. They aren't going to have a banana cake."

His mom glared at him like he had criticized her personally.

"I don't really care what kind of cake we get," Owen said. "Whatever Sadie likes in the end will make me happy."

His dad quickly changed the subject back to the only one that seemed to keep the peace—golf. Jonathan was ready to leave. It had been a long day for Riley and she needed some downtime before bed.

"Hey, Riley, why don't you go inside and get all of your stuff together so when the grown-ups are ready to go, you're all set."

"I don't want to," she whined.

"Maybe we'll do a movie night with Sadie and Uncle Owen if you go get ready," he said, hoping the bribe would work.

"I love movie night with you," Sadie said.

Jonathan kind of loved movie night with her, too. She was not much of a movie buff and it was hilarious to hear her try to figure out the movie's plot while she watched.

"Will you be able to watch without questioning everything that happens like you did last time?" he asked her.

"I did not question everything," she replied with a smile. "I was genuinely curious why they changed so much from the book. The book is always better, by the way."

"Can I pick the movie?" Riley asked.

"If you go get ready."

"I can help her," Sadie offered, getting to her feet.

Jonathan pushed his chair back. "That's very sweet of you. If you can help her find everything, I'll grab her a plastic bag to put her wet bathing suit in."

"I'll help her, Sadie. You should stay with your fiancé," his mom said, standing up and blocking her path.

Sadie seemed a bit taken aback but sat down. Jonathan followed Riley and his mom into the house. They went back into the bedroom and he went to the kitchen to look for a bag.

"Can I use this garbage bag?" Jonathan asked his mom.

She snatched it out of his hands and put the wet suit and towel in there. "You can go back outside, Riley. Grandma needs to talk to your daddy a second."

Riley skipped off, and Jonathan really wanted to follow. He was in trouble for something and if this was about thinking banana cake was terrible, he wasn't going to stick around for the lecture.

"What are you doing?" she whisper-yelled.

"I'm packing Riley up so I can go back to Owen's and put her to bed."

"Don't be smart with me, mister."

"What are you asking, Mom?" He was genuinely confused.

"I know we're both trying to get Sadie and Owen to rethink how fast they want to get married, but what you're doing is very different. Weren't you just telling me that maybe Sadie was good for your brother? That maybe he should marry her?"

"Yes. I said that."

"Then explain to me why it seems like you're trying to steal your brother's fiancée away instead?"

Jonathan was so shocked by her accusation he couldn't even defend himself. He began to stutter and fumbled for his words.

"Do you know what I wanted to happen when you saw Georgina tonight? I wanted to see that old look in your eye that you used to get when the two of you would come over here and hang out on the weekends. I wanted to see that spark, that cute banter you used to do. But you know who put the twinkle in your eye and the smile on your face?" She didn't need to answer her rhetorical question. He knew who made him feel the way he did tonight. "Sadie. Your brother's soon-to-be wife. You're out there giggling about chocolate cake and how much you two love movie nights. What are you doing, Jonathan?"

That question was a bit harder to answer. He didn't know what he was doing or why he was feeling this way. He rationally knew it was wrong to think about her the way he did, but he couldn't stop himself. He had tried.

"It's not what you think. We live in the same house. I can't help it that we're forced to spend a lot of time together. Not to mention Owen's always traveling. She's stuck with me and Riley."

"All the more reason you should be careful about what you are doing, son. I know you want me to believe what I just saw with my own eyes and heard with my own ears isn't real, but it seemed way too real for me."

Jonathan wasn't going to argue with her because his feelings for Sadie were becoming much too real. He needed to heed her warning or things would never be the same.

CHAPTER TWELVE

"I WANT TO live in this pool. I could sleep on this float. You would never know I was here unless you came outside." Mariana splashed some water over her legs as she floated around the pool on the glitter rainbow float that Owen had bought for Riley.

"You can't live here. Your husband would miss you."

"But would I miss him?"

She made Sadie laugh, something she desperately needed to do more of lately. She was stressed about everything that had to be done, stressed about not acting stressed in front of certain people who were bound and determined to get her to postpone the wedding, and stressed about why part of her didn't just want to postpone the wedding but run away completely.

"Any word on your town house? When will you get all your stuff or what's left of it?"

"They had people go in and start digging out items. I got to pick up what I wanted. Owen got me a storage unit. We put most of it in there for now."

"Was there much that could be salvaged?"

"More than I thought. I still lost so much. I feel like I'm in some kind of weird dream. Owen asked me to marry him and it's as if my old life disappeared. Everything that was mine is gone or in a storage container. All I do is obsess about this wedding. Speaking of which, can you come with me to taste cake tomorrow? My mom can't make it and I asked Jonathan to come but ever since this dinner we had at his parents' house, things have been off. I feel like he doesn't want to go anymore but doesn't want to tell me."

Mariana paddled over to the edge where Sadie sat with her feet in the water. "Why would he not want to go eat cake?"

Sadie didn't think it had anything to do with the cake. It was much more likely that his mother had pointed out that Sadie was beginning to cross lines she shouldn't even be close to. It had been more than embarrassing when Beth had to remind Sadie that she was marrying Owen, not Jonathan.

"I don't know. So, can you come?"

"You know I would if I could. I have been hoping you would ask me to do this job, but I have to go to my sister-in-law's house tomorrow for my nephew's birthday. Can you change the appointment?"

Sadie shook her head. "The wedding planner made the appointment. I think it would be bad form to cancel."

"Could your brother go with you?"

"I don't really want to taste cake with my brother. He hasn't been the most supportive person about this wedding. I don't think I could handle his negative energy."

"Then you're stuck with your brother-in-law. It won't be that bad. You'll be eating cake."

Mariana was right. How bad could it be if they were stuffing their face with cake?

"Sadie! Guess what I got?" Riley came running out back with a small shopping bag in her hand. Her hair was up in a ponytail and she had on bright pink shorts and a rainbow-striped tank top.

"Tell me. I can't wait to find out."

Riley put her hand in the bag and pulled out a sparkly pink tiara. "Daddy said I can wear it to the wedding. It will be like I'm a princess."

"Wow! It's beautiful. That reminds me. I need to ask you a very important question. Would you like to be my flower girl in the wedding? It's an important job. You have to sprinkle flowers down the aisle for me. Do you think you could do that?"

"Do I get to wear a pretty dress like you?"

"You do, and we will have to find one that will go with your tiara."

"Then yes. I will be your flower girl." She wrapped her arms around Sadie's neck and gave her a big hug.

"That makes me so happy."

"What makes you so happy?" Jonathan had joined them on the patio. He had on his sunglasses and hadn't shaved in a couple of days, leaving him with a five o'clock shadow that gave him a rugged edge.

"Riley agreed to be my flower girl. I think I'm going to have to bring her to the dress fitting next week with your mom and my mom. In fact, maybe Riley can go to the cake tasting with me tomorrow."

"Cake?" Riley's eyes went wide with excitement.

Jonathan took off his sunglasses, revealing those blue eyes like Owen's. "I thought I was going to the cake tasting with you tomorrow."

"I want to taste cake."

"You and me both, little one," Mariana said from the water.

"I got the feeling you weren't too excited about doing that anymore," Sadie said, replying to Jonathan.

He kicked off his slides and sat next to her at the pool's edge. "I said I would go. We can bring Riley along if you want."

"Yes!" Riley shouted, throwing her arms in the air. "I love cake."

Jonathan's leg brushed up against hers and he twisted at the waist to grab Riley and tickle her. "You want to go get your bathing suit on and jump on Mariana?"

Mariana shook a finger in their direction. "Don't even think about it, chica."

Riley giggled and sprinted for the house. Her ponytail bounced side to side.

"I guess the three of us will go to the bakery."

"It'll be fun." He put his hand on her knee and her whole body felt on fire. She couldn't remember the last time she had such a physical reaction to a man. He got up and went inside to check on Riley. Sadie slid into the pool to cool off. She dunked her head under the water. What was she doing?

"You alright?" Mariana slid her sunglasses down her nose and peered over the lenses at her. "I feel like I'm missing something."

"I'm fine. You're not missing anything."

Mariana laughed. "It's okay. I can wait until you're ready to tell me the truth. I will be here, floating on this rainbow whenever you need me. You have more major stressors going on in your life right now than most people experience in a lifetime. It would not be surprising if you're having some feelings."

Mariana would be waiting a long time because Sadie was never going to speak these feelings out loud. She didn't even know what to call them or how to begin to explain them. What had started out as a desire to get Owen's brother's approval somehow had become something else. Something that gave her a rush half the time and made her feel guilty the other.

This was part of her stress reaction. Mariana was right. Sadie was experiencing several major life stressors all at once. That had to be messing with her head. It was causing her to misinterpret things and to seek out any and all affection and comfort. Jonathan simply made her feel safe like he did for Riley. She was responding to that and getting it mixed up with the growing feelings she was having for Owen.

That had to be it, she told herself. Anything else was nothing but a mistake.

JONATHAN HAD HEEDED his mother's warnings, but he wasn't going to leave Sadie to plan this wedding on her own. He would show his mom that he had no intentions of stealing his brother's wife. Well, his wife-to-be.

"How many cakes do we have to eat today?" Riley asked from the back seat.

"We aren't going to be eating whole cakes. We're going to a tasting. That means they're going to give us little bite of a bunch of different cakes."

Riley seemed satisfied with that answer. "I want to eat all the ones with sprinkles."

Sadie cringed. She glanced at Jonathan. He knew there probably wouldn't be any sprinkles, but he decided not to burst her bubble, hoping that what they did have would be tasty enough for her not to remember that was what she wanted.

Kessler Bakery was one of the most renowned bakeries in the Jupiter/Palm Beach area. Jonathan had looked it up on the internet and it had fantastic reviews for its modern designs, unique flavors and handmade sugar flowers.

It was very posh inside. All the decor was black and white with pops of teal. There were fancy cakes, cookies and colorful cupcakes on display in the case. Pictures of extravagant wedding cakes hung on the walls. There was a little room off to the right that had a desk and two plush chairs in front of it.

Sadie went up to the woman behind the counter. "Hi, I'm Sadie Chapman. I have an appointment with someone named Kallie."

"Wedding cake?" the woman asked. Sadie nodded. The woman pointed to the office. "You can take a seat in there and I'll let Kallie know you're here."

Jonathan picked up Riley and took a seat next to Sadie, who was looking a little peaked. "This is very fancy. Do you want a fancy cake?"

"I don't know. I saved some pictures from

the internet. None of them look like the ones on the walls."

"You don't have to have a fancy cake. You can have anything you like. They just might not take a picture of it and hang it on the wall."

She smiled and her shoulders seemed to relax. "I don't need my cake on the wall."

"Hi, you must be Sadie." The woman they assumed was Kallie came in and sat down. "And who is this cutie?"

"This is Riley and I'm Jonathan."

"Awesome. So let's start with the easy part. How many people do we need to feed?"

"Seventy-five."

"Okay, not too big. Do you have ideas or do you want to look at some ideas about what kind of cake style you want?"

Sadie pulled out her phone and handed it to Kallie. "There are a couple there that I really liked. I don't want anything too extreme."

"These are beautiful. So a simple layer cake, some texture, maybe buttercream that looks like ribbon wrapped around it and some flowers. Are you thinking fresh flowers or edible? We are known for our sugar work."

"I don't have a preference. What do you

think?" Sadie said, looking to Jonathan for some support.

He didn't know what to say. It wasn't his cake. He didn't really care how a cake looked, more how it tasted. He could tell she was feeling overwhelmed even though Kallie was taking it pretty easy on her. "I think the sugar flowers would be cool. What do you think, Riley? Should we get flowers made out of sugar that you can eat or regular flowers?"

"Sugar," Riley agreed.

"Sugar it is," Sadie said.

Kallie and Sadie discussed colors and types of flowers for a bit. Jonathan's stomach started to rumble. He just wanted to get to the tasting part.

"Are we going to eat cake now?" Riley whispered loud enough that everyone could hear.

Sadie laughed. "Hang in there, sweetheart. We're almost done with the boring stuff."

"I want some chocolate cake."

"You sound just like your dad. Have you two been conspiring against me?"

Jonathan defended himself. "I did not tell her to say that. I told you that people love chocolate."

Sadie's lips curled up in that sweet smile. Jonathan would bet they tasted better than chocolate. Not that he was thinking about kissing her. He would never kiss her.

"I'm trying to keep an open mind about flavors and you two keep trying to influence me to get chocolate."

"I want sprinkles, too," Riley added.

"I don't know about having sprinkles," Sadie said. "This isn't like a birthday cake."

"We could put sprinkles inside the cake," Kallie said. "Like a confetti cake. You could do a different flavor on each layer. You could do a chocolate for him, confetti for her and whatever flavor you want. The bride always gets the biggest layer, though."

"Wait, what? I want the biggest layer," Jonathan teased.

"No, I want the biggest layer," Riley said, placing her hands on his cheeks.

"You can't have the biggest layer. You're the smallest one here. You get the top layer. It's nice and small like you."

"No, I should get the biggest and you get the smallest because you're the biggest."

"I think we should listen to Kallie and follow the rules. Brides get the biggest layer and the bride is me."

"You three are adorable. You're going to make a beautiful family," Kallie said.

Sadie's face fell. She glanced Jonathan's way. He didn't realize that Kallie thought he was the groom. He wasn't sure if it would make it more or less awkward to set her straight. He decided not to call attention to it.

"Thank you. Does that mean we get to taste some cake now?"

"Let's taste some cake."

Kallie led them all back into the kitchen part of the bakery. They had a long metal table covered in plates of cake set up for them. It looked as if they had five different chocolate cakes and every other flavor, too. Jonathan's mouth watered.

Kallie explained how the tasting would work. She handed them both a piece a paper with numbers on it and flavors. Each plate had a number written on it. They were to taste the cake on a plate and mark their thoughts by the number on the paper.

Turned out not all the chocolate-looking ones were actually chocolate. There was mocha and cherry cola. One of them was a hot fudge and the other was triple chocolate. There was a green one that had something called matcha in it. Lemon poppy seed and burnt butter. Sadie took a second bite of the chocolate cake with a hazelnut spread frosting and chocolate ganache filling. She wasn't wrong about that being delicious.

"You're going to fall in love with the chocolate hazelnut one, aren't you?" Jonathan asked her, knowing it was going to irk her to admit it.

"You would like me to pick that one, wouldn't you? Well, I also like another one."

"Oh yeah?" he challenged. "Which one?"

"Number twelve," she answered, avoiding eye contact.

Number twelve, according to the sheet, was chocolate cake with a salted caramel filling. "Two chocolate cakes?" He couldn't help but laugh.

Sadie pressed her lips together, obviously trying not to laugh at herself. She punched him in the shoulder. "Which one was your favorite?"

"I actually liked the champagne with the strawberry frosting filling. I never would have thought to choose that before coming here."

"I like the confetti cake the best!" Riley said, finishing off the plate of that one.

And just like that, they ordered a three-tiered chocolate hazelnut, champagne and strawberries and confetti wedding cake. Sadie took one more bite of the chocolate with salted caramel filling.

"Don't look at me like that," she said around her bite of cake. "No reason to let a good piece of cake go to waste."

He laughed and wiped some chocolate from the corner of her mouth with his thumb. "You're a mess," he said.

It was like she stopped breathing. She stared up at him with those soulful hazel eyes and his entire body felt her magnetic pull. Never in his life had he wanted to kiss someone so badly. His mother's voice sounded in his head. This was his brother's fiancée. He could not do anything to hurt his brother.

He stepped back and reached across the table for a napkin. He handed it to her. "We should go."

At the very least, he needed to go outside and get some fresh air. He almost kissed his future sister-in-law and almost did it right in front of his daughter. That would have been way more confusing than the hug she witnessed the other day.

His actions had much bigger consequences than he wanted to admit. He could end up hurting not only Owen, but Sadie and Riley in the process. He couldn't be so careless. He needed to protect everyone, even if what they needed protection from was him.

CHAPTER THIRTEEN

SHE WAS HIDING. Sadie wasn't proud to admit it, but it was what she was doing. She was a terrible person. If Owen knew what had happened or, even worse, what she had wanted to happen, he would break up with her. She needed to stay away from Jonathan and focus her attention on Owen when he was in town. That was the only way she was going to stop transferring her feelings for Owen onto Jonathan, because that had to be what she was doing.

The last few days, she had spent most of her time at her mom's house. She told Jonathan that her mom needed her help, but the truth was she needed her mom to help her get her head on straight.

"When does Owen get back?" her mother asked as they sat at her dining room table and tried to start organizing the seating chart.

The dining room table was covered in a

hand-drawn layout of the reception room at Owen's country club. Each table sat eight people and names of guests were on sticky notes. As guests RSVP'd, their sticky note would get moved to a table until all the tables were full.

Sadie's mom had already taken the liberty of putting herself at the table closest to the wedding party table and Bianca and her father as far away as possible.

"This afternoon. He finished yesterday afternoon, but they have all these events for the golfer to attend. He couldn't leave until today." She peeled off her dad's sticky note and put it at a different table up front. "You can't make Dad sit in the back."

Her mom put her hand on top of Bianca's sticky note. "Fine, but Bianca stays here."

Sadie cocked her head to the side. "Mother."

That was all she had to say. Her mom peeled off Bianca's name and handed it to Sadie. "Make sure wherever she sits, she's not in my line of vision."

"I know it's not easy for you, but I hope you can be civil."

"I'll try. That's all I can promise," her mom replied. "I didn't realize how much professional golfers travel. I hate to think about you apart more than you are together. You'll be able to travel with him next summer, right?"

"No reason I couldn't, I guess. I don't know anything about golf, though."

"You're going to have to learn when you're married to him." Her mother switched the sticky note that had Sadie's godparents names on it with the one labeled with her cousin's and his wife's names.

"I'm willing to learn, but I don't think I need to go to every tournament. He needs to play in at least seventeen every year. That's his job. I wouldn't want him to come to school and watch me teach. I might go to the really big ones, but I don't think I need to be at all of them."

"What do the other wives do?"

Sadie shrugged. She had no idea. She didn't know anyone in that world. The whole thing was completely foreign to her.

"Well, you should find out. That would be one of those things you and Owen talk about before you get married, so you know what he expects from you and he knows what your limits are."

The list of things she and Owen needed to

talk about seemed to be getting longer instead of shorter. Every time she crossed something off the list, she had to add three new things.

"Are there things you wished you had known about Dad before you married him?" Her parents weren't the best role models for how to do this marriage thing right, but maybe she could learn from their mistakes.

"I don't know what I could have asked that would have stopped me from marrying him. He certainly wasn't going to admit that he would put his own selfish needs above those of his family. He probably believed that he would honor his vows. He wouldn't have told me that when we turned forty, he would begin to lose interest."

"Forty?" They had gotten divorced when they had been in their late fifties. Sadie had no clue that they'd spent close to two decades unhappy.

"I thought you didn't know anything was wrong until he said he wanted a divorce."

"Well, I didn't acknowledge that anything was wrong until then, but I may have noticed a few things."

"Do you think if you had admitted something was going on when he first started pulling away, you could have saved your marriage?"

Her mom shook her head. "I have no idea. I can't spend too much time thinking about it because I could play the what-if game until it killed me." She reached over and grabbed Sadie by the hand. "I do think that you shouldn't run and hide from your problems. Whatever is troubling you, you should feel comfortable enough to address it with Owen. And he should feel the same."

Owen never seemed to think there were any problems. He acted like she was silly for stressing over every little thing.

"What's really bothering you?" her mother asked. "I feel like there's something you're not telling me."

"I'm not sure I fit into his life, into his family, into his house even. Sometimes I feel like my life has been flipped upside down and I'm not sure how to get back on my feet because I'm trying so hard to redefine myself in his world instead of mine."

Her mom gave her hand a squeeze. "I don't want you to lose yourself, Sadie girl, but at some point, you have to stop thinking about things as yours and his. You shouldn't have to fit into his world and he shouldn't fit in yours. This is the beginning of something new for both of you."

"He doesn't seem to be thinking about changing anything in regards to how he lives."

"Then you need to say something. Staying quiet won't do you any good."

"Look at you giving advice like a champ."

Her mom tried and failed not to smile. "Are you saying I don't usually give such good advice?"

"Honestly? Sometimes your advice sounds more like a lecture. But this was good. I hear what you're saying and I'm going to heed your advice."

Sadie's phone chimed with a text. Owen had taken an earlier flight and wanted to surprise her, but she had surprised him by not being there.

"I have to go. Owen's home. I should attempt to be open about how I'm feeling." The best thing she could do was learn from her mother's denial. The more she pretended there wasn't a problem, the more likely she and Owen would fall apart.

"Hello?" she called out when she got back

to his house. Not his. Theirs. Soon-to-be theirs. She needed to stop dividing and start combining.

"Why are you yelling?" Jonathan came down the stairs in his swim trunks and no shirt. This was a test. Sadie closed her eyes and willed herself to pass this one with flying colors.

She looked him right in the eye and refused to be attracted to him. "Your brother texted me that he was home."

"I am home," Owen said, coming around the corner. He picked her up and lifted her off her feet. "How are you? Did you miss me?"

She hugged him back and breathed in his cologne. He was happy to see her. He loved her. She was happy to see him.

"Of course I missed you. I always miss you."

Jonathan brushed past them. "I'll let you two lovebirds get reacquainted." His tone had a bite to it.

"What's his problem?" Owen asked, setting her back on her feet.

Sadie didn't want to dissect Jonathan's feelings. That wouldn't end well for her. "I don't know. Let's not worry about your brother."

"I will happily not worry about my brother. What would you like to do instead?"

"Let's do something, just you and me. I feel like we haven't done anything alone since we got engaged."

"Probably because we haven't. Did you have something in mind?"

Sadie figured she'd give a little to get a little. "I know you just got done playing in a tournament, but maybe you could take me mini-golfing or to a driving range. I want to learn to enjoy some of the things you love."

"Aw." He cupped her cheek. "That is so sweet. I appreciate that."

Sadie waited for it to happen. She willed the feelings to come. The other day at the bakery, Jonathan had only brushed her lips with his thumb and she thought she was going to spontaneously combust. The want had started in her stomach and shot through her entire body. Kissing him had been the only thing that would have relieved the burn.

She waited and waited, but the feeling didn't come. Unlike Jonathan, Owen didn't hesitate to kiss her on the lips, and still there was nothing.

"Let's go play some mini-golf. I want to break you in easy."

Easy. *Ha.* There was nothing easy about this relationship.

"Cannonball!" Jonathan yelled as he jumped in the pool. Riley had been a good listener and waited for him to come outside before she swam.

He hoped the water would get rid of the burn he felt after seeing Sadie and Owen all lovey-dovey in the foyer. She was happy he was home. She should be. They were getting married.

Owen stuck his head outside. "We're going out. Don't plan on us for dinner. We won't be back until late."

"Cool. Have fun!" *Did that sound too enthusiastic?* It was definitely too much. Owen didn't notice. Jonathan's brother never noticed that kind of stuff. He was more concerned about getting out of here with Sadie, his fiancée, whom he would be marrying in just over a month.

"I wish Sadie could come swim with us. Maybe when she gets home, she can come out with us."

"Sadie and Uncle Owen are hanging out by themselves today. They won't be home until past your bedtime."

"But we're almost done with *Charlotte's Web* and she was supposed to read it with me."

"I can read it to you." Riley didn't need Sadie. Aunt Sadie wasn't going to be around forever. When they went back to Boston, Riley wouldn't see her more than a couple of times a year.

Riley stared at him. He could see the battle going on in her head. She wanted to tell him something, but she didn't want to upset him.

"What? You can tell me what you're thinking. I won't be mad."

Riley worried her bottom lip with her teeth. "I want Sadie."

"I know you prefer Sadie to read to you, but Sadie wants to spend tonight with Uncle Owen. We just need to accept that. They're getting married in a little more than a month."

That was when the whining began. "We're almost at the end, and I don't want to finish it without her."

"Then you're going to have to wait because she isn't going to be home tonight."

"But I want to finish it tonight."

"Then you'll have to finish it with me."

Riley scowled and splashed water at him. "I don't want to read it with you. I want to finish it with Sadie."

Why did he feel like this conversation was going nowhere? "Okay, you can finish it with Sadie."

"Tonight."

"Good luck with that." Jonathan climbed out of the pool. Swim time was over.

He sat down on one of the loungers and grabbed his phone off the side table. He checked his email and noticed one from Megan the Realtor. She sent him a few listings and an offer to take him to look at anything he wanted to see.

Jonathan had no plans to stay in Florida any longer than he had to. After the wedding, he was going to take Riley back to Boston. It was too much to stick around. Too much money, too much emotional turmoil, too much trouble. Jonathan didn't need any more trouble and Sadie was nothing but trouble. Florida. He meant Florida was nothing but trouble.

His phone rang. It was his mom. "Hello, Mom."

"Is your brother home yet?"

If she wanted to talk to Owen, why didn't she call him? "He's back in town, but he's not home. He went out with Sadie."

"I think you need to talk to him when he gets home. I'm sending you a picture."

Jonathan was done being his keeper. He didn't care if he married Sadie or not. He could rush into this marriage out of spite if that was truly what he wanted.

His mother's text came through. He clicked over and there was a screenshot of an Instagram post from Courtney's account. It was of Owen on the golf course, and it was recent, not some memory from when they were together. The caption read, What a finish! #soproud @owenbradley.

"Why would she take a picture of him and post it?"

"Not only did she post a message to him, but he replied." She sent another screenshot of Owen's first comment and their back-and-forth conversation on her post. "You need to talk to him about this."

As much as he wanted to tell her that he

was done meddling in Owen's business, this was too troubling to ignore.

"I'll talk to him when I can get my hands on him."

"Thank you. I feel like he needs to think about what he really wants."

Sadie was not a piece of property or a possession for Owen to keep or give up. "*Who*, Mom. Both Sadie and Courtney are people. Owen needs to decide who he wants to be with."

"Who. He needs to decide who he wants, Jonathan. And he needs to do it soon."

He hung up with his mom and rubbed his tired eyes. If Courtney was trying to lure Owen away from Sadie, how would Sadie handle that? She would probably not be much of a fan of anyone with the last name *Bradley*. If he chose Sadie, there would no longer be any reason to be concerned about why they were getting married so quickly.

Either way, Sadie stayed off-limits. There was no getting around that. Just like there was no getting out of the massive temper tantrum Riley would throw when she realized that Sadie wasn't going to be home when it was time for a bedtime story.

"I want Sadie."

"I understand that, Riley Marie, but Sadie is out with your uncle, and you have to go to bed. I can read this to you or something else," he said, holding up the *Charlotte's Web* book.

"No, you can't read it. I just want Sadie. Can you please get her?"

This wasn't a typical Riley tantrum. It wasn't because she was too tired or because she had a bad dream. This was next-level.

"Okay, it sounds like you've decided to not read a book with me. I'm going to leave and I will see you in the morning. Sweet dreams."

"No! I'm not going to sleep until I read that book."

"Good night, Riley." He went to the door and shut off the light.

"No! I'm not going to bed!" she shouted, totally unfazed by his words. She not only raised a ruckus, but she literally got out of her bed and opened the door.

This went on until for another thirty-five minutes. Jonathan had almost broke. He was about to tell her she could wait up for Sadie when she finally gave in to her tiredness.

After that battle, Jonathan could have gone to bed, but he was going to stay up until his brother got home. He felt like an angry parent waiting for their teenager to come home after curfew when the two of them finally walked in the door.

Owen's laughter filled the room when he stepped into the kitchen. Jonathan put his glass of water in the sink. Sadie exited the mudroom next. She seemed startled to see him.

"Hey, Jon. What's up?" Owen asked.

"Not much. Did you guys have a good night?"

"Sadie is not going to be joining the PGA tour with me, but she did learn why putting can make or break someone's game."

"I'm sure putting is important, but it's not like you have to hit the ball through a windmill on tour," Sadie said.

"No, I do not have to hit balls through windmills. I have had to hit out of what felt like a forest once. I had to take a shot between these two trees. It felt a lot like what we did tonight."

"Well, I guess we'll have to find a hobby we're both good at if golfing isn't my thing."

"Golf isn't a hobby. It's a lifestyle. It's my lifestyle." Owen went to the refrigerator and grabbed a soda. He didn't even bother to ask Sadie if she wanted something. Jonathan didn't know why that irked him, but it did.

Sadie worried her bottom lip with her teeth. It reminded Jonathan of when Riley struggled to say how she was feeling. He watched as Sadie forced herself to stand up for herself. "It's not your whole life, though. When we get married, start a family, our lives are both going to change."

"Why would things change? Lots of guys on the tour are married and have families. Plus, we aren't going to start having kids right away."

This felt like a very personal conversation. Jonathan wasn't sure how to see his way out of it.

"You want to have a family, though, right?" Sadie asked, looking a bit flush.

Owen took a swig of his soda and shrugged. "I mean, maybe down the road. I'd like to enjoy our time as husband and wife first. Kids change things. Ask Jonathan."

Jonathan wanted no part of this discussion. "I think this is where I say good-night."

"Oh, come on. Be honest. Once you and

Mindy had Riley, there wasn't as much time for the two of you, right?"

"Having Riley only brought me and Mindy closer together actually."

Owen exhaled a laugh. "Whatever you say, brother. If you can promise me that my kids will all be as awesome as Riley, I'll have as many kids as Sadie wants."

"I love my daughter, but tonight, I feel like I spent the evening with the devil," Jonathan admitted.

"Riley?" Concern etched Sadie's face.

"Oh, she was a handful tonight. She wanted to read *Charlotte's Web* tonight and nothing else would do. However, Aunt Sadie was the only one who could read it."

"Oh my gosh. I'm so sorry. We're almost done. I told her I would finish it with her tonight. I totally forgot."

Jonathan shook his head. "It's not your fault. She needs to learn that sometimes things aren't going to go the way she planned and she's going to have to adjust."

"That's a hard concept for a nine-year-old, but you're right. I'll make it up to her tomorrow." She yawned and stretched her arms above her head. "I think I better get ready for bed. I am exhausted."

"Good night, sweetheart," Owen said, kissing her on the cheek.

"Good night." She pulled her hair tie out of her hair. "Good night, Jon."

He was momentarily entranced by the way her hair fell around her shoulders. It looked so soft, he wanted to run his fingers through it. "Good night."

She went upstairs and Owen took a long swig of his soda. "I should go up, too. This weekend was tough. I almost blew it on Saturday."

"Can I talk to you for a minute before you go up?"

Owen's eyebrows lifted. "Why does that sound a little ominous?"

"I need to talk to you about something that's been bugging me."

"What's that?" Owen took a seat at the island.

"I need to talk to you about Courtney."

Owen stood up right away. "I already told you I wasn't going to have a conversation about her. Good night, big brother."

"Owen, the fact that you don't want to even

talk about her makes me even more concerned about what's going on. Do you still have feelings for her?"

"I'm engaged to be married, Jonathan. I think that answers your question." He turned to leave, but Jonathan grabbed his arm.

"It doesn't. I wish it did, but it doesn't. I know that she's engaged to be married. I know that she's still following you and your career. I know that she posted on Instagram about your performance in the open this weekend. I also know that you commented on that post. And the fact that you don't want to talk about it makes me think that you still have some unresolved feelings that could be bad for your impending marriage."

Owen's face flushed red. "Are you really going to attack me in my own kitchen about stuff you know nothing about?"

"Nothing about? Who did you call when you were crying about Courtney breaking your heart? I was the one who was on the other end of the line, in case you've forgotten."

"Yeah, I know you were on the other end of the line. But you've also been the one in my house this last month and you've seen that I have moved on. That I am in love with Sadie and that we are getting married. What are you trying to accomplish here by ambushing me? Did you think I was going to confess to still being in love with my ex?"

Jonathan wasn't going to let him off the hook. "Are you still in love with your ex? Did you ask Sadie to marry you because you heard Courtney was getting married?"

"Good night, Jonathan. You have fun with your conspiracy theories."

It was worse than Jonathan had thought. The fact that he wouldn't talk about it at all meant that his feelings about it all were still too raw. That didn't bode well for Owen or Sadie.

CHAPTER FOURTEEN

"WHAT ABOUT THIS ONE?" Sadie's mom held up a mermaid-style dress that had lace and crystal beading.

"There is no way that's going to fit without needing alterations that will take forever."

Say Yes wasn't a very large bridal boutique, but there seemed to be dresses everywhere. In the back, there were four dressing rooms and two raised platforms almost completely surrounded by mirrors for the bride to get a full view of her dress. As soon as they checked in, a lovely woman named Holly was assigned to them. Her job was to find Sadie dresses and help her try them on. Beth, Mariana and her mom were supposed to be there for moral support, but her mother couldn't help but be involved in pulling things off the racks.

"Since we only have a limited amount of time, Mrs. Chapman, it's important that you let me choose the dresses for Sadie to try on," Holly said, retrieving the mermaid dress. "I'll know what kind of turnaround we can get on a dress, so we don't waste Sadie's time trying on something that won't be ready by August 2."

Candice threw her hands up. "Fine. I can follow directions. I will sit and only offer my opinions on the ones she tries on." She took a seat and folded her arms across her chest.

While she was seeing red, Say Yes was the personification of the color white. The walls were lined with racks of white bridal gowns, and the furniture for family members to sit on was upholstered in ivory leather. The mannequins were faceless and white. Crystal chandeliers lit up the store in bright white light, and the whole place smelled like vanilla and sugar.

Riley snuggled in next to Beth and looked around wide-eyed. Sadie needed to make sure Holly gave her some special attention when they got to the flower girl dresses.

After a brief consultation, Holly went to work pulling dresses for Sadie to try on. Seeing herself in a wedding gown made all this that much more real. This was happening.

She was going to marry Owen in one of these dresses.

Sadie stood in the changing room an extra minute after getting the first dress on. If she went out and showed her mom and his mom, she would be solidifying that commitment to see this through. The anxiety clung to her, heavy and debilitating.

She still hadn't told Owen she loved him. She liked him. She liked him a whole lot. Perhaps it wasn't a bad thing to marry someone she considered a friend. She could learn to love someone she liked. That had to be better than what happened to her parents. They had been in love and when the love faded, there wasn't enough like to keep it going.

Yet, there were these feelings she had for Jonathan. Why did they have to be so much stronger than the ones for Owen? She thought it had something to do with being around each other more often, but the more time she spent with Owen and avoided Jonathan, the only thing that increased was her desire to see Jonathan, to tell him about something funny that happened or to find out how his day had been.

"Is everything okay in there?" Holly asked

from the other side of the door. "Do you need any help?"

It was time to put on her brave face and show off this first dress. She opened the door and let Holly lead her to the raised platform. The sleeveless A-line gown had a scoop neckline with floral appliqués on the bodice that trailed down the front of the skirt. It had a short train and didn't make Sadie feel very fancy.

"That's pretty," Beth said.

"You look so pretty, but you're also very smart," Riley added. Sadie had unintentionally made the little girl superaware that looks weren't everything.

"Eh," Mariana said with a shrug.

"Next," her mom said as soon as she made eye contact with her.

She was right. It wasn't *the* dress. It went like that for the next three dresses. The fourth dress felt different the moment Holly zipped her up.

"We call this a fit 'n' flare style. It looks beautiful on you."

Sadie could only stare at her reflection in the dressing room mirror. This dress was something out of a dream. Closing her eyes, she could picture walking down the aisle. She could almost feel herself holding on to her dad's arm. At the end of the aisle was the man she would spend the rest of her life with, and Jonathan looked so handsome.

Sadie's eyes snapped open. Her heart beat faster than a hummingbird's wings. Why in the world would she have seen Jonathan instead of Owen? What was wrong with her?

Sadie could feel the anxiety attack coming. Pressing her hands to her cheeks, she tried to remind herself to breathe so she didn't pass out. She was marrying Owen. Had she not freaked out, her mind would have conjured up Owen standing next to Jonathan, who was the best man. Of course it would have.

"Are you ready to show everyone else this beauty?" Holly asked. "Come on." She led Sadie out into the main area.

Beth and Mariana audibly gasped.

"That's...wow," Beth said.

"You are so nice Sadie, and that dress makes you look like a princess!" Riley chimed in.

Mariana's hands were flapping. "I'm not going to cry, I'm not going to cry. I'm crying. I'm definitely crying!"

Holly knew whom she had to sell it to. She spoke directly to Candice. "This has the dramatic V-neck you liked on the last dress but the low-back feature as well. This is lace over tulle. I love the flared Chapel-length train. She looks absolutely—"

"Stunning," her mom said, with tears in her eyes. "What do you think, sweetheart?"

"Not going to lie," Sadie said. "I feel pretty glamorous in this dress."

"That's the one, Sadie," her mom said. "It's perfect, and I am so grateful to be on the earth to see this."

The tears ran freely down Sadie's cheeks, as well. Her mom climbed up the platform to hug her daughter. "Me, too, Mom. I couldn't do any of this without you."

Mariana dug some tissues out of her purse and handed one to Beth, who was wiping her eyes, as well. Sadie never imagined this would be so emotional. It was just a stupid dress.

"Beth Bradley, is that you?" A woman dressed head to toe in yellow walked into the dressing area. She was like a walking lemon drop, bouncing over to Owen's mom.

"Debbie," Beth said, getting to her feet.

"It's been a long time." Behind the woman in yellow was the most gorgeous blonde Sadie had ever seen. She was flanked by three almost-as-gorgeous blondes on each side. She had quite the entourage. "Hello, Courtney."

Courtney. That was a name Sadie had heard before. Courtney, as in Owen's ex-girlfriend. The one he never talked about, and now Sadie could see why. If he even thought about this woman, he would probably fall back in love with her.

"Beth, what are you doing here?" Courtney asked, coming over and embracing Owen's mom.

"We're dress shopping," Beth said, motioning to Sadie. "Courtney, this is Sadie. Sadie, this is Courtney."

Sadie was about to step down, be the bigger woman, and shake her hand in greeting.

Courtney's face went through a whirlwind of emotions in a matter of seconds. Interest, confusion, shock, hurt, finally shifting into rage.

"Why is she wearing my dress?" Courtney seemed to be trying to keep her voice calm, but it sounded very strained.

Sadie froze as the group of blondes gathered around Courtney like an army ready to protect their queen.

"Why is she wearing my dress?" Courtney repeated, this time with a bit more vitriol.

"I'm sure that's not your dress." Holly tried to calm her down. "You purchased a dress, Miss Rosewood. Those are kept separate from what's on the floor."

"I know it's not my actual dress, but that's my dress. That's the dress I'm wearing to marry Xavier. She can't wear that dress to marry Owen. She can't."

Sadie's mom was having none of that. "I don't know who you are, but if that's the dress my daughter has fallen in love with, she will most certainly be marrying Owen in it. I don't remember asking for your opinion, especially since we have no idea who you are."

"This is Owen's ex-girlfriend," Sadie managed to spit out. She could feel her face turning seven different shades of red. This was mortifying.

Courtney stepped toward Sadie. "Did you know I was shopping at this boutique? Did you come here on purpose?"

"I had no idea. I never would have come had I known," Sadie said, wishing she could snap her fingers and no longer be wearing this dress.

"Where did you even come from? No one I know has ever heard of you and suddenly you're engaged to Owen? Are you a golf groupie? How can you marry someone you've known for a hot minute?"

Surprisingly, it was Beth who came to Sadie's defense. "Hold on there, Courtney. You know I love you, but you don't have any room to talk about jumping into a marriage right after a breakup."

"You know I was ready to get married, Beth. Your son couldn't commit. At least that's what he said. Was it really me and not him? How could he ask someone so completely out of his league to marry him instead of me?"

"Oh, no, no, no. No one talks about my friend like that." Mariana pushed away one of Courtney's entourage in an attempt to get to her.

Was Sadie back in high school? What was happening?

Her mother dropped her purse in Riley's lap. "Hold my purse, Riley."

"Mom!" Sadie had to jump in between her mother and Courtney before the melee could begin.

"AND THEN MRS. CHAPMAN was waving her finger in the lady's face and said, 'My daughter is better than you!' and Gramma was like, 'Everybody calm down!' and Mariana was speaking in Spanish. I don't even know what she was saying. All these blonde ladies were yelling. I just held Mrs. Chapman's purse because I didn't want anyone to yell at me. They were all yelling so much."

Riley's play-by-play of what happened today at the bridal boutique explained why Sadie had run upstairs as soon as they got home. Jonathan felt terrible.

"That was pretty much the most horrible situation I have ever been involved in. Poor Sadie was having a beautiful moment with her mom and then Courtney showed up and completely ruined it," his mom said.

"They really picked out the same dress?"

"According to Courtney they did. So much for Sadie being so different from her. I feel so bad for Sadie. She looked stunning in it, too.

I don't know how she's going to find something else."

"Why does it matter what dress Courtney wears to her wedding? It's not like they are even going to ever see one another, especially in their wedding dresses."

Jonathan's mother stared at him like he was a complete moron. "Honey, there is no way Sadie can wear the same dress as Courtney. No way."

"Should we warn Owen about what happened?" he asked her.

"I don't know," she said with a shake of her head. "Part of me says we should stay out of it. But you should be ready for him to need to talk about it."

Jonathan didn't care about how Owen felt. Sadie didn't like drama and it sounded as if she had gotten a giant dose of it today. He was worried about Sadie and the impact the entire debacle had had on her.

"I should go talk to her," his mom suggested. "I feel like I need to apologize."

"Maybe you should give her some space. You can call her later tonight." Jonathan knew that Sadie had already felt like his mom liked

Courtney more than her. She would never want his mom to feel bad.

"Do you two want to come over for dinner tonight? Maybe we all should give her some space."

Jonathan didn't want to leave. He wanted to be here when Sadie showed her face. He felt very protective of her and needed to know she would be okay. "How about Riley has dinner and a sleepover at Grandma and Grandpa's? I have a big conference call with my boss and our Chinese client tonight, so it would be superhelpful if I had no distractions."

"Are you sure? You could work in your dad's office if you needed some privacy."

"I have everything spread out in the living room. It would be easier for me to stay."

"Do you want to grab some clothes to stay over with Grandma?" his mom asked Riley.

"Can I say goodbye to Sadie?"

"I think we should probably leave Sadie alone. Maybe we can do something really fun with her tomorrow."

"We could take her to Disney!" Riley jumped up and down. She had been asking to go ever since they got to Florida.

Jonathan was not up for that yet. In fact,

he was hoping that his parents would offer to come with them when the time came, so he wouldn't have to ride the teacups ten times in a row like he imagined Riley would want to do.

"Let's try to think of something a little closer to home. Maybe we could go to the beach. Sadie might need a fun day at the beach to get her mind off what happened today."

Thankfully, Riley was happy with that idea. "Yay! I've been wanting to go to the beach. We'll make it the best day ever."

She ran upstairs and his mother stared at him wordlessly.

"What?"

"That's nice of you to want to do something to lift her spirits, but I have the same concerns I had the other day when you were at my house."

"I'm not falling for my brother's fiancée, Mom. You can relax."

"Good, because that's the last thing your brother needs. One love triangle is enough."

"Yeah, well, according to Owen, he's not hung up on Courtney at all. Maybe she's having second thoughts about calling things off,

but he claims he's only got eyes for Sadie."
Jonathan didn't completely believe him, but
then again, why wouldn't he choose Sadie?
She was so easy to love.

"Well, after what happened today, let's
hope so."

Riley and his mom left, and Jonathan paced
downstairs. He wanted to talk to Sadie, but he
didn't want to bother her. If she wanted to talk
to him, she would come down, right? Maybe
she was upstairs on the phone with Owen,
spilling her guts out about how she was feeling about everything that had happened.

He stood at the bottom of the stairs. He
didn't hear anything. She wasn't talking to
anyone. The only noise in the house was the
sound of the air conditioner working over-
time. What if she wanted to be alone? Would
she be mad if he checked on her?

He went up the stairs. She wouldn't be mad
if he just asked her if she needed anything.
He ran back downstairs to grab a glass of
water. If he came bearing gifts, he might be
better received.

Outside her door, he paused. He could only
imagine how mortified she had been today.
It sounded like Courtney took all her frustra-

tion with Owen out on Sadie. It was unfair and uncalled for.

He knocked on the door and waited. She didn't make a peep. Maybe she had fallen asleep. He knocked again and the door opened. Sadie's eyes were red and her clothes rumpled. She had her hair up in a messy bun.

"What?"

"I brought you some water. Do you want some water?" He held out the glass.

Her eyes went from the glass to his face and back to the glass. "Thank you," she said, taking the water from him. She disappeared back into the room but left the door ajar. He took that as an invitation to come in.

"I'm sorry about what happened today."

Sadie took a sip of water and set the glass down on the nightstand. She sat down on the bed and fell back with her arms above her head. "Not exactly how I wanted things to go."

Jonathan wasn't sure where to sit. The small guest room was painted the most neutral shade of beige and was furnished with a full-size bed, dresser and nightstand. Sadie didn't have a lot of stuff because of her predicament, but what she did have was neatly stored away.

Jonathan sat on the edge of the bed and noticed the television mounted above the dresser was on but muted. *Family Feud* was on and the closed captioning was displayed along the bottom of the screen.

"You and Courtney are so different, I never would have thought you'd pick the same wedding dress. I mean, how many dresses does that place sell? What are the odds you'd pick the same dress?"

"Given the luck I've had this summer, I would say we should have assumed they were pretty good. This is exactly what I should have expected. I bet she looks a million times better than I ever could in that dress."

"Don't do that. Don't compare yourself to someone else."

"Why not? It's true. I'm sure you've met her considering how chummy your mom was with her and her mother. That's the other thing. Your mom even admitted she loved Courtney. I'm fairly certain that she wishes Owen had asked Courtney to marry him instead of me."

If Jonathan had to choose between Courtney and Sadie, there'd be no question whom he'd choose. "My mother feels terrible about what happened today. She wanted to come up here and apologize, but I told her to give you some space."

"That's sweet of her. It's better that everyone leaves me alone, though. I need to wallow because it became perfectly clear today that everyone who knows Owen is confused about why he let Courtney go and settled for me. She's gorgeous."

"For someone who doesn't like being judged on her looks, you're pretty good at doing the judging."

She pushed up on her elbows. "I don't like being defined by my looks, but that doesn't mean I can't acknowledge when someone is prettier than me. And I'm not stupid, I know that kind of thing matters to men."

"Whoa." Jonathan slapped his hand against his chest. "Hurtful. Some men care about things other than how someone looks." She tried to interrupt, but he stopped her. "Not that it isn't something that impacts attraction, but it's not the only thing. And just so you know, I think you are a million times prettier then Courtney."

She lay back down and covered her face with her hands. "Don't lie to make me feel better."

He tugged at her hand. Her cheeks were flushed pink under there. "I'm not lying," he asserted. "You are welcome to your opinion, but you need to let me have mine."

She dropped both her arms at her sides. "I respectfully disagree with you, then."

He smiled. She wasn't just pretty, she was more. She was humble and kind. She was funny and capable. She was patient and thoughtful. She was honest and gentle. It was that *more* that made her so attractive.

"I wish you could see yourself the way I do, but I will agree to disagree."

"I really loved that dress. I could picture myself getting married in that dress. You should have seen my mother's face when I walked out. I felt so beautiful." Her hands went back to covering her face. "That sounds so lame and I know it shouldn't matter."

"But what bride doesn't want to look beautiful on her wedding day?" Jonathan remembered his wedding like it was yesterday. Mindy had never looked so pretty. She had brought tears to his eyes that day. The thought put a lump in his throat.

"I hate feeling so insecure. Why do I even care what Courtney Rosewood thinks about me? She's no one to me. Who cares if Owen used to date her? He didn't want to marry her. He wants to marry me. I'm sorry that hurts her feelings, but I can't help that. She's also getting married to someone else, so why does she care that he's marrying someone else? It's all so stupid."

"It is stupid. Why not buy the dress that makes you feel like a million bucks? Who cares what Courtney wears?"

She moved her hands and looked up at him with those red-rimmed eyes from crying those stupid tears. "I can't wear the same dress. If your brother knew we were wearing the same dress, he wouldn't be able to not think about her when he saw me. Thinking about her would probably make him regret a lot of choices he's made lately."

"Sadie," he said in his disappointed-dad voice. She couldn't possibly think that was true. "If that's what you really believe, then why are you marrying him?"

She bit her lip and the tears reappeared. He wiped the one that slid down her cheek.

"If Owen regrets not marrying Courtney, he doesn't deserve you. My brother asked you to marry him because he wants to be with you. You are someone special. Someone who makes him a better person. Someone who isn't just beautiful on the outside but on the inside, as well. Through and through. If he ever regrets asking you to be his wife, he's an idiot because he's so lucky to have found someone like you and even luckier that you choose him back."

Sadie swallowed hard and reached up to touch his face. The air between them changed, became electric. Jonathan's heart raced and felt like it might explode from beating so hard. His brother was the luckiest man on the planet as far as he was concerned because he would do anything for Sadie to want to kiss him as much as he wanted to kiss her.

Her phone chimed so loudly it made them both jump. The spell was broken and Jonathan stood up, needing to put space between them.

"It's Owen. He wants to FaceTime," she said, but she didn't answer.

"I'll leave you two to catch up, then." He started for the door.

"Jonathan," she called after him. He turned back even though the guilt of what he was feeling for her made him want to run out of this house and get as far away from her as possible. "Thank you."

He smiled and gave her a nod before slipping out and down the hall. Thankfully, he had his own private bathroom attached to his room. He'd never needed a cold shower more in his life. His mother was going to kill him because he was most definitely falling in love with his brother's fiancée.

CHAPTER FIFTEEN

"DON'T PEEK!" RILEY GIGGLED. There was a lot of racket going on in the kitchen. It smelled like bacon, and it was making Sadie's mouth water.

"I'm not peeking, but my stomach is growling. It really wants whatever it is that you just made."

Riley had spent the night at her grandparents but was brought home bright and early. So early, that neither Jonathan nor Sadie was out of bed yet. As an apology for waking her up, Jonathan and Riley offered to make her a special breakfast. Riley wanted the menu to be a surprise.

"Okay, open up!" Riley exclaimed.

The table was covered in platters of pancakes, bacon, eggs and strawberries. Everything looked delicious.

"You helped make all this?" Sadie asked.

Riley nodded. "Daddy made the pancakes

all by himself. We can make them into funny faces. Get the whipped cream, Daddy."

Jonathan gave her a salute. "Yes, Chef."

Riley put a pancake on the plate in front of Sadie and placed two pieces of bacon on it in a V shape for a mouth. Above that, she put two strawberries for eyes and spooned some scrambled eggs on the top of the circle for hair. When Jonathan retuned with the whipped cream, he gave it a shake.

"Do the nose," she said to him. Jonathan squirted a blob in the center. When he finished, Riley looked at him. "Can I?"

"Open up."

Riley tipped her head back, and Jonathan squirted whipped cream right in her mouth. Sadie loved their relationship. It was clear how much they adored each other, and they had a way of making everyday things fun.

They definitely made breakfast more exciting. Sadie's funny-face pancake was delicious. She enjoyed every bite.

"We have another surprise for you," Riley said once breakfast was done.

"Another surprise?"

"Two more actually. Don't try to trick me into telling you."

"Oh, come on. You can give me a little hint."

Riley shook her head. She seemed very proud of herself for not giving anything away.

"You need to go pack a bag. You need a swimsuit and a towel," Jonathan said. "That's all I'm saying."

"So we're going swimming somewhere…" Sadie waited for him to elaborate. He didn't.

"Go pack, Sadie," he replied with a smirk. "We leave in fifteen minutes."

Swimsuit, cover-up, sunglasses, towel, sunscreen. Sadie wasn't sure what else she would need. She threw a maxi dress in her bag just in case the jean shorts and pale yellow cami she had on wasn't nice enough for wherever they were going before and after they went to go swimming.

No one said a word once they were in the car. Jonathan had taken her bag and placed it in the trunk so she couldn't see what was back there. The mystery was high.

Sadie hummed along with the song on the radio. It was a new song by one of those boy bands that all the little girls were enamored with. Riley began to sing. Jonathan turned up the volume and, much to Sadie's surprise, started to sing along, as well.

"You know this one?" she asked with a giggle.

"Know this one? It's my jam." He tapped the beat on the steering wheel and belted out the chorus completely out of tune.

"Dad!" Riley's laughter made Sadie smile. "You're a terrible singer!"

"I am not. You should see my dance moves to this one. It's too bad I'm driving."

Sadie covered her mouth to stifle her laugh. "Feel free to pull over. I think that could be very entertaining."

Jonathan glanced her way. One side of his mouth curled up. "You think so, huh?"

It didn't even matter what the surprise was that Riley had planned for her. Being with the two of them was exactly what Sadie needed today. They were the only people who could make her forget all about what a disaster the day before had been.

Jonathan pulled off the highway and turned down a familiar road.

"Where are we?" Sadie asked, craning her neck to read the street sign they just passed. Before Jonathan could answer, Sadie spotted the sign for Say Yes. All the good vibes evaporated and panic set in. "Why are we here? What are you doing?"

Jonathan pulled in and parked the car. "You are going to buy that dress."

Sadie shook her head, slowly at first and then vigorously back and forth. "No. I'm not going in there."

"You are. You are going to buy the dress that made you feel like you were ready to walk down the aisle because you deserve it. You deserve to feel sure of yourself."

"I can't." Sadie refused to unlock her seat belt. The dress had made her feel sure that it was what she wanted to wear on her wedding day, but not so sure about the groom. In fact, Courtney wasn't the only reason she had a hard time sleeping last night. She also couldn't stop thinking about how she had pictured Jonathan at the end of the aisle, not Owen. Maybe the whole circus yesterday was her bad karma for thinking about the wrong brother.

"You can."

"I can't face those women in there after the scene everyone made yesterday. My mother seriously wanted to fight. Do you know how embarrassing it is to have to hold back your sixty-one-year-old mother from punching someone?"

Jonathan put his hand on her knee and it sent a jolt of electricity up her leg. "The only one who should be ashamed to show her face in there is Courtney. You didn't do anything wrong except probably look better in that dress than she does, which is why she freaked out."

Sadie rolled her eyes. "You forget that I have eyes. I know which one of us is going to look better in that dress, and it's not me."

"My wife told me that she tried on seventy-five dresses before buying one. I can't imagine trying on seventy-five anythings. It blows my mind what women go through. Guess which dress she bought."

"I have no idea."

"Not number seventy-five. Or any of the seventy-three before it. She ended up going back and buying the one she tried on first."

Sadie didn't understand what this had to do with what happened. Her dress wasn't the first one she had tried on.

"I'm not sure how that relates to my situation. All I'll be able to think about is that

Owen's ex is somewhere wearing the same dress. It won't feel good."

Jonathan maintained eye contact, the intensity of his blue eyes keeping her pinned against her seat better than the seat belt ever could.

"Mindy bought the first one because when she had put it on, she said she knew. There had been something about that dress that spoke to her. Her mom wanted her to try a couple more on to be sure, so she tried on seventy-four more and nothing compared. Not even close, she told me."

It was sadly possible that Sadie could try on that many and never find one that made her feel as beautiful as the one inside Say Yes. Everything else would be compared with that one in her head and probably never live up to it.

As if he read her mind, Jonathan said, "You could go to another shop and try on a hundred other dresses, and maybe none of them will feel the way the one you wore yesterday did. What if you settle for another dress? Won't you still be thinking about how Courtney is somewhere wearing your dress while you're stuck in the second best? If you're going to waste a single thought on Courtney on your wedding day, you might as well do it dressed in the gown that makes you look like a princess."

"You really did look like a princess," Riley said from the back seat. "The prettiest princess I ever saw."

Sadie's throat tightened. It couldn't have been easy for Jonathan to talk about Mindy. He didn't do it often. Placing her hands on top of her head, she tried to find fault in his logic. She couldn't. Either way, Courtney won. There didn't seem to be a good reason why Sadie shouldn't wear a dress that made her look like a princess. Who wouldn't want to look like a princess on her wedding day?

She unbuckled her seat belt. "You two better be coming inside with me."

Smiles broke out across both of their faces. "That was the plan," Jonathan said.

Sadie recognized Holly the moment they walked through the door. Every fiber of her being wanted to turn around and run back to the car. She couldn't do this.

Jonathan slipped his arm around her waist and guided her forward instead. "You can do this," he whispered. Seriously, could he read her thoughts?

Holly noticed her and her eyes gave away her shock. She quickly put on a smile. "Sadie! You're back. How are you?"

"We're here so she can get the princess dress," Riley said before Sadie could speak.

"The princess dress?" Holly clearly didn't want to assume.

"*The* dress," Jonathan said. Sadie nodded weakly. "The one that caused all the hubbub yesterday. She needs to put it on again because we think it's the one and we don't care who else might buy it. Right?" He gave Sadie a little squeeze.

"I'm assuming we don't have an appointment." She glanced at Jonathan, who grimaced. Men didn't think about things like dress fittings needing an appointment. "Is there any way I could try the dress on one more time, though? I need to see it one more time before I can make a decision about walking away." Maybe she would put it on again and it wouldn't make her feel the same way. She kind of hoped that was true. If she put it on and the magic was gone, she could go somewhere else and find a new dress.

"I'm not usually supposed to let someone do a fitting without an appointment," Holly said, looking over her shoulder. The other woman working was busy with another bride-to-be and her very loud and opinionated mother. "But I have a little bit of time before my next bride comes in. Let's get you in a dressing room."

Sadie stayed frozen by Jonathan's side. It was like she had post-traumatic stress disorder. What if she went back there and Courtney showed up? She couldn't take that kind of drama two days in a row. She spun around and took a step toward the door.

"Whoa." Jonathan pulled her back. "Wrong way, lady."

"Maybe I can't do this. All I can think about is what if she walks in?"

"You have me and Riley here to protect you from any unexpected drama. No one is going to ruin this fitting for you. I promise."

"Come on, Sadie." Riley tugged on her arm. "Maybe I can try on a dress, too."

Sadie had completely forgotten that Riley hadn't tried on any flower girl dresses yesterday because after the shouting match with

Courtney ended, Sadie couldn't get out of here fast enough.

"You should definitely try on a dress. Can we do that? Can she try on a dress with me?"

"Sure," Holly said, holding a hand out for Riley. "You come with me. I know the perfect flower girl dress to go with the wedding dress Sadie picked out."

Thrilled, Riley went with Holly. Jonathan took Sadie's hand. "You can do this. It's all going to work out like it's supposed to."

Sadie stared at their clasped hands. He had this way of making her feel safe and empowered at the same time. She trusted that he would protect her and appreciated that he believed she was strong enough to do anything. Why did he have to be so perfect? Her heart was clearly not getting the message that it couldn't be his. Would it ever?

"I'M SO GLAD she decided to come back," Holly said while they waited for Sadie and Riley to put on their dresses.

"We sort of had to make her come, but I think she'll be happy she did."

The woman fiddled with the ring of keys in her hands. "It's really sweet that you're here for her, although I'm surprised you're not worried about the superstition that the groom shouldn't see the bride in her dress before the wedding."

Jonathan wanted to cringe. "Oh, I'm not the groom. I'm the best man."

"Oh!" Holly seemed mortified. "I didn't realize. I thought… You guys were so… Riley is your daughter, though, right?"

His chest tightened. Sadie couldn't be his, but Riley always would be. "She's mine."

"Well, it's still supernice of you to be here to help her out. Yesterday was pretty terrible."

"That's what I heard."

"Are you ready for us?" Sadie's voice came from behind the mirrored wall in front of him.

"We're ready!" Holly answered. Jonathan needed a minute that he wasn't going to get. Seeing Sadie in a wedding dress—the wedding dress—would make everything undoubtedly real. The feelings he had developed for Sadie over the last month would have to be squashed.

Riley skipped out first, looking as adorable as ever. The ivory dress had a lacy top and a big tulle skirt that he could tell Riley loved. She stood on the pedestal and spun in a tiny circle.

"You look darling," Holly gushed. "That dress is perfect."

Jonathan couldn't speak. His little girl looked so grown up. Her mother would have been in tears. He wasn't sure he would get through this without shedding one or two either. He swallowed down the lump in his throat.

"You are the prettiest princess in the whole world," he said.

Grinning from ear to ear, Riley beamed with pride. "Thanks, Daddy."

She went on to say something about needing shoes and how perfect her pink tiara would look with this dress, but Jonathan stopped listening because Sadie had stepped out of the dressing room and the rest of the world seemed to disappear.

"I shouldn't have put this on," she said.

"Why?" Holly asked. "You look amazing!"

Amazing didn't do her justice. Sadie was stunning. Her beauty made his heart feel like it could explode out of his chest. His eyes were glued to her. He was afraid to blink, fearing he'd lose even a millisecond of seeing her absolutely glow.

"Because I love it even more." Sadie had her back to him as she looked at herself in the mirrors. She ran her hands down her stomach and finally rested them on her hips. "I love it so much."

She took his breath away. Standing on the raised platform, she was a perfect bride without a groom on the top of a wedding cake. Jonathan just stood there, gaping. He was never going to get over her. He might have to be secretly in love with his brother's wife for the rest of his life.

Sadie turned around to face him. "Tell me it's not that great. That I can find something else."

Jonathan began to blink over and over. Had she lost her mind? Surely she'd look good in anything, but there was no denying that this dress was made for her. It fit her like a glove. It was perfect. He could completely understand why Courtney had a meltdown yesterday. If she saw Sadie looking like this in that dress, she knew she'd never compare.

"I think he's trying to say that it looks so good on you that he's speechless," Holly said.

"But if you want to try some other dresses on, we can make you another appointment, and I can see if there are some other dresses with a similar design and style."

"My brother will never regret asking you to be his wife because you're an amazing woman. When he sees you in that, the only thing he'll ever regret is not asking you the moment he met you."

Sadie's gaze held steady as she worried her bottom lip with her teeth. He had to fight the urge to climb up there with her and kiss her until she never doubted herself again.

"Buy the dress," he told her.

"Buy the dress, Sadie. We're a perfect match!" Riley said, hopping from one step down to another.

"Are we going to buy the dress?" Holly asked.

Sadie took a deep breath. "I'm going to buy the dress."

Tape measures came out and numbers were written down and Sadie put a deposit down on her dream dress. Riley was disappointed that she didn't get to take her dress home. The nine-year-old didn't understand the concept of not buying off the rack.

"You and I will come back in a couple weeks and get to try them on again," Sadie assured her. "If everything fits just right, you'll be able to bring it home."

"Fine." Riley climbed in the car. "Is it time for surprise number three?"

Jonathan helped her with her seat belt. "It's time."

"Okay, where are we going?" Sadie asked. "I feel like being blindsided once was enough for today, and if we're headed to a bathing suit competition, I want to know so I can jump out of the car right now."

He felt guilty for making her uncomfortable, but laughed at where her paranoid brain took her. "I'm sorry you felt blindsided, but I knew there was no way I was getting you here unless I didn't tell you. I promise we are not taking you to a bathing suit competition. The next stop is all about relaxing."

"Do you think we should tell her, Dad?"

Jonathan didn't want to cause any more anxiety. It was time to put on their flip-flops and have some fun. "Go ahead."

"We're going to the beach! We brought all the stuff we need to make a giant sandcastle. Will you help me make a sandcastle?"

Jonathan could see the relief on Sadie's face. Her whole body relaxed into the passenger's seat. "I would love to build one with you. I'm kind of an expert at building sandcastles."

Why didn't that surprise him? One thing Jonathan knew about Sadie was she was one of the most capable people around. Just another reason she was the best. His brother was the luckiest guy in the world, and he better know it. Things had definitely changed over the last month. Instead of being the protective older brother, Jonathan was now thinking he needed to talk to Owen about how he'd be there to take him down if he ever broke Sadie's heart.

CHAPTER SIXTEEN

A TRIP TO the beach was exactly what Sadie needed. It had been awhile since she spent some time by the ocean. She loved the sound of it and the way the waves felt as they lapped against her shins when she stood at the shoreline.

"Bring the bucket of water, Sadie!" Riley stood by their sandcastle. Sand clung to her knees and her lopsided ponytail needed to be tightened.

"Come here," she said. "You've got to see this."

Riley didn't hesitate. She scampered over and took Sadie's outstretched hand. "What?"

"See that in the sand? I think we should put that on the top of our sandcastle." She pointed at the large cockle shell that was perfectly intact. They had collected some smaller ones, but that would be the pièce de résistance.

Riley picked it up and went running to her

dad. Jonathan oohed and ahhed just as Sadie expected. He was good like that. Always so good with Riley. She bent over and filled the pink sand pail with water and joined father and daughter on the beach.

"I think this is the best sandcastle that I've ever seen." Sadie poured the water into the moat that Riley had dug around their castle.

"We need one more tower," Riley said, filling one of her buckets with sand. Jonathan had come prepared with pails of all shapes and sizes, sand shovels and sand sifters.

"She's very good at this architecture stuff. Has a real eye," Sadie said to Jonathan, who sat on his AC/DC beach towel. She had no idea he was into rock 'n' roll until today.

"My girl has many talents," he replied with a charming grin. He adjusted his baseball cap and stretched out his long legs, crossing them at the ankles. "She takes after her dad."

Sadie quirked an eyebrow. "You have many talents? Like what?"

"I am awesome at making pancakes, I do the best cannonballs into the pool, there isn't a crossword puzzle I can't solve."

Laughing, Sadie shook her head. "You

are way more impressive than I thought you were."

"Are you telling me you didn't find me superimpressive the moment you met me?"

When she first met him, she was too worried about what he thought about her to ponder what she thought about him. Once she was sure he hated her, the only impressive thing about him was how mean he could be to someone he barely knew.

"Maybe not at first, but you've been impressing me for some time now," she admitted. He had done quite a turnaround. She wasn't sure why, but ever since she had to move into Owen's house with him, she'd seen a different side.

Jonathan had treated her with such kindness and compassion the last couple of weeks. He was exactly what she needed when she needed it.

Riley placed the shell on the tallest of the towers. "It's awesome. Dad, take a picture."

Jonathan pulled his phone from the beach bag and had them kneel behind their masterpiece. Sadie put her arm around Riley, who was grinning ear to ear. Jonathan didn't need to tell either one of them to smile. Sadie hadn't felt this happy in a long time, and it should be making her miserable. Why was everything better when she was with Jonathan and Riley?

"Would you like me to take a picture of all three of you?" A woman appeared behind Jonathan, offering to help.

He hesitated a second before answering, "Sure."

He came around and got down on bended knee beside Riley. The woman generously took a few pictures for them.

"You have a beautiful family," she said as she returned the phone.

That familiar knot in Sadie's stomach reappeared. Jonathan thanked the woman, not bothering to correct her. It was understandable for people to be confused. It wasn't as easy to explain why Sadie was. Being with Jonathan and Riley was effortless. It was too easy, like putting together a puzzle with only three pieces. Jonathan wasn't the Bradley she was engaged to marry, though.

Sadie watched as Jonathan scrolled through the pictures on his phone. She noticed the way one corner of his mouth curled up when his gaze lingered on one of them.

"You're going to have to text me those," she said, as he put his phone away.

"Of course. Sorry I didn't correct our friendly photographer. I wasn't sure how to explain that you're Riley's aunt-to-be. Figured it was just easier to let her think what she thinks. She's a stranger we're never going to see again, so it doesn't really matter what she thinks, right?"

He was so nervous. She couldn't tell if it was because he was worried about how she felt about being called a family or because the misconception had made him uncomfortable.

"I wouldn't worry about it. I mean, we are family. Or almost family. In a month, we'll be brother and sister."

Jonathan sucked in a breath and held it a moment before blowing it out. "That's true. You're so wise, sis."

The word sounded wrong to her ears. Sadie had a brother and she knew the feelings she had for Jonathan weren't anything like the love she had for Paul.

Riley pulled on Jonathan's arm. "Maybe after Sadie marries Uncle Owen, she can marry you."

That was unexpected. Sadie was glad that

Jonathan had to figure out how to explain to her that wasn't possible.

He bent down so he was eye to eye with Riley. Placing a hand on her shoulder, he said, "Honey, that's not how it works. When two people get married, they make a promise to stay married until one of them passes away. Like me and Mommy. We were married until she went to heaven."

Riley's expression turned serious. "I don't want Uncle Owen to go to heaven yet."

"Uncle Owen isn't going to heaven anytime soon. Don't worry." Jonathan pulled her in for a hug.

"So you can't marry Sadie?"

"I can't, honey. But she gets to be your aunt. That's still cool, right?"

Sadie wished she could say something, but her throat was so tight. She hadn't realized how attached she had become to the little girl as well as her father. Having these two in her life had somehow become reason number one and two for why she should marry Owen at this point. There was probably something very wrong with that.

"It's cool," Riley agreed. "Can I get some more water for my moat?"

"Sure."

Riley dashed off to fill her bucket while Sadie sat down on her beach towel. Jonathan sat next to her. "Did we manage to take your mind off your troubles for a bit?"

"You sure did." She wasn't going to admit how being with them created a few more problems for her, though.

Riley and another little girl were chatting by the water. Riley was giving her some advice on how to make the perfect sandcastle.

"That child could make friends anywhere," Sadie commented.

"It's funny, but that wasn't really the case until we came to Florida."

"What?"

"I'm serious. She's been pretty reserved the last few years. Losing her mom took a huge toll on her."

"On both of you, I'm sure." Jonathan was nursing wounds that he didn't let anyone see, but she knew they were there.

He nodded. "Losing Mindy nearly destroyed me. If it wasn't for Riley and needing to be here for her, I'm not sure how I would have survived it."

Sadie reached over and placed a hand over his. "I'm glad you had each other to live for."

Jonathan stared down at their hands. "It's been so hard. Mindy was a great mom. She was like you. Dealing with kids came naturally. When Riley needed something or had a meltdown, Mindy just knew how to console her. I'm clueless half the time and totally clueless the other."

"That's not true. You are very good with her."

"I've had to learn. Usually the hard way. Things were really difficult back in Boston. She had a lot of trouble sleeping at night. She would wake up having these horrible night terrors. I used to sleep on her floor, so I'd be there right away when she woke up screaming."

"Oh my goodness, Jonathan. That's terrible. Poor Riley."

"It was bad, but you know what? She hasn't had one nightmare since we got here. She hasn't had trouble going to sleep and I haven't needed to be in her room. I don't know what it is."

"Maybe Owen is right about Florida being the right place for you," Sadie said, wishing it was true. She couldn't imagine what it would be like not to have Riley and Jonathan in her day-to-day life.

Jonathan ran a hand through his hair. "I don't know. I think it has something to do with being here. Mindy hated Florida, which is why we stayed in Boston. I wanted her to be happy, so I agreed to stay. I think I've been resisting coming home because I worry it will make Mindy unhappy, which is dumb. I don't think she can even be unhappy where she is now."

Sadie placed a hand on his back, needing to comfort him. "It has to be so hard for you. I'm sure you want to respect her wishes, but at the same time, do what's best for you and Riley now that she's gone."

"We never talked about it, you know? What we would do if one of us died before the other. We didn't even have a will. We talked about how we should write one when she got pregnant but never got around to it. I have no idea what she wanted for Riley or me. It's not like we had a heart-to-heart about moving on after one of us died. We imagined we'd be old and gray by then."

"I think she would want you both to be

happy. However, wherever and whoever that happens with." Sadie knew that was what she wanted for him since she couldn't be that person. She hoped that Jonathan would find love again. He deserved it even though the thought made her heart ache a bit.

"Can we get some ice cream?" Riley asked, forgetting all about her moat. "I'm so hungry."

"How can you be hungry already?" Jonathan asked.

"Hey, building sandcastles isn't easy," Sadie said in support of the ice-cream idea. "You can really work up an appetite." Sadie was a stress eater, and fighting her feelings for her brother-in-law was creating a tad bit of stress.

Jonathan jumped up to his feet and held a hand out to help Sadie up. "Then I guess we should pack up and go get some ice cream."

Ketterman's was an adorable ice-cream shop a couple of blocks from the beach and built inside an old train service car. Fun train memorabilia filled the display case by the entrance and photos of old train cars hung on the walls throughout.

The three of them were seated and perused the menu filled with colorful pictures of mouthwatering sundaes and ice-cream concoctions.

"What's this one?" Riley asked, pointing to one of the sundaes.

Sadie moved her finger to the written description. "What does it say?" Jonathan started to read it, but Sadie stopped him. "She's got it. Let her try."

Riley kept her finger on the glossy menu and moved it from word to word in the sentence just like Sadie had taught her when they read together at night.

"Two sh-...two sc...oops of vanilla ice cream."

"Good job. Remember to use the picture to give you some clues if you get stumped."

"Cov...ered in hot fudge and peanut butter? It has peanut butter on it?"

"That's what it says."

Riley struggled to phonetically sound out the word *sauce*, so Sadie helped her with the letter sounds. She managed to read the rest of the description herself.

"I want that one," Riley said.

"Chocolate and peanut butter does sound

good. Maybe we can split it," Jonathan suggested. "Because it also sounds huge."

"You did an awesome job reading that by yourself. Have you been practicing?" Sadie asked.

Riley nodded proudly. "I've been reading those books you gave me to Uncle Owen's tiger."

"You've been reading? By yourself?" Jonathan seemed surprised. He shifted his gaze to Sadie. "I didn't know you gave her books."

Sadie knew Jonathan was sensitive about Riley's reading struggles, but she had hoped it would be okay to encourage the child to read. He couldn't be mad about that. "I gave her some books I thought she could handle on her own. I wanted to build up her confidence. I'm glad it seems to be working."

"Did you like the books that Sadie gave you?"

Riley nodded. "There was one about a girl who loves the color pink like me. That was my favorite."

"That was really nice of Sadie to do that. It's pretty awesome that you've been reading. I know it hasn't always been your favorite thing to do."

Riley gave a little shrug. "Sadie made it fun."

"That's all it took? It was never fun before?"

"Plus Sadie's a good teacher. If we move here, can you be my fourth-grade teacher?"

"Sorry, girlie. I only teach third-graders. But if you move here, I will help you anytime you need it."

"Let's move here, Dad. I really want to live here." That was the first time Riley had been assertive about what she wanted. She usually deferred to whatever he said about it.

Sadie waited for Jonathan's response. His worries about what Mindy wanted or thought about them moving to Florida had been holding him back, but would they continue to when Riley made it so clear this was what she wanted? Sadie wasn't sure what she wanted him to say either. If they stayed, she'd get more time with them. Could she fight off these feelings she was having if Jonathan continued to be a constant in her life?

JONATHAN'S FEELINGS ON moving to Florida were still mixed. Maybe even more so the closer he got to Sadie. These moments together were this combination of the best time and something that felt very forbidden.

Being in Florida meant he and Riley could spend time with his parents and Owen and Sadie. There were pluses and minuses to that reality. Being around Sadie had not only helped Riley heal, but it had also given him a new perspective on life. For the first time since Mindy's death, he believed he could feel love again.

Sadie wasn't someone he should be in love with, though. His feelings for her made every alarm bell go off in his head. If he could let go of this infatuation with her, maybe they could make it work living near one another. If he couldn't, Boston was the safe alternative.

"I don't know, sweetheart. Moving is a big deal. I'm not sure we're ready for all that just yet."

"Didn't Owen set you up with a Realtor?" Sadie asked before taking a sip of water.

"Yeah, I think he was setting me up with her for reasons that had nothing to do with buying a house."

"I noticed that, but she still sells houses."

"She texted me. I've kind of put her off. Like I said, it's a big deal to move. Not sure

I'm up for all that upheaval. Plus, there are things in Boston." He didn't want to mention Mindy's grave, but he was thinking about it.

Mindy was probably up in heaven shaking her head at him. Losing her had been so difficult. It was something he would never completely get over. His heart didn't work that way. It was also something he hadn't talked to anyone about until today. Sadie had a way of getting him to open up about things he wasn't willing to share with anyone else.

Jonathan didn't think he could ever fall for someone else after Mindy, and he certainly never thought he would be interested in someone who was unattainable. Someone who, the more he let himself care about, was destined to break his heart. His heart wasn't in good enough shape to take more damage.

"I get it. I'd love to have you guys close, though. But I understand Boston has been home for a while and it was where Riley's mom wanted you guys to live."

When she said she'd love to have them close, Jonathan didn't just hear those words, he felt them. How could he be so foolish as to develop feelings not only for a woman who was spoken for but for a woman who was engaged to his own brother? She was off-limits in every way possible. Yet, here he was sitting across from her at an ice-cream shop, thinking about how tempting it would be if they lived in the same state.

"I would miss my friends," Riley admitted. That was exactly why he didn't want to move her. She had lost enough; she didn't need to lose more. "But I could make new ones. I want to live by Gramma and Sadie more than I want to live by my friends back home."

That was unexpected.

"I'm sure your dad will make the best choice for both of you. He always takes good care of you, doesn't he?" Sadie asked.

"Yep," Riley answered happily.

It made his heart happy to hear them both say that. Sadie had a way of doing that, making him happy. It was just her way, he tried to tell himself. She did that for everyone. It wasn't like she was trying to do it for him because he was special. Owen was the only one who held a special place in her heart. He needed to remember that as he sat across from her, staring at those pretty lips that he'd wanted to kiss for much too long.

"I think we should come back to the beach

on the Fourth of July to see the fireworks," Jonathan said to Riley. "I heard they're pretty awesome."

"Yeah! Will you come with us, Sadie? It's more fun when it's all of us."

"I would love to come with you, but we have to bring your uncle with us. He told me he's going to be home for the holiday."

Jonathan had to force himself to smile. Hearing his brother's name was like a bucket of ice water being thrown in his face. He needed to wake up and smell the coffee. Owen was going to marry Sadie in a month. He had to get right with that and get right with it now.

With their bellies full of ice-cream sundaes, they headed home for the day. Sadie and Riley were playing the license plate game, trying to be the first to find plates from other states.

"I can't believe you saw one from Oregon. Those people drove a long way to come to Florida," Sadie said as they walked into the house.

"Is that the farthest you've ever seen?" Riley asked.

"I once saw a plate from Alaska," Jonathan said.

Sadie didn't believe him. "No way. You did not. Where?"

"When I was in Alaska," he replied with a grin.

She gave him a playful push and laughed. "You're a goof."

"Yeah, Dad. You're a goof."

"I'm a goof? You're a goof," he said, reaching for her to give her a tickle. She giggled and ran into the kitchen. Jonathan chased her, and Sadie chased him.

"Run, Riley! I got him," Sadie said, tugging on his arm.

"You sure you want to join this battle?" he asked, giving her a chance to get away. "I will take you out if I have to." He wiggled his fingers at her.

She narrowed her eyes, deciding her fate. "You wouldn't."

"Is that a challenge?"

She took a step back, and he reached for her waist. Her laughter filled the room. She spun out of his reach and took off after Riley. He followed her into the living room, where they came to a dead stop.

"Well, hello there," Owen said, getting up off the couch. "I was wondering where in the world everyone was. I was about to text Sadie and here you all come."

Sadie glanced at Jonathan before going to Owen and giving him a hug. "You're back early. What happened?"

"I was worried about you, so as soon as I finished my round today, I headed back," Owen said, letting her go. He stared right at Jonathan. "But I guess I was worried about nothing, looks like my brother and niece cheered you up."

Guilt flooded Jonathan's body. Not for cheering Sadie up but for enjoying his time with her so much when it was Owen's place to do that, not his.

"This morning we had funny-face pancakes and they were so yummy and we went to the beach and we built a sandcastle and we had ice cream that was also so yummy," Riley said, giving him a play-by-play of the day. Jonathan noticed she left something out.

"Wow, that sounds like a very fun day. A lot of sugar was had by all."

"And we got dresses for the wedding, too. Sadie looks like a princess!"

"You found a new dress? That's great." Owen smiled and wrapped his arm around her waist, causing a new feeling to replace the guilt. Jealousy wasn't much more pleasant.

"I went back and got the dress," Sadie answered. She clearly was nervous about his reaction. She wrung her hands.

Owen's eyebrows pinched together. "Which dress?"

"*The* dress. The one that Courtney ordered from the same shop."

"You bought Courtney's dress?"

Did he really just call it Courtney's dress? Jonathan wanted to punch his brother in the face. Maybe that would knock some sense into him.

"She bought *her* dress," Jonathan said. "The one that makes her look like the most beautiful bride you're ever going lay eyes on."

"Right. I didn't mean to say... I just meant..."

"If it bothers you, knowing that she is wearing the same dress on her wedding day, I can cancel the order," Sadie said. Jonathan wanted to scream absolutely not, but he restrained himself.

"No, it doesn't bother me. Does it bother

you? It seemed to bother you yesterday. What changed your mind?"

"Your brother reminded me that I shouldn't compare myself to anyone else, and that the only thing that mattered is how the dress made me feel while I was wearing it."

"Sounds like Jonathan was superhelpful."

"I'm sure you would have said the same things if you had been here," Jonathan said.

"I'm going to go shower and wash the sand and salt water off me," Sadie said, breaking the tension. "I'm glad you're home." She kissed Owen on the cheek.

"Riley, why don't you go clean up, too," Jonathan said. "You can use my bathroom."

She started to protest until Sadie reached for her hand. "Come on, little one. We deserve a shower after a hard day building the world's greatest sandcastle."

Without hesitation, she took Sadie's hand and went upstairs. The woman was magic.

"Thanks for being there for my fiancée when I couldn't," Owen said when they were alone.

"Yeah, no problem. Riley was there yesterday and saw how upset Sadie was by the whole thing. She really was the mastermind behind cheering her up." Blame the kid. That seemed like the smart play.

"I can't believe Mom took her to the same bridal shop as Courtney. And what are the chances that they would pick the same freaking dress? I can only imagine what a shock it was for Courtney seeing Sadie in that dress. She was probably completely devastated."

Anger bubbled up and out of him. "Why are you worried about how Courtney felt? How about how Sadie felt when Courtney told her to take the dress off and that she couldn't figure out what made Sadie so special that you would choose to marry her? Can you imagine how devastating that was for Sadie? Because she was pretty devastated. I was here. I saw how red her eyes were from crying and I heard her tear herself down and say she couldn't compare to someone like Courtney."

"I know how upset she was," Owen shot back. "I talked to her last night on the phone. I saw her on our video call. I didn't mean that it wasn't hard for her. No one should have made her feel that way."

"Well, I don't know about you but I couldn't care less about how Courtney felt about the whole thing. She'll get over it, just like she got over you."

Owen puffed out his chest. "Wow. You're really going to go there, are you?"

"I just don't want anyone to make Sadie feel like she's anyone's second choice. Whoever Sadie marries should make her feel like the only woman who matters."

"She's not my second choice. She's the only person I ever asked to be my fiancée. Why do I feel like you need to remember that she said yes to me? She's marrying *me*. We're clear about that, right?"

Owen didn't need to use his fists to punch Jonathan in the gut. His words did a good job of that. Sadie was marrying him. There was no confusion, but there was disappointment.

"Why wouldn't we be?"

"I don't know. I'm sitting here, wondering where everybody is and you guys come in laughing, playing and acting like one happy little family. She's my family, though. She's going to be my wife."

Jonathan understood that better than anything else. He wanted his brother to be happy and knew Sadie could make him more than that. What was beginning to worry him was that Owen might not make Sadie as happy as he should. Jonathan couldn't stop himself from caring about that, too.

"I know she is. Deserve her."

CHAPTER SEVENTEEN

"So YOU AREN'T going to register for gifts?"
Mariana was checking over Sadie's to-do list.
The days were flying by and the wedding
felt like it was right around the corner. There
were only a few more things to do.

Owen had been home to meet with the flo-
rist, even though her mother had been the
only one to do the talking at that appointment.
They had hired a photographer and chosen
the menu for the reception before he had to
leave to go to his next tournament.

"Have you looked around?" Sadie replied.
"Exactly what would we need to register for?
He has a huge house full of stuff. I don't think
we need guests to buy us silverware or towels."

Mariana leaned back in her lounger. "I
guess you're right. What could people get a
couple who have everything?"

"Well, he has everything. I barely have

anything." Ever since Courtney accused her of being with Owen for his money and celebrity status, Sadie had been self-conscious about how much he had compared with how little she had.

"Hey, that's not your fault. And if you needed a new house, which you don't, your insurance would be buying you a new one. It's not like you didn't have a life before Owen came into it."

She was right about that. Sadie used to live quite comfortably. "My mom thinks we should ask people to donate to a charity of our choice. Supposedly that's what the rich and famous do."

"If you'd like to start a college fund for my children, I will happily accept."

"My mom didn't say it, but I'm sure she'd appreciate it if we raised money for cancer research."

Mariana reached over and patted Sadie's hand. "I think that's perfect."

At least something about this wedding was perfect. Everything else felt completely off. And if she was being honest with herself, she knew why but had been trying to deny it.

She and Owen had spent Fourth of July

with his parents, Jonathan and Riley. The fireworks had been spectacular, but the real ones were still the only fireworks she'd seen when she'd been with Owen. The truth was becoming clear. She would probably never see fireworks when they kissed, she would never get butterflies when she saw him. The spark wasn't there. Not like it was with Jonathan. The man only had to smile in her direction and she wanted to melt at his feet. He'd brushed against her when they were standing on the beach watching the fireworks, and her whole body had felt like it was on fire.

Truth be told, she was going through with this wedding because she thought the only way she could have Jonathan and Riley in her life was to be married to Owen. She was a terrible person.

"What's the matter?" Mariana swung her legs over the side of the chair so she was facing her friend. "For someone who's getting married in a few weeks, you don't seem very excited."

Excited wasn't a feeling Sadie had associated with this wedding since the beginning. *Terrified, anxious, overwhelmed* and *incompetent* had been reigning supreme. Then there was *confused. Extremely confused* because the Bradley brother who was winning her heart wasn't the one she was getting ready to make a vow to love and honor from this day forward.

"Can I tell you something?"

"Of course."

Sadie sat forward and faced her friend. "I need you to promise that after I tell you, you'll forget that I ever said it."

Mariana took off her sunglasses and wore a serious expression. "I am your best friend. There is no judgment here. Whatever you tell me stays between you and me."

Even though Owen was on tour and Jonathan and Riley had gone to look at some houses with Megan the Realtor, Sadie still glanced at the closed patio door. She was about to say something out loud that she had been holding inside for too long.

"I'm falling in love with Jonathan."

Mariana's eyes widened and her jaw dropped open. No words came out of her mouth.

"Okay, now is a good time for you to forget what I just said. Pretend you never heard it."

"Sadie. *Sadie.* Sadie!" Mariana stood up

and sat back down on Sadie's lounger. "What do you mean you're falling in love with Jonathan?"

"I don't know." She hung her head in shame. "I'm sure it's because we've been spending so much time together since Owen's been on the road. Plus he's got Riley, and she's the sweetest kid, so maybe I'm confusing my affection for her as affection for him."

"Sadie."

"I'm sure that it also has something to do with the fact that I'm stressed and vulnerable after everything that happened to my house and planning this wedding. His kindness is messing with my emotions."

"Sadie."

Panic was setting in because she clearly wasn't convincing Mariana nor was she persuading herself. "I can't be honest about this. It's not like I can be with Jonathan when I'm engaged to Owen. If I call off the engagement, Jonathan would never want anything to do with me. Owen is his brother. He is way too loyal to go after his brother's ex." She fell back on the lounger. "Oh my gosh, I don't know why I just said all that."

"Sadie." Mariana grabbed both of her

hands. "You're in love with your fiancé's brother."

"No, I'm not in love with him. I'm falling in love with him but probably not. It's just that he's so good to me and to Riley. He's such a good dad, and you know how important that is to me. And he's funny and easy-going. He's also so humble and understanding. Sometimes it's like he can read my mind, he's so in tune with what I'm feeling and thinking."

"Amiga, be honest, do you feel the same way about Owen?"

"Owen?"

"Yeah, the man you agreed to marry. Tell me what you love about him."

It was like she was having a flashback to the night Owen asked her to marry him. Why did she agree to marry him? There were several good reasons. "He's a good man. He's financially stable. He has good taste?"

"Are you asking me or telling me?"

Sadie covered her face with her hands. This was embarrassing. If someone asked Owen why he was marrying her and all he could say was she was nice and had good taste, she would be mortified.

"My mom wants me to get married. She's

wanted me to get married for years now. She almost died and I thought she wouldn't be around to see me in a wedding dress. I said yes to him because I believed there was enough good in him that eventually I would fall in love with him."

"But you were never in love with him?"

Sadie dropped her hands and looked Mariana in the eye. She shook her head. "I've been trying and my heart just doesn't want to go that extra mile."

"What about with Jonathan? When you think about him, what does your heart tell you?"

"That it's willing to run a marathon," she admitted. "That it will break into a million pieces if he goes back to Boston, and that I'm one hundred percent in love with him."

"You're such a liar," Mariana said, tipping her chin down.

"I'm not lying. I wish I was. You have no idea how much I wish I was, but I'm in love with Jonathan instead of Owen."

Mariana shook her head. "Not about who you're in love with. You've been trying to tell me that you're confused, but that's a lie. You aren't confused. You know exactly how you feel about both men. The only thing you're confused about is what you're going to do about it."

"What in the world am I going to do about it?" Tears began to well in Sadie's eyes. "I don't want to hurt Owen, but I don't want Jonathan to break my heart either. That sounds so selfish saying it out loud, but that's what would happen if I tell him how I feel. I just know it."

Mariana gave her a hug. When she pulled back, she said, "It's not selfish. No one wants to get their heart broken. Owen is a good guy. He lives in this amazing house. He'll be able to provide for you and your future family together the rest of your life. There are lots of women out there who would kill for that kind of arrangement."

"Interesting word choice—*arrangement.*"

"Because that's what it would be. It wouldn't be the same as marrying the man you love and sharing your life with him. You need to decide if you want to settle for a good arrangement or risk it all for the amazingness that comes with true love."

"How can I break up with Owen and ask Jonathan to be with me instead? They are brothers. How would that work exactly? I just don't see how it ends well for any of us. If I give up what I have now, I could easily lose them both. I can't lose Jonathan. I would rather be his sister-in-law than never see him again."

"You cannot be his sister-in-law when you have feelings this strong. Do you think that Jonathan feels the same way that you do?"

Sadie answered honestly. "I have no idea. I want to say yes because he says things that make my heart want to explode. I also feel like there have been a few times when he's wanted to kiss me, but maybe I'm just projecting."

Mariana smirked. "You are not projecting."

It would be nice if Sadie felt a bit more confident about that. "What do you think I should do?"

"This is only my opinion. You're going to have to decide what to do for yourself."

"I get it. Lay it on me."

"I think that you shouldn't marry someone you aren't in love with. I don't want that for you and I don't think that your mom would really want that for you. She wants you to get married, but I'm almost positive she wants you to marry the person you're in love with."

Sadie knew that was true. Her mom kept saying that it didn't matter if this engagement happened so quickly or that the engagement would be short. If they were in love with each other, they didn't need to worry about how long they'd been together.

Mariana continued, "So, my thought is you need to end things with Owen no matter what, then you need to be honest with Jonathan and see if he feels the same way."

"And he could say no, and I could lose both of them."

"He could and you could. That's the risk you have to take for love. At the same time, if you decide that you're not willing to do that, I will absolutely pretend that we never had this conversation. I will not judge you for choosing Owen. I will stand up in your wedding and I will pray that over time, you find some love for him."

Sadie appreciated her frank assessment and her willingness to let Sadie make her own choices without judging her. Mariana really was the best friend she could ask for. Sadie had an extremely difficult decision to make. She would be praying, too. Praying that she'd make the right one.

"THIS ONE IS a little smaller, but I love that it's been updated so there won't be much for you to do before you move in." Megan had taken Jonathan and Riley to three houses today. The first two were a complete bust. They were outdated and not in the right location.

This house had the most promise. It was under budget, didn't need to be gutted and wasn't on a busy street. He also liked that it was near the elementary school in the only district that Jonathan would consider for Riley to attend.

"It's a three-bedroom and two-and-a-half-bath. They recently put in new appliances in the kitchen and it had a new roof put on two years ago." Megan unlocked the front door and held the door open for Jonathan and Riley.

"Three bedrooms means that you get one, I get one and there's one for Sadie when she comes to visit us," Riley said as she skipped inside.

He hadn't thought about how confusing things might be for her. After having everyone under the same roof for a few weeks now, it shouldn't have been surprising that she would assume they would continue on like that. "If we move to Florida, Uncle Owen and Aunt Sadie will live close enough that they won't need to sleep over. They can come over for dinner, though."

"But Sadie likes when I read to her before bed."

"That's cute. She gets along well with Owen's fiancée?"

Anyone who knew Sadie got along with her. It wasn't hard to do. "She can't wait for Sadie to become her aunt."

"It's great that you and your brother have a good relationship. I have an older sister who I haven't talked to in like over a year. We're just so different and her husband thinks women should be seen and not heard. He hates me because I talk. A lot."

Jonathan had noticed. "Well, maybe it's a good thing that you don't talk to her often. He probably likes you more now."

Megan's laugh seemed a bit exaggerated. She had been doing that all day. It was like everything he said was the funniest thing she had ever heard. He had a good sense of humor, but he wasn't that hilarious.

"I still think you're lucky to be so close to your brother. Family is important. You only get one, right?"

Jonathan couldn't disagree. Riley, his parents, his brother—they were the most important people in his life. He had suffered a loss that he wouldn't wish on anyone. It taught him not to take anything or anyone he cared about for granted.

"You only get one," he replied.

And he was risking everything, everyone he cared about, by being so selfish. His feelings for Sadie had clouded his judgment time and time again. He could never act on those feelings because it would hurt his family. It would hurt Owen and it could hurt Riley in the end. He had confused her enough. She had lost her mother and if he wasn't careful, he could cause her to lose Sadie, too.

"Well, won't it be nice if you and Riley can settle down here and see your brother and his new wife all the time?"

Suddenly, everything was clear. It was like the fog was lifted and he knew exactly what he had to do. "I really appreciate you taking us to look at houses, but I don't think we're going to be moving to Florida. I'm sorry for wasting your time. Come on, Riley. We're going to go back to Uncle Owen's."

Megan's expression shifted to confusion. "Are you sure? Was there something about this house that you didn't like? I can show you some other listings. There were a couple that were a little bit outside of your budget but are bigger and have some nicer amenities if you want to look at those."

"We aren't going to move to Florida, Megan. It's not about the houses." It was about family and keeping his family from falling apart. The only way to do that was to put some space between him and Sadie. It was what was best for everyone.

When they got home, Sadie was nowhere to be found. That was a blessing. He let Riley watch a movie while he went upstairs to his room to make a call.

"Everything okay?" Owen asked right away.

Jonathan never called his brother. If he needed to tell him something, he sent a text. That was just the norm between them. Surely,

Owen feared something terrible happened if he had to pick up the phone.

"Everything's fine. I just needed to tell you something and I didn't think it was right to do it over text," he explained to ease his brother's anxiety. "I saw you finished in the top ten today. Nice job."

"Thanks, but I'm pretty sure you didn't need to tell me that you saw my score for the day. What's up, Jon? I'm supposed to go to this dinner thing in a little bit."

Jonathan took a deep breath. "Riley and I are going to head back to Boston. I know you had us come out here to house-sit while you were traveling, but since Sadie is staying here now, I don't think you really need us."

"What are you talking about? The wedding is in a couple weeks. Why would you leave before the wedding?"

"We'll come back for the wedding. I just think that we need to get back to our lives in Boston."

"I thought you were still thinking about moving to Florida. What is going on?" Owen's tone clearly expressed all of his concern. "Mom is going to be really upset."

Jonathan paced in front of his bed and

pushed his hair back off his forehead. "Mom will be fine. I come to visit for all the holidays. Riley loves you guys. I love you guys, but we belong in Boston."

"I don't know what happened, man. If I did something, if I said something. I know you've been questioning my judgment ever since you walked in my house and found me proposing to Sadie, but I want you to know that I heard you about being the kind of man who deserves Sadie, and I will. I will be the man she needs me to be."

Jonathan's already battered heart took another hit. This was what he wanted, wasn't it? Owen would step up. He would be the man Sadie deserved. She would be happy. Owen would be happy. Eventually, Jonathan would be, too.

"That's good. I'm not leaving because of you. I'm leaving because of me. I'll be back to be your best man. I hear it's going to be the wedding of the year. I wouldn't miss that for anything."

Owen was quiet for a second. "Thanks, brother. I hope that whatever it is that you're going through, that you know what you're doing and that you'll be okay. You know that Sadie and I are here for you guys if you need us."

Hearing her name was another jab. "I know."

Breaking the news to Owen was one thing, telling Riley they were going home would be another. She wasn't going to like that idea at first, but it was clearly what was best. Even worse would be lying to Sadie about why they had to go. He couldn't tell her it was because he was in love with her. That wasn't fair to her or Owen.

When he got downstairs, he wasn't expecting to find Sadie sitting on the couch next to Riley, but there she was in all her sweet glory.

"Hey, there you are. Riley said you guys looked at some nice houses today. Find anything you'd want to buy?" Sadie asked.

This was it. He might as well kill two birds with one stone and tell them both at the same time. Maybe Sadie would help soften the blow for Riley.

"We did not find anything that I wanted to buy. In fact, I realized that I've been giving Riley some mixed messages lately. On one hand, I've been taking her to look at houses and entertaining the idea of moving while saying over and over again that making a move would probably be too stressful."

"But when we move here, we'll be happy," Riley said.

"We're not going to move here, honey. In fact, I've decided that we're going to go home."

"You're going to go back to Boston at the end of the summer?" Sadie asked. She pushed her hair over her shoulder and shifted her position closer to Riley. His daughter leaned against her. They were presenting quite the united front. It was making this all that much harder.

"We're going back to Boston tomorrow."

"Tomorrow?" Sadie's voice rose a couple of octaves.

"I don't want to go back to Boston tomorrow," Riley whined on cue.

"I know you don't, sweetheart, but Sadie is here to watch Uncle Owen's house. They really don't need us to be living here when they are just about to start their lives together. We'll come back for the wedding. You are still going to be flower girl."

Riley started to cry. There was nothing worse than being the reason for her tears.

"Honey, we'll come back and visit. I bet your friends in Boston have been missing you and will be so happy to get to have a playdate when we tell them we're home."

Typical Riley, he could see her warring inside, but she wouldn't fight him when she knew this was what he wanted. She was too much of a pleaser for that.

"I'm really sad," she said.

Sadie gave her a hug and kissed the top of her head. "Can you do me a favor? Can you give me and your dad a minute to talk alone? Maybe you can go upstairs and read for a little bit. Reading always makes me feel better when I'm sad."

Riley hugged her tighter. "I found the best house today. It even had a room for you. Dad didn't like it and now we have to go to Boston."

"You are so sweet. Thank you for thinking about me while you were looking for houses. It proves to me that I really need to talk to your dad."

Riley let her go and ran right past Jonathan and upstairs. No hug for him, but at least she understood they needed to leave. Sadie, on the other hand, didn't seem so convinced.

"I know you probably have questions, but I need you to know that I am doing what's best for my family. Owen understands. I talked to him on the phone."

Sadie stood up and put her finger on his lips to stop him from talking. "You can't leave. I'm in love with you, Jonathan."

CHAPTER EIGHTEEN

THE PLAN HAD been to talk to Owen and then talk to Jonathan, but things were not going as planned. Sadie had no other option than to drop the bomb. The fear of losing him forced her to speak her heart.

"You can't leave. I'm in love with you, Jonathan."

Saying those words to him was sort of freeing. Like letting go a weight she didn't know she had been carrying. She dropped her hand to her side, so he would feel free to respond to her confession.

Jonathan blinked and blinked again, but no words left his lips. She could practically hear the wheels in his head spinning.

"I've been trying to deny these feelings, but I can't anymore. I have to be honest with myself and with you."

His blue eyes were fixed on her. It looked like he had been manhandling his hair earlier.

It was sticking up a bit in the front in the most adorable way. She wanted to run her fingers through it and smooth it out.

"Sadie, you're marrying my brother."

She was ready for him to say something about Owen. She needed to assure him that they both wanted to protect Owen's heart in all of this. "The last thing I want to do is hurt Owen. I care about him. I do."

"I would never hurt my brother. Never. I don't even know what you're doing right now."

Sadie's cheeks began to burn and her stomach ached. There were two ways this was going to go, and this was beginning to feel like it was headed in the wrong direction. She needed to get him to acknowledge the connection. To help him see she felt it, too.

"I know how much you care about your brother, but I need you to be honest with me. That night when we were here by ourselves and you were in my room, did you want to kiss me? It definitely felt like you wanted to kiss me."

Jonathan's shoulders stiffened and he stood a little straighter. "I don't know what you're talking about."

This was verging on the most embarrassing moment of her life. "The night I was in my room crying over that stupid wedding dress. You sat on the bed with me and there was a moment right before Owen called where it felt like we were going to kiss."

Jonathan took a step back and rubbed his forehead. "I don't know what you thought was going on, but I was trying to comfort my brother's fiancée because I felt bad that someone had made you feel like you weren't the right person for him. You are the right person for Owen. You challenge him in all the right ways."

He thought she was the right person...for Owen. Not for him. He hadn't thought about kissing her that night. These feelings she had were not going to be reciprocated.

"Listen," he said. "If I gave you the wrong impression and made you think that there was something going on between us, I apologize. I don't think about you that way. I think about you being my brother's wife and the future mother of his children. I think maybe you got confused. We've been spending time together and you've been under a lot of stress. Maybe you thought me being nice to you meant something other than friendly feelings, but please know, I am not in love with you, Sadie."

Her breathing was more labored than usual and her head spun. This felt very much like an anxiety attack. She sat back down before her legs gave out on her.

"I'm sorry if I gave you the wrong impression. I really think you were mixing up your feelings for Owen with your feelings for me. My brother is an amazing guy who loves you. He can't wait to marry you. You guys are going to have a great life. I won't say anything to him about this." He started to back out of the room, and Sadie was about to hyperventilate. "I think this is another good reason why Riley and I need to go back to Boston. Some distance will help you see that you're not really in love with me. You'll see."

Complete humiliation. Sadie had never been so humiliated. Not only did she make a fool of herself by confessing her feelings, but she had taken it a step further and tried to convince him that he felt the same way.

He didn't.

She needed to get out of this house. She couldn't wait until Jonathan and Riley left tomorrow, she needed to put distance between them this minute.

Deep breaths were the only thing that were going to help her see straight. Well, at least she was no longer conflicted. She knew where he stood and could move on with her life. Things didn't work out the way she wanted, but what was new about that? Once she could stand without fearing she would pass out, she headed right up to her room to pack what little she had there.

She was homeless and loveless. She wasn't even sure where she should go. Bursting her mother's happy-wedding bubble wasn't high on her priority list today. Maybe Mariana would let her crash on her couch.

"Sadie?" Riley's voice from across the hall stopped her cold.

She turned and hitched her duffel bag up on her shoulder. "Hey, sweetie."

"What are you doing? Are you coming to Boston with us? Is that why you're packing?"

Cue total destruction of her heart. "No, honey. I am not going to come to Boston with you. I am really sorry I couldn't change your dad's mind about that. I hope that you remember all the things we talked about when you read your stories, okay?"

"Are you going to still want me to be your flower girl even if we don't live together?"

Sadie did not have the heart to tell her that it was quite possible no one would be the flower girl at her wedding because there wouldn't be a wedding. "You are the only one I want to be my flower girl."

Riley hugged her hard. She squeezed Sadie so tightly, she thought she might burst. "I love you, Sadie."

There were the three words she had wanted to hear, only they were coming from the wrong Bradley. What a fool she had been to think that Jonathan would be in love with her. She had misread his kindness for something stronger and allowed herself to think there was a possibility the two of them could overcome impossible odds.

"I love you, too. Don't forget that you are smart, you are sweet and you are loved. Anyone who tells you different is a liar."

"You are smart and sweet and loved, too."

That felt very much like a big fat lie. She wanted only one person to feel that way about her, but he maybe agreed with the first two. In fact, he probably wanted to take back all the nice things he had ever said about her after she basically told him she wanted to cheat on his brother with him. She was a terrible person. She was kind of an idiot. And the only one who loved her was a nine-year-old who didn't know any better.

"I have to go, Riley. I'm…um…having a sleepover at Mariana's. You have a good night and a safe trip."

"Bye, Aunt Sadie."

What was left of her heart instantly disintegrated. Mariana better have some tissues ready because she was going to be able to hold back these tears only until she got out of this house.

WHAT HAD HE DONE? That was not what he expected her to say. Mostly, because that was not what she was supposed to say.

Sadie was in love with him? Sadie. In love. With him.

And what did he do when she dared to be honest with him? When she stood there more vulnerable than he'd ever allowed himself to be? When she bared her soul and handed him her heart on a silver platter? He lied and told her he had no idea why she would feel that way. He lied and told her he had never once thought of kissing her. Even though there were about a hundred times over the last few weeks that he wanted to kiss her. Lately, it was all he ever thought about.

That was why he needed to leave. This house, this town, this state. He needed to get as far away from her as possible so he didn't give in and act on these feelings he was having. She belonged with Owen. Hopefully, he had helped her see that.

He stomped around his room, tossing clothes into his suitcase. He would help Riley pack up after dinner. Yanking shirts off hangers and slamming drawers shut did nothing to help him regulate all this negative emotion swirling in his body. He was angry with himself, frustrated with the situation and sad for Sadie.

It was shameful the way he had treated her. This was the woman he loved and he made her feel like the dirt on his shoe. It was unforgivable. That was what he had to do so she would never give him a second thought.

His phone rang. It was his mother, who had most likely talked to his brother. He could try to ignore her, but she would only keep calling until he either shut his phone off or answered.

"Hello, Mother."

"What is this about you and Riley going back to Boston? Why would you leave right before you brother's wedding? That makes no sense."

"We'll come back for the wedding. Don't worry."

"Don't worry that my son decides to completely change his plans and run back to Massachusetts with no explanation or warning."

She was not going to be so easy to trick. "Mom, I'm leaving because I need to leave. I have been giving Riley mixed messages and making her think that we were going to live with Owen and Sadie the rest of her life. When we went to look at houses today, she actually said it was good that we were in a three-bedroom because then Sadie would have a room."

"Sadie? Not Sadie and Owen?"

No, even his daughter had forgotten that the two of them were a package deal. "She is getting too attached and I need to get her back to our life in Boston."

"You need to get her back to Boston because she's too attached to Sadie or because you need to get back because you're getting too attached to Sadie?"

Leave it to his mom to see right through him even when she couldn't actually see him. He flopped on his bed and covered his head with his pillow. What was he supposed to say? Admit that he was in love with her and she was in love with him? His mother would hate her. How could he be with someone whom his family didn't like? That would never work.

"I don't know what your obsession is with me and Sadie, but hopefully you will let it go once I am back home. Sadie is marrying Owen in a few weeks and that's that," he said from under his pillow.

"Does she know how you feel? Did you tell her you were leaving?"

"She knows that we're leaving. We said goodbye. I told her we'd be back for the wedding and she said she would see us then. It was very uneventful." It was the exact opposite of what happened, but his mother seemed to buy it.

"So the wedding is still on?"

"Of course it is. Owen is committed to this

relationship and Sadie is head over heels for him." He was never going to be able to lecture Riley about the evils of lying without feeling like a total hypocrite.

"Are you and Riley going to stop by before you leave and say goodbye to me and your father?"

"If that will make you happy, I will come by your house on our way out."

His mother let him go and he was left with nothing but the guilt of all his lies. Whom didn't he lie to today?

This was supposed to make everything better, but he felt anything but. There was a knock on his door and he sadly hoped it was Sadie, there to give him one last chance to admit he felt the same way as she did. He wasn't sure he could lie to her face again.

"Daddy?"

Riley. "Come on in, sweetheart."

His little girl came into his room with the saddest look on her face. She climbed on the bed and snuggled with him.

"Sadie's having a sleepover at Mariana's. She won't be able to read with me tonight. Will you read with me since she can't?"

He held her tighter. "Of course I will. I love to listen to you read."

"Do you not like Sadie anymore?" she asked in all her innocence.

"Why would you think I don't like her?"

"Because we had so much fun this summer and now you don't want to have any more fun with her. You just want it to be me and you."

He couldn't do it. He couldn't tell any more lies. "I like Sadie a lot. And I'm so glad that you had fun with her this summer. My hope is that after she gets married to Uncle Owen, you'll have lots of chances to have fun with her and Uncle Owen."

"And you? Sadie has the most fun when it's all of us."

Maybe with a little distance he'd be able to be around her without wanting more than he could have. Great, now he was lying to himself.

"I have the most fun when it's all of us, too."

"Me, three. I'm going to miss living in Florida. We didn't even get to go to Disney World."

He gave her little back a rub. "I'm sorry.

I promise the next time we come to visit Grandma and Grandpa, we'll go there."

"Can Sadie come with us? Everything is more fun when she's with us. Remember?"

She was making this so much harder. He wasn't the only one who fell in love with the schoolteacher with the long brown hair and the big hazel eyes.

"I remember." He would never forget.

CHAPTER NINETEEN

"A GOOD NIGHT'S sleep makes everything better. Am I right?" Mariana asked as she fell into the recliner next to the couch. "Are you feeling like a new woman?"

"Had I actually slept, I might be able to answer that question. But seeing that all I did was toss and turn while replaying the moment Jonathan made it clear that I was completely delusional, I'm probably not the one you want to ask."

The pity on Mariana's face was almost too much. Sadie closed her eyes so she didn't have to see it as well as hear it in her voice.

"What's on the agenda for the day? Do you need to go back to the house to get anything? Do you need a place to 'not sleep' again? You know you're welcome to stay here as long as you need to."

"I don't want to impose on you. After I call the wedding off and return my engagement ring to Owen, I will need to break the news to my parents. I'm sure I can stay with my mom once that happens."

She had declined both her mother's and Owen's calls yesterday. She simply ignored her mom. She texted Owen that she was at Mariana's and couldn't talk, which was true, but made it seem as if Mariana had needed her, not the other way around. She selfishly needed to nurse her own wounds before she could take wounding him by returning the ring.

"I'm so sorry everything went down like this. I know you were hoping for a different outcome."

That was an understatement. At the same time, it was what Sadie had known would happen all along. She had fought her feelings for him the entire time because she knew he would choose to protect his brother over being with her.

"If it's any consolation, I still believe that everything happens for a reason. Maybe you had to fall in love with Jon to realize that you weren't ever going to fall in love with Owen. This way, you didn't make the mistake of marrying the wrong person. It's very possible that you just haven't met the man you're going to marry yet."

Or maybe she was destined to be alone. She should probably start adopting cats so she could fit the stereotype better. Owen returned home today, and that looming conversation was also a valid reason she didn't get any sleep.

"I can't believe I still have to talk to Owen and explain to him why I need to back out of this wedding that he's already paid thousands of dollars to throw. Maybe I can use some of my insurance money to pay him back. I don't know what else to do."

Mariana shook her head. "There's no way Owen is going to make you pay back anything he put a down payment on. He doesn't seem like that kind of guy."

"He's not, but I've learned that people don't always act the way you think they will when you drop a bomb on them. He also has a little bit of an ego. He may not be so happy about me breaking it off and want me to pay."

"We'll see at the end of the day. Do you want some breakfast? I can make us some eggs. I also have cereal."

Sadie sat up and stretched her arms over

her head. "Don't worry about me. I'll be out of your hair before it sinks in that I was here."

"Well, if you change your mind, I will be in the kitchen."

Sadie wanted this day to be over more than she wanted food. It would be nice if there was a fast-forward button in life to zoom past the bad and pause the good stuff. Owen was supposed to text when he was back in town. It was a waiting game until that came in.

Her mind began to drift unconsciously to Jonathan and Riley. When were they leaving? Had anything changed after Jonathan slept on it? She missed them so much already that her chest ached. Maybe with time that would lessen and she could move on. It seemed so impossible right now. Who would make her laugh the way they did? Who would make her funny-face pancakes the morning after a rough night?

Her stomach growled. Maybe she was hungrier than she thought. She got up and went to find her friend and some food. It might not be funny-face pancakes, but it would be something.

OWEN TEXTED AROUND two o'clock. Sadie had spent the whole morning overthinking about what she was going to say. Now that she was standing outside his house, her head was empty. She couldn't remember how she was going to start this conversation or end it.

She rang the doorbell like she hadn't lived there for the past month and a half.

"Oh, it's you! Did you forget your key?" Owen asked when he greeted her. "How are you?" He pulled her in for a hug.

All the guilt she'd been trying to keep at bay sat on her shoulders like a two-ton boulder. "I'm not okay, actually," she responded.

He pulled back and took a good look at her. "Is Mariana okay? You look like you were up all night. What happened?"

"Maybe we can go sit down?" She motioned toward the living room.

His face was pinched in confusion. "Yeah, sure. I hope you're asking because you want to tell me what's going on."

"I definitely want to tell you what's going on," she assured him.

"Good, because I can't stand any more secrets. Can you believe my brother? He practically got up at the crack of dawn and drove home. What was that about? I still don't feel like I got a straight answer from him."

Sadie sat on the couch in the same exact spot she was sitting when Jonathan informed her and Riley that they were leaving. She got up and sat on the loveseat instead.

"I feel really bad that he did that to you. I feel even worse because I'm going to do the same thing."

He took the seat next to her and reached for her hand. "What do you mean?"

"I'm moving out," she blurted. "I will probably go live with my mom until I figure out what I'm going to do next."

"You're moving out for three weeks? What's the point of that? We're going to get married and it's not going to matter where we lived before the wedding."

"I'm not moving in after the wedding."

He shifted in his seat to better face her. "Well, now I'm really confused. Where are we going to live if not here? Or are you trying to tell me something else? Is there even going to be a wedding?"

The tears were already rolling down her cheeks. She used her free hand to wipe at them before they started to drip off her chin. "I'm so sorry, Owen. I thought I could go through with this. I thought that maybe with a little more time, I could be one hundred percent sure that I wanted to marry you."

He let go of her hand and moved a tiny bit away from her. "You haven't been one hundred percent sure this whole time? Why did you say yes if you weren't sure?"

"Because you seemed so sure and I wanted you to be happy and I knew an engagement would make my mom happy. I care about you. I care about you a lot. It wasn't like there weren't feelings there to begin with, it's just that I was hoping they would blossom more and instead they kind of closed up."

Owen needed a moment to process that. He rubbed his forehead and closed his eyes so he didn't have to look at her anymore. She wasn't sure how else to explain what happened. She wasn't sure if she should mention how she felt about Jonathan or not. She didn't want to cause any problems between the brothers.

"Let me see if I have this straight—you weren't totally sure you wanted to marry me when I asked you to, but you knew it would make me and your mom happy if you said yes, so you did."

She nodded even though hearing it back made it sound so much worse.

"Then you hoped you'd fall in love with me before the wedding, but that didn't happen. I somehow made you fall out of love with me."

Shaking her head, she reached for him. "You didn't do anything." He pulled away and stood up. She wiped away more tears. "This is all me. I wasn't ready for this and I should have been honest with you from the beginning. We've barely spent any time together since we got engaged. I feel like I know Jonathan and Riley better than I know you at this point."

"Jonathan and Riley." Owen nodded his head. "Did my brother know about this? Did you tell him you were calling off the wedding and that's why he left? Did he not have the courage to tell me? To give me a head's-up at least?"

"He didn't know how I was feeling until I told him yesterday *after* he told me he was leaving. I'm just as confused about why he was in such a rush to leave."

Owen moved around the room with his hands on his hips. "We have all these plans made. Before I left, you and I picked out flowers with your mom. You seemed happy."

There was no reason to beat around the

bush, to have him stand here trying to guess where things went wrong when she could just cut to the ending. "I'm in love with Jonathan."

He froze. His head turned slowly until their eyes met. "You're in love with Jonathan?"

"I didn't set out to fall in love with him. It just happened. In fact, if someone had told me that was how this story was going to end when I first met him, I would have told them they were crazy. I wanted him to like me. As a sister-in-law. Obviously. I was worried that he thought I was all wrong for you. I didn't think I could win him over, but somehow I did, and I thought his feelings for me were like the ones I have for him."

"Did something happen between you while I was gone? Did lines get crossed and that's why he left? Just tell me, Sadie, because it's kind of a big deal that my brother left."

"Nothing improper ever happened. He was always a complete gentleman. Even when I told him how I felt he was clear that he did not feel the same way and that I should remember that I was marrying you. He was always concerned about what you thought. He didn't want me to hurt you. He told me that the first night I met him actually and again last night."

"He told you he didn't have feelings for you? None?"

Sadie's whole chest hurt. She nodded her head, unable to answer with words.

Owen began to laugh. His laughter grew into something almost maniacal. "You believed him. Didn't you?"

"Why wouldn't I? I pretty much was standing there with my heart in hand and he swatted that thing across the room without a second thought."

Owen sat down on the couch across from her and held his head in his hands. "My brother is such a martyr."

"What?"

He didn't reply to that question. "I've been having doubts, too. I didn't want to say anything because I thought it was just normal cold-feet kind of thoughts."

That got her attention. "For how long?"

He shook his head. "I don't know. A while. Jonathan got on my case a couple times about things I said to him and it made me want to try harder, to prove to him that I was right to ask you and put you in this pressure-cooker situation. I do care about you. I think you're a great person."

"I care about you, too. This was never about not thinking you were a good person. Just not the right person for me."

"I get that better than you can imagine. I think I'm still in love with my ex-girlfriend. I don't think I really ever got over losing her. When I found out she got engaged so soon after we broke up, I think I jumped at the opportunity to do the same thing, thinking it would somehow prove to her that I was just as over her as she was over me."

Courtney. Sadie wasn't wrong to feel so insecure about her. Courtney also wasn't as over Owen as she wanted everyone to believe. "I think if you were sort of unconsciously trying to make her jealous, it worked. It also helped that she saw me trying on dresses. She was very hurt that you had asked me to marry you after such a short courtship but wasn't ready during your relationship with her."

"She's been following my social media very closely. Even posted some things on Instagram and tagged me. She's been trying to get my attention, and if I'm being completely honest, I think I've been trying to get hers."

It made sense why he'd been so adamant about having the wedding so soon as well as everything being top of the line. He wanted to outdo Courtney in every way so she would regret not coming back to him.

"It sounds like you have some soul-searching to do. Maybe once I give you this—" she slid the engagement ring off her finger and held it out for him "—you can decide if you want to fight a little bit harder to get her to reconsider."

He took the ring and rolled it between his fingers. "Maybe. I'm really sorry about not being honest about my feelings and trying to push something on both of us instead of taking the time to figure out my real truth. I didn't mean to drag you into an engagement when I knew that I didn't have one hundred percent pure intentions."

She appreciated his honesty now. "I forgive you. I'm sorry I didn't voice my concerns earlier."

"But maybe it allowed you to find someone better. If you hadn't been engaged to me, you wouldn't have met my brother."

"Your brother who does not have feelings for me. I don't know how productive falling in love with him really was. Feels a little more like unnecessary heartache than a gift from the fates."

"He hurt you."

Sadie stared down at her hands in her lap. He had hurt her worse than anyone ever had. She nodded.

"He would never hurt you unless he thought that by not hurting you, he would hurt me. Maybe you need to have another conversation now that you and I are on the same page about this engagement."

Sadie was not up for the abuse. She couldn't deal with the rejection one more time. "I know you know your brother better than anyone, but he was really clear last night."

"I'm sorry for that, too."

"It's not your fault. People feel what they feel. You couldn't have made him care about me any more than you could force yourself to fall in love with me."

The sad reality was Sadie couldn't get either Bradley brother to fall in love with her.

"I'm still sorry. You deserve someone who loves you with his whole heart. Someone worthy of you loving him back that much, as well. I don't know that I ever deserved to be the one you fell head over heels for. I'm awesome, but I'm not the one."

She thought Jonathan was, but she was wrong. "Good luck to you. If you need me to pay some of the deposits, I'm happy to take care of my share of the costs."

Owen shook his head and helped her to her feet. He wrapped Sadie up in his arms. "I got it. I can do one thing right."

That went much better than she thought it was going to. Maybe it wouldn't be so bad to tell her mom. Whom was she kidding? The end of this engagement was not going to sit well with Candice.

"Mom, WE NEED to leave. We were going to leave four hours ago, but you tricked my daughter into running to the store with you. Then we had to stay for lunch. Then you needed us to wait for Dad to come back from the barbershop. We need to hit the road so we can get at least get to North Carolina."

"Why do you need to leave today? If you don't want to stay with your brother, you two can move in here. We have plenty of room for you."

Jonathan had been sitting at his parents'

house for too many hours that should have been spent on the highway. After an extremely rough night that included his own sleeplessness due to overthinking everything that happened with Sadie as well as Riley waking up screaming from her first nightmare in months, Jonathan had to get going or he would fall asleep behind the wheel.

"Mom, we need to go home. I just want to go home."

Really, he just needed to put more space between him and Sadie. Because if he were to accidentally bump into her right now, he might not be able to stop himself from telling her he was a fraud who really was madly in love with her. That couldn't happen.

The front door opened and Jonathan sighed with relief. "There you go. Dad's home. We can go now. Riley! Grab your stuff. We're leaving in five minutes!"

"I want to finish the puzzle," she shouted from the other room. The puzzle had been his mother's other stall tactic.

"Five minutes? Oh, come on," his mom complained.

"Look who's still here. I was hoping I would find you here. Good job, Mom." Owen walked in and gave his mom a kiss on the cheek. It reminded Jonathan of the way he always did that with Sadie. Sadly, Jonathan hadn't had a chance to kiss her cheek even.

"When did you get back in town?" And why was he congratulating his mom on a job well done?

"Couple hours ago. Sadie came over and we had a real heart-to-heart. I heard you two had one of those as well yesterday."

Sadie. She told him that they had a talk? Jonathan prayed she didn't say anything about the silly feelings she thought she had. She would fall for Owen if she had enough time. Women always did. "We said our goodbyes. I told her we'd see her at the wedding. There's still a wedding, right?"

"We've decided to call off the wedding, actually. She's not in love with me, and if I'm being totally honest, I'm still in love with Courtney."

Jonathan's jaw dropped. "You're still in love with Courtney? What are you talking about? You told me that you were over her. That you weren't going to hurt Sadie by carrying around unresolved feelings. I trusted you."

"You trusted me? That's rich, brother."

Jonathan was seeing only red. How could Owen be in love with the wrong woman? "You have someone like Sadie, and you would give her up for Courtney? Do you even realize how amazing Sadie is? There's no comparison between the two of them! Sadie is kind and generous, but also strong and smart. She is so smart. And she's funny. She makes me laugh all the time. Being around her just cheers me up, but she also allows me to feel what I need to feel. She doesn't hold it against me if I'm having a moment and she just sits with me when I need comfort instead of a distraction. She is one in a million, man."

"Spoken like a man in love with my fiancée. Well, my ex-fiancée."

Jonathan scoffed at his accusation. He hadn't meant to go on like he had. He simply couldn't understand what his brother was thinking. Especially after Jonathan had turned her away solely to give his brother a chance at a wonderful life. "I'm not in love with your ex-fiancée," he said, trying his best to keep up appearances. "I told her last night that she needed to focus her attention on you and everything would be fine."

Owen's cocky smirk was annoying. "You were wrong. She and I aren't meant for each other, and I think you love her, but you're afraid that makes you a bad person or at the very least a bad brother."

"He's absolutely in love with her," their mother chimed in. "I called him out about it weeks ago. The night you were all here and I was trying my best to get him back together with Georgina. It was crystal clear that he only had eyes for one woman at the table."

Jonathan shook his head. He was not the kind of man who stole his brother's wife away. He wouldn't be able to live with himself if his brother distrusted him.

"Jonathan, come on. Admit it. How many times did you challenge me to treat her better, to think about her feelings, to deserve her? That wasn't because you were looking out for me. You were looking out for her because you were in love with her and you were worried I wasn't going to be good enough for her."

His mom touched his arm. "Honey, it's okay. I know I gave you a hard time earlier, but now Owen is being honest about his feelings and doing the right thing. You don't have to hide your feelings anymore."

Jonathan's head was spinning. He wasn't prepared for this ambush. "You're still in love with Courtney?"

"And Sadie is in love with you," Owen said like it was no big deal. "Sounds like we both have some work to do to win the woman we love back."

"You don't hate my guts? You don't want to punch me or tell me I'm a jerk for getting in the middle of you and the greatest woman in the world?"

"Of course I don't hate you. I can't really blame you for falling for her. I think she's pretty awesome, but she should be with someone who thinks she is the greatest woman in the world. That would be you, in case you're having trouble following."

Jonathan pressed both hands to the sides of his head. Was he imagining all of this or was this real? Owen didn't want to marry Sadie. Was it really possible that Owen wanted Jonathan to be with her?

"Where is she?"

"She went to her mom's," Owen said, pulling out his phone. "I'll text you the address. I suggest you get going so you avoid rush hour. Mom will watch Riley."

"Go get Sadie," his mom said.

They didn't need to tell him twice. He started for the door.

"Jon," Owen called after him. He stopped and turned to face his brother. "Deserve her."

A smile spread across his face. "I do."

Jonathan took off running for his car. He was no longer in a rush to get to Boston. Instead, he needed to go tell the woman he loved that he had been a fool for not being honest.

Owen had sent him the directions and led him right to a house with Sadie's car parked in the driveway. All the adrenaline that had helped him drive like he was on the NASCAR speedway suddenly disappeared and a ball of anxiety sat in his stomach.

What if she wouldn't talk to him? What if her mother wouldn't even let him in the door? He resolved not to let anything stop him from telling her exactly how he felt.

Candice Chapman looked like she had just gone to the salon and had someone do her makeup as if she was going to be going to some big social event.

"Hi, Mrs. Chapman. I'm Jonathan, Owen's brother."

"I know who you are."

"Of course you do. No reason you would forget." His palms were sweating like they used to when he was a nervous, awkward teenager. "Is Sadie here? I was hoping I could talk to her."

For such a slight woman, she managed to block the opening in the doorway enough that he couldn't see if Sadie was inside the house. She had to be because her car was parked outside. "I thought you were headed to Boston. Why haven't you left yet?"

"I was going to leave this morning, but then my mom wanted me to come over to say goodbye and she spent the rest of the day holding me hostage."

Candice's eyebrow quirked up. "Your mother held you hostage?"

"Well, not actually. I could have left, but you know how moms are."

She titled her head. "No, tell me how moms are."

Oh man, he was not winning her over. "They're persistent and they love their kids something fierce."

"Fathers don't love their children that fiercely?"

"No. I mean, yes, yes, fathers love their children, too. Fiercely. I just mean that moms are better at holding us hostage. Could you not hold Sadie hostage? I really need to talk to her."

"Mom, what are you doing?" Sadie's voice was like ice on a burn. Cool and soothing. Candice opened the door wider and there she was. She looked tired and sad. Her eyes were red like they were the day at the bridal shop. He hated that he might have something to do with that. "Jonathan, what are you doing here? Where's Riley?"

"My mom is watching her while I'm here because I needed to talk to you alone."

"I'm pretty sure you said everything I needed to hear last night."

He was definitely at fault for those tears, and that hurt his heart. "I didn't. I know you met with Owen and called off the wedding. I need to talk to you about that."

She held up a hand to prevent him from coming in. "I know that you think Owen and I should be together, but we talked it out and realized that we're both not in love with each other. It's okay. I did not break his heart. You don't have to worry about me hurting him because I misread our interactions."

"You didn't misread our interactions. In fact, you read them perfectly. That night in your room, I wanted to kiss you so badly that when I left, I needed to take a cold shower. In fact, there were a lot of times I wanted to kiss you. Pretty much all the time the last month or so."

Sadie frowned and the crease between her eyebrows deepened. "What? But you said you didn't…"

"I know what I said last night, and it was all a lie. I didn't want you to know the truth because I thought you should be with Owen. I love my brother and I couldn't live with myself if I stole his fiancée away. Brothers shouldn't do that to each other."

"Why don't you invite the man in, Sadie," Candice said. "The whole neighborhood doesn't need to know your business."

Sadie opened the door and welcomed him inside. Her mother's house looked a lot like his mother's house. They had very similar aesthetics. Lots of gray and cream with pops of blue.

"But Owen doesn't want to be with me. He's not in love with me."

Jonathan could only hope that the collapse of her relationship with Owen didn't ruin his chances to be with her. "He's not, but I am. I have been for quite some time. I tried to deny it to myself, to my mom, who could tell right away, to Owen, to Riley and to you last night. But I'm done lying and hiding how I feel. I'm in love with you, Sadie Chapman, and if my brother doesn't want to marry you, I need you to know that I want the chance to sweep you off your feet. I know that your feelings may have changed after what I said last night, but I hope you'll give me a chance to—"

"Jonathan, stop," she pleaded. "Just stop."

He could feel his whole world collapsing around him. He had lost one love to death. He couldn't imagine losing another to his own stupidity. "I can't stop, Sadie." He took her by the hand. "I love you. I love your smile and your laugh. I love that you don't take off your flip-flops until you walk all the way to the edge of the pool and then put them on the second you get out. I love that you love chicken nuggets almost as much as my nine-year-old. I love that you love my daughter.

That you have always made her feel important and loved. You have no idea how much that means to me."

"I do love Riley. With my whole heart." Sadie had tears in her eyes, but this time, they seemed like the good kind.

"She loves you, too. Riley told me last night that everything is better when we're all together—you, me and her. The beach is more fun, the ice cream tastes better and movie night is more entertaining."

"I talk too much during movies," she said through a giggle.

"That's okay, I love that, too." He reached up and placed his hand on her cheek. "I love you, Sadie Chapman. I love you so much that I don't think I will survive without you. Don't make me even try."

Her skin was so soft and warm. He wiped a stray tear that had fallen down her cheek. Her breathing was a little irregular, but he was counting that as a positive. He was having an effect on her, the kind he wanted her to have. Her pink lips parted ever so slightly.

"I love you, too. I've been so afraid of losing you, I was willing to marry someone I didn't love just to have you in my life," she said before lifting up on her tiptoes to place the softest and sweetest kiss on his lips.

Kissing Sadie was like flying—exhilarating and scary at the same time. He never wanted it to end and he feared it would all too soon. Guess he was going to have to make sure he stuck around so he could do it again and again. Forever and always.

CHAPTER TWENTY

"LET'S SEE," HER mother said. Her patience was wearing thin.

She stepped out of the dressing room and into the bridal suite where Riley and Mariana were getting ready and her mother was micromanaging. Morikami Museum and Japanese Gardens was a unique wedding venue that offered one of the most gorgeous backdrops for their special day.

"Is the veil okay?"

Her mother's eyes filled with tears so quickly, there was no way she had time to see what Sadie looked like before her vision was blurred.

"You are the most beautiful bride I have ever seen, Sweetheart, you blow me away."

The emotion in her mom's voice sent her over the edge and her eyes watered.

"Crying alert!" Mariana screamed. "Get me the tissue!" Riley pulled one from the box and handed it to the matron of honor. "Dab, do not wipe."

Sadie did her best to follow instructions. Her makeup had taken almost an hour to apply. She did not want to mess it up. Not today, not seconds before she walked down the aisle.

"You look like a real princess," Riley said, her right front tooth missing just in time for all the wedding photos. The tooth fairy had shown up even though everyone in charge of reporting to the fairy had been very tired after the rehearsal. Money had been transferred to the tooth fairy pillow perhaps more so in the early morning than in the middle of the night, but Riley was none the wiser. These little milestones were just as important as the big ones.

"You also look very much like a princess. That tiara is perfect."

"Thank you," she said with her toothless grin.

Sadie's father knocked on the door before coming in. "Are we ready to go in here?"

"Come on in, Dad. We're ready."

Dressed in his tuxedo, her father stepped in the room with a gasp. He reached in his pocket and pulled out a handkerchief right away. "Oh, Sadie. You are a vision. I don't think I'm going to make it down the aisle."

"Hold it together, man. Your daughter needs you to be on your game today," her mother said as if she wasn't just crying herself.

He ignored her and kept his focus on Sadie. "You're not my little girl anymore. You really have become an amazing woman. I could not be more proud of you."

"Thank you, Dad."

"Crying alert!" Mariana lunged for the tissues. "Dab, do not rub."

Sadie did as she was told.

"I'm here for Mom. Mom, we're up," Paul called into the room. "Are you ready to go?" He froze when he laid eyes on his sister. "Whoa. Jonathan is not going to know what hit him when you come down that aisle. You look gorgeous, Sadie."

"Thank you."

Her mother gave her two air kisses and then left with her brother to be escorted down the aisle. Mariana handed Riley her basket of flower petals and led her out of the room.

"See you on the other side. You are breathtaking."

"Thank you, Mariana."

That left Sadie and her father. "Are you sure about this? I've got a car waiting outside with a full tank of gas. We could be in Chicago by the morning."

"I've never been more certain about anything. I am ready to become Mrs. Jonathan Bradley." She loved the sound of it. She couldn't wait to go to school and have everyone call her Mrs. Bradley instead of Miss Chapman. Being in love had made her more excited about everything in her life.

"I feel like this one is different from the first one. I could tell right away that you were happier. Dads know these things."

This one was different. From the moment Owen had asked her to marry him to the moment they broke it off, she hadn't felt that special something for him. With Jonathan, it was the exact opposite. Once he showed up at her mother's door, professing his true feelings, she knew she could never be without him. "Jonathan is the right one. Never fear."

"Bride time." Chelsea the wedding planner popped her head in.

Since Sadie and Owen had everything already set up for an August wedding, instead of giving up all of those deposits, Owen decided to gift Jonathan and *his* bride-to-be all the arrangements. Honestly, Jonathan and Sadie had nearly picked everything out together. He had helped with the cake, the dress and the string quartet that would be playing at the reception. It had been more their wedding than hers and Owen's from the start.

Sadie and her dad walked outside where everything was set up on the terrace. The wedding ceremony would take place under a flowered arch overlooking the lake.

"Cue the music," Chelsea said into her headset. "You guys are good to go. Just like we practiced last night."

Sadie took her father's arm and a deep breath.

"Let's do this."

JONATHAN'S HEART WAS beating so fast, he was afraid he was going to wear it out before Sadie even came around the corner and down the aisle.

"You good, brother?" Owen asked. "You

need this?" He held out a handkerchief. "You're sweating like you're in a sauna."

Jonathan could feel the perspiration beading up on his forehead. He took the cloth from his brother and wiped himself off. He didn't want Sadie to think he was nervous. He wasn't nervous. He was thrilled. He could not wait to make her his wife and spend the rest of their days together.

He had gotten a bit choked up when Riley carefully spread the flower petals down the carpeted steps of the aisle. For days leading up to the ceremony, she couldn't stop talking about how she was going to be able to call Sadie Mom as soon as they said "I do." All his fears about bringing another woman into Riley's life had vanished when he met Sadie. She wasn't there to replace Mindy. She was someone extra. She gave Riley extra time, extra attention and extra love. There was no reason Mindy wouldn't want that for their daughter.

The music changed and Jonathan knew he was about to see her. He just needed to see her face and he knew his heart would calm down and his entire body would relax. She had that effect on him. She made things safe and comfortable. It was just her way.

Sadie and her father appeared at the top of the stairs. All of their family and friends were seated theater style in white wooden folding chairs. As soon as she came into view, and what a view it was, it was like no one else existed. He had been blown away that day in the bridal shop, but that was nothing compared with the real thing. Sadie was a stunning vision in ivory lace. A sheer veil covered her face, but he could still see her. Those eyes of hers were locked on him and her smile was bigger than he'd ever seen.

She was going to be his wife and there was no luckier man in the world. Bruce, her father, shook Jonathan's hand and then gave her over to him. Now that Jonathan was a father, he could understand the gravity of that kind of trust. He knew he had to live up to that and take care of and love Sadie all of their days because that was what he would expect from the man who wanted to marry Riley someday.

The minister started talking, prayers were read and candles were lit. The most important part, the only part that mattered to Jonathan, was when the minister asked him, "Jonathan, do you take this woman to be your lawfully wedded wife? Do you promise to love her in good times and bad, for richer or poorer, and in sickness and in health?"

"I sure do," he replied.

"Sadie, do you take this man to be your lawfully wedded husband? Do you promise to love him in good times and bad, for richer or poorer, in sickness and in health?"

"I do," she replied and Jonathan's heart leaped.

"Do you have the rings?"

Jonathan turned to his brother, the man who had asked Sadie to marry him just a few months ago. Owen reached in his pocket and with a playful grin held out the rings, only to close his hand around them before he could grab them.

"Just kidding," he joked, opening his hand back up and letting Jonathan pick them up. "You two deserve each other. Be happy, brother."

It was nice to have his brother's blessing, but he didn't need to get permission to be happy. Sadie made him happy every day. Like Riley had said on that sad day in July, Sadie made everything more fun.

"Repeat after me," the minister said. "With this ring, I thee wed."

Jonathan repeated it and placed the ring on Sadie's finger and then she did the same. When both of them wore their bands, the minister announced, "By the power vested in me by God and man, I pronounce you husband and wife. What God has joined together, let no man put asunder. You may now kiss the bride."

No one needed to tell Jonathan twice. He wrapped one arm around his bride's waist and tugged her close. With the other hand, he gently cradled her cheek.

"I love you, Mrs. Bradley." Before she could reply, he pressed his lips to hers and kissed her until they both needed to breathe.

Breathlessly, she replied, "I love you, too, Mr. Bradley."

* * * * *

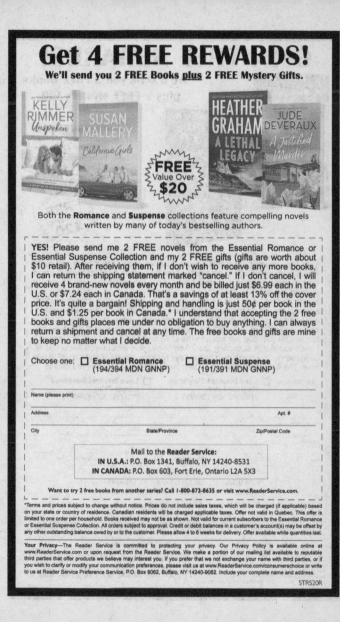